ONCE UPON A PRINCESS

THE LOST ROYALS: BOOK TWO

AINSLEY WYNTER

Ainsley
Wynter
Press

ABOUT ONCE UPON A PRINCESS

A vengeful rebel...

Forced to live in hiding after his family is assassinated, Prince Callum of Embury leads the rebellion to restore his family to the throne. Knowing only grief and revenge, Callum searches for a chance to destroy the king and rebuild his alliances.

A protective princess...

For Princess Zara of L'Ortagia service to her people comes first, while hiding her magical abilities. When the queen commands her to wed the Emburian heir, Zara flees the night before the ceremony—ready to aid the rebels, protect her country from a madman, and discover whether the dashing man who helps her escape is truly who he says he is.

Two passionate hearts...

On the run from the king's forces, Callum and Zara form a

fragile alliance while fighting a growing attraction. Torn between their allegiances and their passion, they find solace in each other. But can the magical princess and the rebel prince find a way to build a kingdom together?

PRAISE FOR AINSLEY WYNTER

and the first novel in her The Lost Royals series,
KISSED AT MIDNIGHT

Unique, intriguing magic system, and the regal drama and the super steamy sexytimes were A++

— AMAZON REVIEWER

Court intrigue and magic and dancing and drama! Instantly sympathetic, complex main characters trying to do their best with their many conflicting loyalties.

— GOODREADS REVIEWER

Such an entertaining read!

— BOOKBUB REVIEWER

DEDICATION

For my wonderful, amazing husband.

Royal apartments, Blackthorne Castle
Kingdom of Embury
Spring 1775

Prince Callum pressed his face to a crack in the door, counting the seconds. The narrow space in the seam between the heavy boards allowed him a view of his parents' sitting room. A large oak wardrobe stood along the wall straight across from him, one of its doors slightly ajar. To the left, a set of painted chairs, a small table between them, and a long velvet settee were neatly arranged over an intricately patterned rug.

As his counting neared fifty, he braced for the moment his older brother, Duncan, would find him. His younger sister, Quinnah, hid somewhere in the labyrinth of rooms that made up the personal apartments of the royal family.

Callum rolled his eyes at his predictability, choosing a favorite hiding place. This was the last summer the three siblings could play such a game. Duncan was already immersed in his studies and trainings as the crown prince, and Callum, as the second son, was similarly, although not as seriously, right behind him. At twelve years of age, Quinnah should have been the only one to hide. But Callum loved games.

He wiped his palms on his thighs, ready to be found so he could finally outrun Duncan.

Several sets of footsteps and shouting sounded from the hall outside. Callum couldn't make out the voices at first, but none sounded like his brother. A chill snaked across the back of his neck.

"Take your hands off me!" his father's voice boomed through the chamber. The sickening slide of metal into flesh silenced his father's outrage. His pained gasp turned into a low groan.

A group of guards dragged his parents into the sitting room, mere feet from him. The men wore masks, partially concealing their features. Callum recognized members of his father's royal guard, still dressed in the MacKinnon emerald and black.

His father jerked against the men's hold, his head tucked against his chest, a crimson stain spreading across his lower belly. The guards split their attention between subduing his parents and watching the door. Callum pressed his lips together and balled his fists.

"No! Stop!" his mother cried. Her powdered wig had been yanked off. A small linen cap covered her head, brown wisps of hair spilling out from under it. Her dress was torn at one shoulder, the delicate fabric hanging loosely. Red scratches marked her upper arms.

Another guard backhanded his mother. "Silence. You are on trial for crimes against the kingdom."

"Unhand her," his father gritted out. "She is your queen, and you will treat her with respect."

The guard smacked his mother again. She cried out and again pulled against the men who held her.

Callum swallowed, fear like smoke streaking through his lungs, nearly cutting off his air. Tears ran down his cheeks. He pressed his face against the door, gaze locked on the scene in the other room, instincts screaming at him to do something. He wanted to rush to his parents' aid, but how?

He rubbed a sleeve over his face, clenching his jaw to keep from crying out. His father slouched against the guards' hold, blood dripping onto the carpet from the sword wound on his torso. He stood in profile to Callum, his features haggard, his tanned skin pale. The queen was closer to Callum, both cheeks a mottled red, one eye starting to swell. Blood smeared along the corner of her mouth.

Callum searched for his siblings amid the group of guards, but he didn't see them. Were they hiding or being held somewhere else? Dorine, one of the chambermaids, stormed into the room and flung open the wardrobe.

"They have to be here somewhere," she growled, pushing aside his mother's dresses. "You two, come with me." She snapped her fingers, and two of the guards followed her out the door. She began calling his siblings' names. And his own.

His limbs trembled. He stepped back and covered his face with his hands, his breaths hiccupping for a panicked moment. The sounds from the next room covered his soft squeaks, but eventually, they'd hear him or look for him in this room. He had no weapons and was completely outnumbered.

I have no way to help them.

The king's guards were chosen for their loyalty to serve the royal family. Callum had known many of the men for years. Why were they doing this? He slowed his breaths and quieted, then went back to the crack in the door, unable to look away for too long.

Felix, one of the footmen, strolled into the room. His head was bare, his face flushed and sweating. He wiped a hand over the Embury crest on his coat, and leaned forward to spit on the king.

"Gracchus is on his way, Your Highness." Felix smiled menacingly. He approached the queen, raising a hand to strike her on the other cheek. "We're rounding up the royal brats while we wait for your cousin."

"Don't you dare!" his mother demanded. "They're children!"

Felix shrugged and clapped his hands together.

Callum feared desperately for Duncan and Quinnah. The hallway was eerily quiet, save for Dorine calling their names. Other members of the guard would likely capture them soon.

His favorite hiding spot had become a trap. He could rush out weaponless and try to help his parents, or cower, knees shaking.

His father groaned and sneered at Felix. "Gracchus always liked to let others do his dirty work."

"It's hardly dirty work. We're helping restore the kingdom to the rightful king, the rightful line." Felix pulled a dagger from his belt and stepped up to the king.

"How...? Why would you do this, Felix?" the queen asked. "And the rest of you—what does Gracchus have over you?"

Felix eyed the guards and waved a finger. "They work for me now."

The king gave him a disbelieving look before his features froze in a mask of pain.

Felix rubbed an arm over his sweating face. "I convinced them, persuaded them, with my magics," he said in a strange voice. "They do what I command."

He clenched his hand into a fist, and the guards shook Callum's parents until they cried out. "Enough. I am in command here," Felix said.

Callum turned over Felix's words, his mind seizing on the likely scenario that Felix was a nocturne. He'd admitted it, but it was so bold a claim, Callum couldn't quite believe it.

Bile rose in Callum's throat at the sight of the blood staining his father's breeches, adding to the pool at his father's feet. The wound wouldn't be enough to kill him immediately, but Callum knew from his sword training, a knife to the gut was painful and likely deadly.

Crashes and screams came from the corridor outside. A hand clamped over Callum's mouth and an arm wrapped around his waist, pulling him away from the door. He struggled, rearing back against the person holding him. He'd been alone in the small study when he'd hidden from his siblings. He was dragged to the side of the room next to a high bookshelf. Kicking out but unable to break the hold on his body, Callum strained to hear the traitors' assault on his family.

"Come with me, Highness," Sir Edmund, one of the royal guards, whispered in his ear. The soldier dragged Callum into a niche behind a shelf set against the wall.

Callum froze, paranoia gripping him. His stomach twisted like a sinking ship. The other room had filled with servants and guards who betrayed his parents. Could he trust Edmund?

The retainer confided at his temple. "We have to get you out of here. Felix has more than a dozen men from the king's guards. The rest are loyal to the MacKinnons. Gracchus staged a coup."

Callum shook his head. "Please help them," he pleaded.

"We must go." Edmund squeezed Callum, pulling him backward.

"Don't do this, Felix," his mother called in a voice broken by sobs. "It will stain your soul. Spare our lives."

Callum flinched. Maeve, the queen, stood as the face of calm against his father's storms.

"My people will never unite behind Gracchus!" his father called out.

Felix laughed. "With your family gone, he'll be the rightful king. The people follow the will of the crown."

"They will never follow a coward such as he." His father groaned.

"Spare my children," the queen begged. "We'll do what you want, but don't harm them."

Armor clanged and sharp smacking noises echoed from the other room, peppered with grunts of pain. Callum shook in Edmund's hold, helpless while the guards beat his parents.

The knight yanked Callum to the side of the room. "Your parents charged me with keeping you safe," Edmund said at his ear.

One of the bookshelves by the window stood at an angle to the wall, the rug below pushed aside as well. The stone behind it exposed an open archway with a staircase. In all the years Callum had hidden in this room, even hiding his favorite toys behind the books so no one else could play with them, he'd never known about the secret passageway.

Callum swallowed, took one last look at the connecting door, and let Edmund hurry him down a narrow, winding stairway. A hinge attached the shelf on one side, likely hidden in the front by the drapes next to it. Callum turned, catching Edmund swinging the shelf back across the entrance to the passageway, leaning forward to straighten the rug as he did so.

Once it closed, darkness shrouded them. Only a faint light shone from below, the rough stone steps slippery with mold. Edmund pulled at Callum's arm, leading the way.

When his parents' screams echoed down to them, Callum stumbled, hitting the side of his head against the wall and crashing to his knees. Blood dripped down his cheek, and his knees throbbed. Grief and terror vibrated within him until he trembled.

Edmund cursed and raced ahead, returning with a torch.

"Come, lad."

He pulled Callum to his feet and held the torch high to light their way before the silence swallowed them up.

CHAPTER ONE

Mondelac Castle
Kingdom of L'Ortagia
Winter 1784

Crown Princess Zara took a deep breath and paused before the tall doors to the small throne room. While it was designed to be less imposing than the grand throne room, its layout still gave visitors a distinct disadvantage.

Zara was familiar with her mother's practiced intimidation. Shoulders back, chin high, she stepped into the room. Much longer than it was wide, a full bank of windows ran along one side while busts of previous queens of L'Ortagia were displayed atop a row of pillars along the other. The queen sat at an ornate throne at the far right end. Isabeau's portrait hung on the wall behind her, flanked by a tall case clock that had been in the D'Arles family for six generations.

It took thirty-six steps to reach the queen, each of which Zara counted under her breath.

"Your Majesty." Zara bent into a deep curtsy then rose

slowly, clasping her hands in front, and keeping her gaze lowered until she was acknowledged.

"Daughter," Isabeau called from her gilded throne.

"Mother." Zara raised her eyes, noting the queen held a letter.

"I received a request from King Gracchus."

Zara's eyes widened before she could check her response. Gracchus was a fierce leader of their neighboring country. They had a few trade agreements with Embury but diplomatic relations were stilted since he had taken the throne several years ago following the royal family's assassinations.

"Gracchus seeks to form an alliance with L'Ortagia." A wry smile passed over the queen's lips.

"What kind of alliance?" Zara asked carefully.

Isabeau picked up the letter and squinted slightly to read. "He says, 'It is time for our countries to establish firmer ties. Embury is a land rich with agriculture and industry. L'Ortagia has a flourishing center of arts'...yes, yes...'and provides trade routes.'" Isabeau continued, stopping now and again to peer at Zara. "So, those are his reasons why one of my daughters should wed his son. This day has been inevitable in many ways."

"It doesn't have to be. Have you decided which one of us?" Zara asked. She concentrated on taking slow breaths, but her panic was like being tied into overly tight stays, cutting off her air.

Isabeau folded the letter in her lap, her slow intake of breath a warning. "*You* will marry Prince Torwyn."

"Marriage to Gracchus's heir doesn't have to be inevitable. Mother, I don't even know him." Zara squeezed her laced fingers and quelled the desire to express her outrage. Despite her mild outburst, she worked hard not to react overtly during her mother's tête-à-têtes. Comportment, achievement, and control were the path to her mother's admiration. Someday.

For now, Isabeau seemed to enjoy when Zara got off balance, and Zara tired of her mother's ensuing lectures on *the demeanor of a future queen*.

"You are lucky, indeed, that anyone would even want you. The king seems to favor nocturnes, but I'd ask that you not bring shame to our house." Her mother's expression was pinched.

"Of course, Mother. Only a few people even know about my... aberration." Zara was used to the scolds and had been ever since the queen discovered that long-dormant features of their bloodline had emerged in Zara, making her a nocturne, one of a feared and scorned group, shunned for their magical abilities. Her mother forbade her, and any other L'Ortagian, from using their powers openly. There was a time when she'd bound her powers. Zara rubbed her wrist with her thumb.

She relaxed her fingers and tried to recall what pressing information Gracchus's letter contained. Aside from marrying her off, what was it about this particular suit that Isabeau took so seriously?

"How would such an alliance benefit L'Ortagia?" Zara asked. She knew her mother usually had multiple motives for doing something.

Isabeau gave Zara an assessing look. "No pleas for me to let you choose someone else?"

Zara shook her head. "No, ma'am. Better it's me than Sidony."

"Good. Now that that's out of the way." Isabeau dropped the letter with a sigh. Had she been anticipating a refusal? When had Zara ultimately refused any of her mother's commands?

Zara pressed on. "How would an alliance with Embury benefit our citizens? Why should we ally ourselves with a ruler whose own people call him the usurper?"

Isabeau leaned forward, clutching the arms of her throne, rings winking in the candlelight.

Zara had found the underlying test. It wasn't enough to promise her to a man not of her choosing, who likely shared traits with his domineering father—a marriage that would make her as miserable as her parents had been. In every interaction, her mother tested her, prodding and manipulating her reactions. Zara dreamed of the day she would be trusted to form an opinion of her own.

"Once Gracchus quashes the rebellion in his own country," the queen responded, "he will finally have the resources to become a threat in the region."

Zara lifted her hands, unable to still the gesture. "Then L'Ortagia can renegotiate our trade agreements. Why should marriage be on the table?"

The queen raised a brow. "It is the most effective means of securing our safety against a ruthless leader."

"This can't be our only choice."

In a rare moment of candor, the queen sighed and looked out the bank of windows. Without turning her head, she said in a grim tone, "Gracchus is a man who seizes power. I believe we either ally with him soon or face his retaliation in the future."

"But, Mother, if he's threatened us in some way, we can't simply give in to his request." Zara raised her voice just enough to make her point. Years before, she'd met the former MacKinnon royals on a rare visit. She and their middle son were the same age. They were a gregarious bunch. The king a bit stern, perhaps, but their court had been lively and cheery. Rumors of Gracchus's court were that it was wildly different: polished but cold, mercenary.

No doubt her mother's training had prepared her to do well in such a place, but it sounded like a living hell. She wanted to use her royal powers to improve her people's quality of life. If she were stuck in Embury during the rest of her mother's reign, she'd spend her time watching over her shoulder, likely placating two tyrants. "We would be losing more than we'd gain from this, Mother. Let him make a request. We don't have to grant it."

"But we *must*. Gracchus may be volatile, but we, and L'Orta-gia, are better off with him on our side. We don't have a choice. Installing you in his court gives us an advantage."

"How could I have an advantage over a man I've never met?"

"I'll arrange a meeting before the ceremony."

When their wedding would be a forgone conclusion?

"You promised me and Sidony that we could choose. You promised us we wouldn't be forced to wed someone we didn't know like you were."

"Zara, I have to do what is best for L'Ortagia. And I have raised you and your sister to be able to handle any man."

Zara waved a hand at her mother's hollow words. Her mother handled men because she was the queen. She used her power over them and expected her daughters to employ the same tactics.

Strategy, tactics, and power were not words Zara wanted to apply to her marriage.

"What if Torwyn is just as ruthless as his father?"

"If he is, it would be your duty to teach him to be better. To guide him, soften those edges, bend them to what we need them to be."

She'd never escape this.

The case clock in the corner chimed the dinner hour.

Duty prevails.

Despite her efforts, she was still just a pawn.

Zara straightened her spine, ignoring the sickening slide of dread that settled into her belly. "It appears I'll be getting married, then." Zara's voice carried the perfect, modulated tone, barely dropping off at the end.

Isabeau regarded her, the earlier pinched look replaced by a flash of pride in her eyes. "Yes. Your country demands it."

"If that will be all, Mother?" Zara stared at a spot just to the queen's left, darting a glance at her face at the last second.

"That will do for now. We'll begin the formal negotiations right away. I anticipate a wedding by early summer. You may go."

Zara turned to leave, her strides measured and even. She made it twenty-three steps until she had to dash a tear from her face.

Sidony, her sister, waited outside the doors. Zara waved her forward, unwilling to speak until they were out of the guards' range.

"Was it what you were thinking?" Sidony asked. She matched her shorter stride to Zara's.

"Yes. She's marrying me off to a man I've never met," Zara said in a low voice. "He's likely as much of an overbearing tyrant as his father."

"I was sure she'd want you to make your own choice of a husband," Sidony replied. "She was miserable with Father."

"That is what I'd hoped for, what she'd as much as promised me—a chance to choose someone." At her door, Zara's shoulders slumped. She waved off another set of servants, waiting until they left before opening her door with a flick of her fingers, not needing the handle.

Sidony gasped. "Did you just…?"

Zara closed the door behind them, again without touching it. She kept her movements small, grateful using her nocturne abilities had begun to feel more natural to her. "I did. Although I seem to have more control when you are around."

Sidony's eyes were huge. "I thought you stopped using your powers as a child."

Zara rubbed at a spot on her forehead, unclear whether the headache had started after meeting with her mother or that brief burst of telekinesis. "Now and again I like to see what I can do."

"Wouldn't we all," Sidony murmured. Zara had the feeling she was talking about something else.

Zara hugged her, dashing at a tear before it could fall. She would not cry over this. At least Sidony would keep her secret.

She waved to the set of chairs by her fireplace, but stood at the back of one, too agitated to sit. "Mother's marrying me off to appease our northern neighbors. This will be disastrous. His own people live in fear of him."

"Is she marrying you to Gracchus?" Sidony asked, eyes wide.

Zara appreciated her sister's solidarity. "Not the king." She shuddered. "Torwyn, the newfound heir."

"Oh." Sidony must have read the look on her face. "Not terribly better?"

"A younger version of his father," Zara said. "With a more refined sense of fashion." The king was known for his gaudy penchant of wearing enormous, bejeweled rings on every finger. He'd done costly renovations on the royal seat, Black-thorne Castle, going so far as to rename it a palace. A monument to its new supposed grandeur. A waste of resources better spent on his people.

"*Oh.* That one." Sidony frowned. "Is it... better or worse that he's only a score and five years of age?"

"All of it's terrible." She eyed her perfume bottles on a tray nearby, imagining the satisfying smash of them against the far wall. She shook out her hands instead. "Torwyn likes to play with his father's cannons, against his own people."

"What did Mother say about that?" The compassion in Sidony's eyes was almost her undoing.

"She said my marriage would keep L'Ortagia safe." Zara shuddered. "That it was our only option."

"I'm assuming the wedding will be at Mondelac?" At Zara's shrug, Sidony continued. "We'll make it a grand occasion."

"Early summer." Zara knew her sister liked to plan such things. She was a natural hostess. "After the Tulip Ball."

"At least we can attend that together." Sidony gave her a half smile. Her sister loved the masquerade ball and happily dragged her to it every year.

"She has to finalize the negotiations, but I imagine I'll return with Torwyn to Embury after the ceremony," Zara said. The reality of knowing she had mere months left of living in L'Ortagia struck her. Again she contemplated the crystal bottles. Several had been given to her by Sidony. She also couldn't justify making a maid clean up the results of her tantrum. Her eyes stung. "I'd hoped to dissuade her from making such marriages for us. I tried, Sidony."

"I know." Sidony pressed a fist to her mouth. "I don't know what I'll—I miss you already."

"I have to find a way out of this." Zara rubbed at her temple again. "This is the wrong course for L'Ortagia. But she wouldn't listen to me."

"You tried. I'm sure you made a compelling argument." Sidony hugged her tightly before going to the door. "As much as she's trained you to take her place, you would think she would listen to your objections."

"And you would be wrong. Her mind was made up."

Sidony left and Zara collapsed on the bed.

She mashed her face into the elegant mound of pillows to muffle a scream. She threw one on the floor. It made a dissatisfyingly soft thump on the carpet. When she pushed herself up, her hand brushed against a letter tucked behind her favorite pillow.

Her back to the door, in case any of her maids should enter, Zara carefully broke the seal and read the contents.

CHAPTER TWO

Rebel camp
Kingdom of Embury
May 1784

Callum led his horse straight to the camp's water trough. Thunder rumbled in the distance. Dark gray clouds filled in the pieces of blue sky. Exhausted and hungry, Callum was grateful he'd made it back before it rained.

The raid had not gone well, with the rebel forces losing two men. Callum had secured provisions for two villages but he was not sure how much longer the rebellion could hold that particular crossing. He'd left it secure then ridden for three days straight to get back to the newer camp that sat closer to the southern edge of the kingdom, which bordered L'Ortagia.

He rested his forehead against his horse's neck, closing his eyes and patting the gelding. He'd changed horses but had still ridden hard to return as fast as he could. The royal wedding was mere weeks away. Callum was determined not to let Gracchus achieve an alliance that would cement his sovereignty.

Two children approached him as he splashed water on his

face. One took the reins and led the horse away. The other handed him a crust of bread and a meaty leg of some kind. Callum thanked them both and headed in the direction of the officers' tents for General Jeffors Millerton, the rebellion's top officer.

Callum ducked under the flap and nodded in greeting to his men.

"Sire, welcome back. How did the mission go?" Jeffors asked.

Callum made his way to his seat at the end of the table, several soldiers clapping him on the back in welcome. He answered questions about the raid on Gracchus's envoy. As he spoke, raindrops fell on the tent in dull thuds.

Jeffors, seated at his left, remained silent throughout Callum's recounting but seemed to shake himself near the end. The general stood and smoothed his coat. It was a few shades lighter than his dark brown skin. Jeffors had served under Callum's father, and his military bearing, complete with close-cropped hair, added to his air of authority. Callum knew the rebels respected him, some even joked with him, but Jeffors had earned their admiration as a soldier and a strategist and now as the leader of the rebellion.

"We have news," Jeffors said. "And we have a plan and a means for stopping the wedding, although it is not without considerable risk."

Callum nodded, his appetite fading at another potential risk to their numbers. "These days, they all have such risk. Let's hear it."

"We considered another assassination attempt, of course, but Gracchus has tripled his guards and rarely leaves the palace. Our spies have given us conflicting information as to whether he will even attend the ceremony."

The rain pounded harder and flashes of lighting shone along the bottom of the tent.

"No, he won't be at the wedding," Callum stated grimly. Thunder rumbled outside. "Even if the guards are divided between the king and the crown prince, there's still too many of them to get close enough for what we need to do."

A leak opened in the roof of the tent, pouring water on Callum's head and the rest of his half-eaten dinner. He shot out of his chair, but still got soaked. One of the men brought him a towel. He took it and turned to the group of soldiers, sighing and chuckling. The rest of the group joined in his laughter, some with gusto. How long had it been since they'd all had a good laugh?

"Don't tell me you've let a hydrokinetic nocturne into our camp," Callum joked, waving to the only spot at the table that had gotten drenched.

One of the camp boys brought pots to catch the dripping water. Another soldier worked to repair the leak. Everyone moved to the other end of the tent to continue the discussion.

"Only the first of many," Jeffors answered. Jeffors and Callum differed in their beliefs about allowing nocturnes to aid the rebellion. The general was all for it, but Callum was cautious, given the usurper's use of nocturnes in staging his coup. "But that does bring up a good point. We could use more nocturnes to aid us."

"Fine. Let's get to that after we solve the issue of the wedding." Callum slung the towel over his shoulder, too impatient to change out of his wet clothes. He needed some good news, and it didn't look like Jeffors had any.

"We believe the princess would be the easiest to intercept." Jeffors looked around at the other officers present. Several heads nodded.

Callum's throat tightened. He'd hoped not to involve her more than he already had, but they were desperate. He'd sought Zara's assistance in intervening with her mother for L'Ortagia's aid, secretly exchanging letters with her for months.

The timing of his letters and the royal wedding announcement had been coincidental. Just as he'd been desperate enough to reach out to Zara, the usurper had done the same with Queen Isabeau.

"I hadn't expected the ask to be so steep."

Jeffors pressed on. "Would she be amenable?"

"Possibly." Callum's hands fell to his lap and he dug his fingers into his thighs. He knew Zara was opposed to the marriage with Torwyn. The princess was protective of her people, understood the threat that Gracchus posed. She would be risking a lot to help them, but she would benefit too. She'd expressed hesitancy to go against the queen. Callum couldn't help but empathize with her sense of allegiance. In this crisis, would she stand on her own? "I'll send her a letter tonight."

"We need to consider this strategy in order to turn the tide of the rebellion. The king is close to taking two more towns at the southern end of the kingdom," Jeffors continued. "If he does, he will cut off supplies we need for the north. Having the princess—in person—to persuade enough wealthy, connected Emburians to help our cause would be invaluable. She can also vouch for your identity."

"She could." The courts had refused his petition, calling him an imposter. He went by an alias, Ash. His lack of confirmed identity was another problem for bringing sponsors to their cause. While the king was wildly unpopular, his policies benefited many of the wealthy. Few of them had reason to go against him. "Bring me a paper and quill. Tell me you have a plan to get her out."

Jeffors grinned. "I do. It's dangerous, but you'll like it."

"I'll like denying him something he so desperately wants." Callum chuckled and reached for a tankard of ale. "Stealing a bride is not on the table."

Gracchus wouldn't have stopped at kidnapping to achieve his ends. The man had arranged the assassination of the entire royal family. *His* family. He would have used every weapon, every scheme, every advantage.

To stop the wedding, Callum had to persuade Zara to help them. His honor—what remained of it—was all he had left. If she didn't agree, they'd have to find another way to thwart Gracchus. But if she did, Callum needed to ensure Zara's safety. He knew what could happen to people who stood in the usurper's way.

He worried that for all his efforts to restore his family to the throne of Embury, he was the last one alive.

There were rumors his siblings had survived. Yet after eight long years with no sign of them, all he wanted was to overthrow the king. Zara was innocent. They'd met as children during a rare royal visit. Zara had been protective of her younger sister, watching over Sidony the entire time.

From their correspondence, he knew she'd listen to his plea. Was she as desperate as the rebels were? Would she risk the queen's wrath?

Callum stared at Jeffors, his gut churning like a river during a storm. There were no other options. They could proceed as they had, steadily losing numbers and resources until there was nothing left of the rebellion. His family would lie cold in their graves, unavenged. His survival would have been for naught.

Or, they could change course.

"Tell me enough so I can prepare her."

Jeffors cleared his throat. "The fastest way inside Mondelac Castle would be with a nocturne's help."

Callum rubbed a hand over his face. In for a penny, in for a bloody pound. His father had been a traditional man who didn't trust nocturnes. Gracchus actually courted them, welcoming them to Embury. Another fact that grated on Callum, though there had been plenty of times he questioned his father's beliefs.

"This nocturne will do what, exactly?" Callum asked.

19

"She's providing us with transport abilities. She'll open a portal into the castle so we can capture the princess."

"And how do you know she can do this?"

Liam, one of the rebels, chimed in, "'It's true, sire. Just this morning, five of us got from one side of the river to the other, all in a mere blink, through a window of sorts."

A muscle ticked in Callum's jaw, matching the tempo of the dripping water.

"Then, we have our plan. Let me be clear: We are *asking* Zara to accompany us out of her castle. Once we get the princess safely away, she can help us bring in more allies among the nobles and merchants who don't support the usurper."

"Asking the princess," Jeffors said. "Agreed. And you'll use the nocturne's portal?"

Callum laid his hands flat on the table. "If it helps us steal Zara out from under Torwyn's nose I will."

"Then it's decided." The general nudged the parchment in front of Callum. "Be your charming self, Ash."

CHAPTER THREE

Zara's rooms
Kingdom of L'Ortagia
June 1784

Princess Zara's slippers shushed along the carpet as she hurried to her chamber. She had gone over Ash's last letter again and again before sending a reply a week ago. She didn't know how the letters traveled so quickly, though Ash had told her he'd used a nocturne's help. Zara placed her replies under her pillow, and they disappeared by the next morning.

Reaching her door, she paused with a hand on the doorknob. This was the right thing to do. The drama and abruptness of running away the night before her wedding gave her pause. Ash granted her a lifeline—for herself and for her people. She felt like she'd stepped out across a wide crevasse. She would escape her wedding and—as her mother saw it—her responsibilities. But the queen would likely not forgive her for doing this. Perhaps in time, she'd come to see Zara's reasons?

That she'd agreed to the wedding because she hadn't had a choice in the matter.

Her heart hammered in her chest. Helping the rebels, shoring up their support, would be the best way to free her country from an encroaching menace. She trusted a man she barely knew for causes she held very dear. Ash, as she called him until she had proof he was truly Prince Callum, shared her beliefs about how dangerous a marriage to Torwyn would be. In one of his letters, she picked up on an air of concern for her... a note of *care*.

Sidony would gently chide her for holding on to a youthful tendre for the prince from when they'd met years before. Perhaps that's all it was. The real Callum died long ago anyway.

But she had many more compelling reasons to take such a leap and trust Ash and the rebels. She had to do this.

Zara stepped inside her rooms and leaned against the door. The air was stifling.

"Your Highness, you need to come with me," a male voice said from the corner of her room by the window. He was tall, his shoulders nearly spanning the distance between the two windows. Someone had pulled the drapes shut. One of the maids, perhaps, as Zara had said she needed to rest before the prenuptial dinner in the banquet hall later that evening.

"It took me longer to get away," she said. Her voice quavered the tiniest bit.

He strode toward her, and Zara made herself step away from the door. Light from a break in the curtains caught the right side of his face. Laugh lines skimmed the corner of his eye. His brown hair was dark, not quite black like hers, and he wore it shorter than most men of late, though a stray lock fell across his forehead. In any other scenario, she would have found him rakishly handsome.

She surreptitiously wiped her palm against a fold in her skirt before offering him her hand. "Zara D'Arles."

He grasped her fingers, bowing over them. "Ash, at your service." He raised his head, revealing whiskey-colored eyes.

She had fond memories of meeting Prince Callum, whom Ash pretended to be, but that had been twelve years ago. The man before her bore a strong resemblance to the prince, certainly. She could see why the rebels resorted to using the story of a surviving child as a member of their group. It couldn't be true. A L'Ortagian delegation had attended the family's funerals. The boy she'd met was long gone.

Ash reached for her elbow, gripping it firmly. "We're grateful for your assistance. I give you my word that you'll be safe with us."

"I'm counting on it," Zara said. Standing before him, it hit her anew that she placed an enormous amount of trust in a group of strangers. She'd never really gone anywhere on her own. She touched his sleeve. "We have a lot to gain from working together."

They stood in silence for a moment before one of the soldiers by the door coughed. Zara startled, breaking away from Ash. Her thoughts jumbled together. She was really doing this, leaving on the eve of her wedding.

"You won't regret it. Let's be off." Ash steered her toward the door, gesturing to the soldier. He ducked his head into the hallway for a brief moment.

"It's clear."

Shouts sounded from the courtyard below. Carriages and wagons had been arriving for days. The courtyard had been nothing but commotion, especially today.

All five of the soldiers tensed at the noise.

"We need to hurry. Torwyn has men all over the castle, including the courtyard." Zara had told Sidony the plan last night. She had her sister's support, but they didn't have much time before her absence would be noticed. Prince Torwyn, if he could pull himself away from his contemplation of his own attire—"is this not the finest leather you've ever seen?"—would not respond to her absence tonight unless it somehow reflected badly on him. She could have been betrothed to a worse man, possibly, but the prince was insufferable on the few occasions she'd been in his company.

She'd danced with Torwyn last night, in a ball arranged by Sidony. He'd been a graceful partner, but he'd bragged endlessly to her about his accomplishments. She heard first-hand his excitement over a new order of cannons "that will blast those dirty rebels out of their nests."

He'd done nothing to endear himself to her, her family, or her people. Torwyn was loathsome.

"Come with us." Ash held out his hand.

This was truly happening. She could still change her mind, be the dutiful daughter.

Zara placed her hand in his, expelling a breath of relief.

CALLUM LED the soldiers down the corridor and to a room across the hall. Zara's disappearance was timed to occur during the rush before the evening meal. Most of the castle servants were working in the kitchens, the two wings allotted to guests, the courtyard, and the stables, greeting guests as they arrived. Callum shook his head at their luck in not running into any of Zara's personal attendants.

Silent and grim, they slipped past several closed doors, making their way to the portal. The spell had cost the rebel army dearly, but they had been able to transport five soldiers into the castle and would make a return trip with the princess. Bargaining the price, they'd been able to cast the portal only a few doors down from her chambers. Callum was relieved by the portal's proximity, given the size of the castle, but conscious of the short duration of the spell. He had barely settled into the princess's window alcove, trying to get some fresh air after the nauseating experience of going through the portal the first time. They planned for the mission to take at most thirty minutes.

Five doors down and across the hallway, Callum opened the door and let his soldiers pass through. As an unlit interior room in the castle, it was dark and silent. His arms prickled with goosebumps. Perhaps it was merely a reaction to being so close to the portal again. The nocturne doorway's outline shimmered, the oval shape partially obscured by something.

"Liam, a light," Callum commanded softly.

A small flicker lit up the room. Liam held a taper toward the portal and slightly above his head. Callum squinted at the shape that stood across the room from the portal. A shiver had passed over his skin when he saw it the first time.

"Is that your wedding gown?" Viola, one of the rebels, asked Zara. "What's it doing in here?"

A dress form with a formal, intricately embroidered gown stood in the middle of the rug at the foot of the bed.

"It's being stored here for easier fittings," Zara said simply. "There's work left to be done on the train."

"You won't need it now. Your Highness, over here please." Callum led Zara to the portal and spoke the words to unlock it. Nothing happened. *Damn nocturne magic.* He tried again and the shimmering outline of the portal grew brighter, indicating it was open.

Callum stepped through with Zara. His soldiers filed in behind him. Although they'd made the initial trip without incident, the soldiers did not like the strangeness of being between two locations. Physically, they stood in a sitting room in Mondelac Castle, but once they'd crossed the portal they could also see, superimposed on the room, the image of where they were returning: the woods off the southern end of the castle.

The number of people inside as well as the exact timing needed for the spell limited the portal's distance.

With minutes to spare, Callum recited the phrase to lock the portal, so they could complete their journey back. Again, it did not work on the first try. Taking a breath to tamp down his frustration, he repeated the phrase.

As he finished, the door to the chamber opened and a man dressed in courtly attire stepped through. The outline of the portal sizzled and crackled but remained open to the room, again not working. Behind him, Callum's soldiers drew their weapons, responding to the threat from both the man crossing toward them as well as the portal's erratic edges. Sparks illuminated the room. Even the silk threads on the gown glowed.

Gracchus's nephew, Prince Adrian, had found them.

"Halt!" Adrian drew his sword and rushed the portal. He stopped at the edge, examining it intently. His face remained impassive aside from a brief uptick of an eyebrow.

Callum tucked Zara behind him, willing the portal to close and work.

At Callum's right, Viola muttered, "Wonder if his powers can reach us in here."

Adrian's gaze flicked to her before returning to study the portal.

Of course he heard that. The bastard hears everything.

Callum's fingers twitched around the hilt of his sword. Adrian was a powerful nocturne and a skilled swordsman. Gracchus had traveled to far away Daeso to get his nephew and bring him back to his father's home of Embury. In return, Adrian served Gracchus by using his powers to locate traitors to the crown.

The portal continued to flash and crackle, wavering down the middle. Callum had to get the princess out of the castle, had to stop the wedding. Adrian was an enormous threat to this mission, and his larger endgame of reclaiming the throne for his family.

"Ranulf, guard her. Viola, repeat the spell. I'll meet you." Callum handed Zara to Ranulf, pleased the soldier's body was big enough to block Zara from Adrian's view and reach. His gaze snapped back to Adrian, who reached a hand to the outer edge of the portal.

"The nocturne said you needed to be the one to activate the portal," Viola said at Callum's ear.

"I needed to make the trip into the castle. You can do the spell."

Ranulf grunted. "This is why we need more of 'em on our side."

On the other side of the portal, Adrian pressed closer. Not certain the portal would work under less than ideal circumstances, especially if Adrian's powers could somehow affect it, Callum stepped out to block Adrian. He couldn't take the chance that the portal would break.

Callum crossed into the chamber and drew his sword, the scrape of metal soothing him in its familiarity, unlike the fizzing noises behind him. He lunged at Adrian, his saber slashing in a downward arc. Adrian parried the blow and retreated two steps. Pressing his minor advantage, Callum thrust again. Their swords locked together and Adrian spun to the side, forcing Callum to sidestep to stay in front of him. He turned, readjusting his stance and attempting to keep the portal behind him.

Viola repeated the spell. The portal sputtered and sizzled, but remained open.

"Don't hurt him!" Zara cried.

Could she be scared for him? Who was Adrian to her?

Adrian pressed toward him with short, hacking blows. His "cousin" was only a couple inches shorter than him, but his speed more than made up for his reach. He landed a cut across

Callum's forearm and then a quick stab into his left shoulder. Callum staggered at the swift pain.

Needing to end the fight as fast as possible, he launched an attack at the prince. He feinted right and then stepped out and swung left, pulling his thrust at the last second. His sword sliced along Adrian's side. Blood flowed from the wound, as it did from the cuts along Callum's upper body, but he clenched his jaw, reining in his impulse to attack further. He needed to incapacitate the prince, not kill him.

Jeffors had been adamant about keeping Adrian alive, despite the threat he posed. He'd summarized their mission: *stall Adrian if he finds you, close the portal, and get out of the castle with the princess.*

Adrian pressed a hand to his bleeding side and glanced at the portal behind Callum. "You cannot have her, rebel."

The crackling intensified and Viola murmured the spell again. Despite the nocturne's promise that the words, spoken at all, would operate the portal, Callum knew what he had to do. Viola was right. He had to be the one to close it.

"Unhand me!" Zara yelled. "Put me down!" One of his men groaned.

After more shuffling noises, Callum risked a quick scan. Ranulf held Zara in front of him. She struggled against his hold.

What is she doing?

If she'd changed her mind, he wouldn't stop her.

When he turned back, Adrian lunged him. Callum parried and blocked, circling around, while calling out the spell. His arm and shoulder ached from the strain, but it took nearly all his focus to chant and dodge Adrian's blows.

Work, useless magic. Work.

He lunged and got in another hit along the top of Adrian's shoulder. It wasn't his sword arm, but it bled immediately. There was more noise behind him, but he couldn't risk looking back again. Something thumped on the floor. Callum kept attacking Adrian.

The clanging of their swords got louder. It was the only remaining noise in the room. His adrenaline surging, he parried another blow but pivoted away from the corner of the room he'd blocked from Adrian's path.

He stepped around to the side, trying to draw Adrian toward him, and instantly regretted it. Not only was he was standing on the train of the overly wrought silk wedding dress, Zara now stood where the portal had been. Caught in the filmy material, he shifted his stance with a rustling noise. The slippery train was snagged on the heel of his boot, effectively telegraphing his moves.

Damn dress.

"Princess Zara, stay there," Adrian said from his corner of the room. Zara's eyes darted between the two men.

Callum turned to the side, using his other arm to block Zara, who moved toward him. He saw an opening and took it, grabbing Adrian by the arm. A weight landed on his back, and he almost lost his hold on the swordsman.

"Let him go! He's only trying to protect me! Stop!" Zara clung to him, raining blows across his head and shoulders, pulling at his hair, and screeching in his ear. Was she putting on a show for Adrian, making it look like she was trying to get away from the rebels? As long as she didn't block his view of Adrian, he didn't care that her hits could have been gentler.

Her proximity to him threw Adrian off because he backed up a step.

Callum grunted and brought his sword down again, turning his wrist, so his blade kept to the side of his target. Wincing as Zara landed a smack to his left ear, he slammed the hilt of his sword into the back of Adrian's head. Checking the impulse to hit him again, he smiled when Adrian slid to the floor, blood from his arm seeping into the carpet.

Callum sheathed his weapon and grabbed Zara by the waist, pulling her around to his front. She froze at the site of Adrian slumped on the floor. He used her shock to catch his breath and press his neckcloth against the wound on his arm.

Zara bent over the prince and shifted him so he lay flat on the floor.

"He was trying to kill me," Callum said.

"I'm not so sure about that," Zara said primly. She held a hand to Adrian's nose before nodding to herself. "He pulled back several times. Did you have to hit him so hard?"

"Yes."

Callum took stock. His crew had made it out and was safely away from the castle. There was that, at least. Adrian was subdued, not dead. Jeffors would be pleased. Savoring the small victory, Callum looked down at the prince. "She's coming with me."

"No need to boast about it. He's been a gentleman, to my sister in particular. I had to make sure you didn't kill him."

CHAPTER FOUR

Zara checked Adrian's breathing. The wound on his arm dripped blood onto the carpet. She went to a chest by the door and pulled out a folded cloth to press against his wound. He was only trying to protect her. Thankfully, he hadn't succeeded. She'd jumped on Ash's back in order to maintain the illusion she was being kidnapped. She wasn't ready for the Emburian guests to know she planned to leave.

"We need to get out of here," Ash said behind her. He squatted and disentangled her wedding gown from his boot. The gown was her mother's design, elaborate and very traditional. Zara loathed it but hadn't bothered to complain. Why bother arguing over a gown? It was only the beginning of the nightmare.

The taper Liam left shone over Ash's shoulder. She stared at him, fresh from the fight. A flash of heat stole over her. There was something so familiar about him.

"Have we met?" she asked, unable not to.

He avoided her gaze. "Why did you jump out of the portal?"

This time, she flushed with embarrassment. "I couldn't leave you here to get out by yourself."

Ash nodded and tucked his sword away. "You'll be wearing that dress tomorrow if they stop us."

"I'm well aware."

He ran a hand through his dark hair, and Zara caught the flash of a dimple as he grimaced at the movement. She grabbed another cloth and handed it to him. "Here. You can't leave a bloody trail for them to follow."

A flicker of a smile crossed his face. "Thank you."

There. That smile.

It couldn't be *him*. Prince Callum had died, his whole family along with him. But as a boy, he'd had a smile that never left his face.

Zara shook her head.

"We're leaving." Ash's eyes narrowed. "If you have a solution for getting out of here undetected, tell me now."

"I've never left with this many people all over the castle," Zara said. "That poses a challenge."

"You've lived here all your life. Except for a servant or lady-in-waiting, no one will look for you for a while." He spared Adrian a glance. "I've made sure of it."

Ash had plotted an alternate route. He'd told her in their letters. He was giving her a chance to change her mind.

She pictured the faces of the tradesmen and shopkeepers, artisans, soldiers, and merchants she'd met over the years, people who filled the square in Cadeau to greet her with flowers and songs for her eighteenth birthday. She imagined what it would do to them to be under Prince Torwyn's thumb.

That would not be happening.

"This way." She went to the door.

Ash blew out the candle as they left the room.

CHAPTER FIVE

Zara led them through Mondelac Castle's winding hallways, her strides swift and sure. Callum followed, familiar with the layout of the rooms and corridors from poring over maps of the castle.

The D'Arles family and servants generally used one main staircase and corridor to access the personal apartments of the royal family. The rooms had been part of a former, intricately designed keep, the effect being that there were rooms and hallways winding around this section of the castle and multiple entrances created over the course of several remodelings. Callum had agreed to use nocturne magic for expediency, but he was glad he'd memorized the layout.

"Wait." Callum paused by a bench in a corner alcove. "There's one more level until we reach the courtyard, right?"

"Yes."

"We need a disguise for the courtyard."

"Hurry. Dinner starts soon, and I'm never late." Zara frowned. "They could be looking for me already. Back here."

They entered the short stairwell in the back of the royal apartments. Thankfully it was empty. He spotted a cloak hanging in one of the smaller rooms and grabbed it, leaving two coins on the dresser. He held it up for Zara.

She wrapped the cloak around herself. Her dress was modest in style, but likely recognizable. The cloak's plainness worked well.

"Let's go."

Walking behind her, he had a chance to study her. She moved with the same surety she had as a child. At the time, he'd envied her innate confidence. He'd seen her as bossy but sincere. Zara was much like the girl he remembered.

Yet there were subtle differences between Zara the girl and Zara the woman. As a girl, her hair had trailed behind her in curls, bouncing on her shoulders. But on this Zara, her dark hair was pulled up and back, pinned and tucked in a well-controlled pouf the ladies fancied. No loose curls dared escape.

Footsteps sounded in the stairwell. He stepped in front of Zara. She slipped the hood forward, her face a shadow beneath, her eyes wide.

They couldn't just be standing there. Callum wrapped an arm around her back and pulled her close to him, turning so her body was hidden.

She stared up at him with her violet eyes, ridiculously thick lashes lending her vulnerability. This woman had charged at him, apparently for show, but he had a nagging sense that was Zara's way: forward but protecting those in her path. He wasn't sure if he liked it.

He tried to ignore the soft press of her body along his front. Heat rose in his chest, and he tamped it down, listening.

Three sets of footsteps rushed past.

"I don't know why we had to draw a bath for Lady Dieford! P'shaw! Who takes a bath before supper?"

"Nathalie! Stop complaining and run along. We've extra bathing tubs in one of these rooms."

The footsteps trailed off, and Callum eased back. Zara blinked, pressing her lips together primly.

"Well done, Highness." He grinned at her.

She stared back, eyes searching his face. He let her look, caught by the directness of her gaze. Did she recognize him? If she did, she didn't yet let herself believe it to be true.

"And you as well."

He and his council had made decisions about this mission, and Callum would carry them out, but he couldn't stop himself from reacting to her attention, to her.

Each moment he wasted gave everyone more time to notice she was gone and start searching for her. Adrian would not stay unconscious forever.

"Let's go, Princess," he said softly.

Zara put her hand in his and let him lead her back into the stairwell. They crept down yet another deserted hallway that contained a little-used door to the outer bailey. Before she and Callum could reach it, the door swung open.

Two L'Ortagian guards stood on the other side.

CHAPTER SIX

"Your Highness!" The guards looked shocked for a moment before hastening into deep bows. As they bent, Ash moved behind Zara, keeping a hand at her back.

"Good evening." Zara lowered the hood of her cloak and faced the men, keeping her expression as neutral as she could.

"Ma'am, may we escort you somewhere?"

Ash shifted behind her. Was he drawing his sword? With two-to-one odds, he could still take two guards. She couldn't let that happen. He'd already fought with Adrian. She wanted to get out without any more violence.

"No need to bother. I'm leading the earl here"—she waved over her shoulder at Ash—"on a quick tour. Such a busy night for us all."

She looked them each in the eye and raised her chin. Her hand trembled at her side, but she hid it in her skirts.

"Of course, of course, Your Highness."

Ash pressed his hand into her back. *Get rid of them.* She stepped out into the courtyard, Ash following, with one of the guards holding the door.

"Weren't you heading this way?" Zara asked.

"Yes, yes," both guards said and went through, practically knocking shoulders in their haste to leave.

Once the door closed behind them, Zara shook out her hands.

"Put your hood back up. We don't want to call attention."

She followed Ash's command and scanned the bailey. "Did your backup plan include a horse?"

"And a wagon," he answered. "This way. Head down, if you please."

She followed him across a section of the bailey where it connected to the back of the stables. The sun was minutes from setting, the yard already growing dim. Torches had been lit, but the light did not reach this end of the bailey.

Ash hoisted her into the back of a small covered wagon already hitched to a team.

"Perfect timing," He said. "There's a space across from Viola."

Zara scrambled forward and picked her way around a cache of barrels. In the space between them, a soldier waited. She was the woman who had repeated the portal spell.

He closed the back flap and, a few moments later, the front bench creaked as he climbed onto it.

Viola stared at Zara as if taking her measure.

"Hello again," Zara whispered.

Viola nodded, apparently satisfied, and touched a finger to her lips. Zara wanted to offer assistance. Perhaps staying out of the way would be the best course.

Viola rearranged various tarps, covering more barrels and blocking Zara's view of the back of the wagon. Then she pulled open the front curtain to speak with Ash. She handed him a satchel from behind the curtain. From the sound of sliding cloth, it was likely a disguise to go over what he had been wearing.

He said something to Viola in a low murmur. Zara scooted closer, picking up "forest" and "alarm" but not much else. There was a commotion outside, and Ash set the team in motion, calling out to someone in the courtyard.

Viola ducked back into the wagon and eyed Zara. "Are you going to give us up?" she asked.

"Never," Zara said.

"Then why get out of the portal?"

The last time Viola had seen her, she'd escaped Ranulf and jumped on Ash. "I was trying to help. If we were stopped, I didn't want them to know we were working together."

"The queen was already forcing you to wed." Viola sniffed. "What else could she do?"

"I didn't want to find out how it could get worse."

Viola tipped her head then, again putting her finger to her lips. Though the light was fading, Zara caught the flash of a ring on her finger. There was something familiar about it.

Zara pointed to her own rings, tapping one. Grudgingly, Viola held out her hand. Zara squinted and leaned over to get a better look at the jewelry.

She ran her thumb across the top of the ring. A carving was etched into it, but she couldn't quite make out the design.

"Highness?" Viola barely spoke above a whisper.

The wagon rolled forward, causing the front curtain to sway open briefly. In the dimming evening light, the ring's design was clear. It was an intaglio crest ring, featuring a lion rampant on top of a shield. The shield itself also held a lion, a stripe, and two stars, the MacKinnon crest belonging to Angus, the former king.

Zara blinked and squeezed Viola's fingers. "It's him, isn't it? Callum's alive."

"Yes," Viola said softly.

Zara touched her fingers to her chest.

The wagon lurched to a stop. The guards at the gate were

likely checking each carriage and wagon as they passed through.

Realization crashed into Zara. Her heart thudded hard, pounding the truth in steady beats. Viola moved her hand back infinitesimally, her wide brown eyes solemn and concerned.

From his seat at the front, *Callum* spoke to the guard, his voice gruffer than she'd heard it. Zara vibrated with shock and relief.

Prince Callum of Embury is alive.

After the assassinations, the crown had passed to Gracchus, the king's second cousin, and the nation of Embury mourned the loss of its royal family. The mourning had continued to the point that there were rumors implicating the new king in their deaths. Gracchus had initiated a new family crest marking the turn of his rule. The rebellion started once he assumed the throne.

Zara huddled in the wagon, flashes of her visit with the MacKinnons turning over in her mind. From the best apple tart she and the other children shared at an informal tea, to observing the young princes march in a military exercise with the king's guard, Zara recalled that young Callum had been energetic and particularly close to his older brother. He'd talked about family in his letters to her as well.

Her hands shook with the knowledge that an old friend, one of the lost princes of Embury, had come back from the dead.

~

CALLUM CLIMBED down from his seat. He adjusted the gloves he'd taken from Viola's bag, but resisted the urge to cover his face beyond the low tip of his felt hat.

The guard walked around the wagon. "A bit late to be traveling. Big festivities tomorrow. What's your hurry?"

"I've another stop to make," Callum answered and spit on the ground.

"What business did you have at the castle?" The guard looked bored, and Callum guessed he'd been asking various merchants, delivery persons, and coachmen the same list of questions for the past few days. Viola had probably answered them when she drove the wagon in. She had come through a different gate, but he hoped the guards had seen so many deliveries and arrivals, they wouldn't question a wagon entering and leaving in a short span of time.

"Delivered wine for tomorrow. Said they had plenty." He gripped the back wheel and tested the spoke, attempting a nonchalance he didn't feel.

"Here now. That cannot possibly be true." The guard had a thick mustache and a thicker frame. He hitched up his belt and seemed to come to life at the mention of extra wine leaving the castle grounds.

Callum could have kicked himself. Granted, a wine cask generally only held wine, and bringing in wine had been the plan in order to gain entry more easily. But having extra casks would make this inspection take longer.

"Aye. Got a message from the kitchens there was plenty of wine, although I did get rid of a few. I have another village I can get to tonight."

"No need to be in such a rush." The guard eased back on his heels before rocking forward and proceeding to the back of the wagon.

Callum met him there, dabbing at the beads of sweat on his upper lip with a kerchief. "Here, let me." He reached into the back and drew forth a small cask of wine. The guard actually snorted, refusing it at first. Callum scanned the interior for Zara. She sat still as a crow on a fence post across from Viola, the hood of her cloak shielding her face.

Sweat trickled down the back of Callum's shirt. She'd

surprised him earlier by pretending to attack him to fool Adrian. Would she improvise again? What had she been whispering about with Viola?

He eyed the guard. "I could make a gift to the princess's guards of a few casks of wine." Callum handed one over and grabbed two more casks.

A grin split the guard's face. "I'll thank Yves and the rest of the men on watch tonight for your remembering them."

"A blessing on you all."

Callum passed over the wine, tied the back curtain, and returned to the front of the wagon, careful to moderate his stride and his posture to that of a vintner, not a soldier.

The wagon rumbled forward, under the gate, and across the drawbridge. He kept his posture relaxed, eyes forward, but his hands shook. He tightened his grip on the reins to stop their shaking. They'd made it out of the castle, with the rebels' newest accomplice perched quietly in the back of the wagon.

CHAPTER SEVEN

They traveled for an hour, the sun sinking behind the trees lining the road, and Zara shivered in the cooling mountain air. Her borrowed cloak was made from a rougher wool than she was used to. It scratched against her neck and arms. She counted the slats of wood that formed the wine barrels.

She'd done it. Maybe if they got far enough away from Mondelac, it would feel more real and relief would set in.

No one from the castle had called out as they'd passed the gatehouse, or sent riders looking for her, so she hadn't been missed yet. Perhaps Sidony was stalling for her. She felt a twinge of guilt at leaving her behind to face questioning about Zara's disappearance. It wasn't fair to do to her sister, but she trusted that Sidony could handle it.

Thoughts of her sister made her chest ache. The royal family and any important guests dined together most evenings. But after, Zara loved to take to her room with Sidony, who always knew how to make her laugh. The longer the wagon trundled along without being chased, the reality of who Zara was leaving behind sunk in. Beyond her future odious husband, Torwyn, there was her mother. She'd miss her, but it was Sidony she was the closest to.

Leaving Sidony had been the most difficult part of her decision to escape with the rebels. Maybe she should have made more of a plan with her sister, given her advice on how to handle their mother in her absence.

Zara stopped herself. In truth, neither of them had an easy relationship with the queen. Zara trusted Sidony to keep her secret.

Viola left her to her musings, climbing up to sit next to Callum at the front. Zara curled up in the middle of the wagon in silence, her mind churning over what she'd done and what could have happened with Callum. How had he survived? She'd heard rumors, but had grown to expect those, especially with an unpopular king.

The wagon stopped, and Zara straightened. Callum pulled the curtain aside and peered down at her.

"We're meeting up with the others."

"Is anyone following us?" she asked. She assessed his face again with the knowledge of who he was. At least as much as the starry night sky would allow. High cheekbones, straight nose, perfect jaw, and dark hair. The features that had made him almost pretty as a youth had hardened into more angles as an adult. He was certainly more... brawny.

There was something elemental about Callum, almost earthy.

He yanked off his gloves and reached for her, grabbing her under the arms and pulling her out the front of the wagon. "Not yet," he said grimly.

"That's quite—if you'd let me get my bearings. Just a moment," she sputtered, never having been handled in such a way. She didn't need to be treated like porcelain but this was too much.

"My apologies." Callum, however, wasn't looking at her and

seemed focused on another task. As he helped her down, two men ran out to them.

"Sire, are you all right?" one of the soldiers asked. The other was busy moving the wagon farther into the woods and unhitching the horse.

"Yes." Callum shot her a look of gratitude. "We found our way out."

Zara shook out her skirts and moved to the side of the road. She wanted to talk with Callum, but everyone around her was busily unloading the wagon and seemingly taking it apart. They could talk once they got going again.

Through their letters, she and Ash—Callum—had planned to get her safely away from the castle, then organize meetings for her to assist the rebels in getting support from other powerful Emburians. As the crown princess, she had sway in her country, but she and Callum seemed to disagree about how much.

A part of her feared she was merely a pawn between the two—counting Gracchus, that would make three—sides. Her mother used her to secure an alliance, and Gracchus used her to achieve further legitimacy. At this point, she needed the rebels' help and they clearly needed hers. Theirs was the side she trusted more.

They were traveling north to Embury, but she wasn't sure where they'd make the crossing. Soldiers from the group who had snuck into her castle came out of the trees leading horses.

Viola had gone a few feet down the road. She hurried back and grabbed some supplies out of the wagon. She had told Zara the rest of the barrels were empty stand-ins. Callum had given all the real wine to the castle guards. The group's coordination was admirable.

The rebels were ready to leave again in mere minutes. The wagon no longer looked like the one they had ridden in, the rebels having dismantled the covering. She couldn't help but be impressed. Aside from Callum and Adrian's injuries, there'd been no bloodshed, another impressive aspect of Callum's small force.

Callum approached her as the group began mounting their horses. The wind picked up, swirling her skirts around her ankles and making her shiver. She strove for patience, but when he stood before her, the rush of knowing he'd survived came back to her.

"Callum." She couldn't help the wonder in her voice. "It's *you*."

He gripped her shoulders, concern in his gaze. "When did you know?"

"Viola had your family ring. I saw it before we left Mondelac."

"Ah. I gave it to her for safekeeping during the mission." His big hands were warm. He ran his thumbs up and down her arms, the effect heartbreaking.

She leaned closer, wanting to give him comfort, and he dropped his hands. "You could have told me yourself," she said.

"You wouldn't have believed me," he said softly. "Any real chance we had to gain your trust had to come from me as Ash. And, obviously, your... distressful situation."

He gave her a rueful smile, and Zara mentally rolled her eyes at herself, wishing for immunity to his charm. Callum the rebel fit with her memory of Callum the dashing young prince, especially the hint of roguish charm.

"Probably true," she said.

"Let's be off." With that, he grabbed her hand and led her to his horse.

"Are we to ride... together?" The rest of the soldiers were already mounted.

Viola eyed the road.

"Apologies. I'm out of practice with my manners. We are. Here you go." Callum boosted Zara up onto his horse and followed, sitting behind her. He laid a hand on her waist, settling her back against him.

"Oh!" Her mind blanked at the feel of him along her back. He was warm and hard. She wriggled in the cloak, wishing she could have brought one of her own.

"Hush, Princess," he said against her temple. He nudged his horse forward, and they took off, settling into the middle of the group of riders.

She kept her eyes on the road but placed one of her hands over his where it curled around her waist.

Nothing was quite as she'd imagined it would be. It was much more exciting. Even though she was alone with the rebels, she'd found an old, and dear, friend.

In the eight years of his reign, Gracchus had opened trade routes and sent emissaries to neighboring countries, expanding Embury's foreign relations. Every couple years, rumors would spread that one of the lost princes or the little princess had been found. But as of yet, none had been returned to the court or been reinstated on the throne. They were presumed to lack the resources and support to retake Embury, or, more likely, were imposters. Except the one behind her was very much real and alive.

"I'm glad it's you," she said, turning her face to him. She took in his almost boyish features, especially his tousled short dark hair and the dimple in his chin. His eyes were deep set, their color like old bronze.

"I wanted to tell you."

The scents of rock jasmine and pine drifted from the clusters of trees at the side of the road. Taking the reins in one hand, he ran the other down her back, tucking her into his chest.

"When can I meet with members of the guilds who support you?" Zara asked. Her insides were a jittery mess. The rebels' desperation was so real to her. They'd risked so much to help her. She needed to do whatever she could for them.

"We have to get someplace safe tonight. I promise I'll answer your questions, and we'll go over the plans then."

The horses took off into the night, farther and farther away from the nightmare her wedding was to be. She leaned against Callum, letting out a breath she'd held for months.

CHAPTER EIGHT

As they rode from Mondelac, Callum began to relax. He had the princess, she was unharmed, and somehow no one was after them to get her back. Yet. He barely noticed the cuts from his swordfight with Adrian. Viola had bandaged him up when they'd ridden together.

The route they planned to get across the border to Embury would have them back at camp by tomorrow evening. It was too bad the nocturne they'd purchased the spell from couldn't have the portal empty back into camp. The initial trip in was successful, but the second trip had almost not worked. When they met up with the other soldiers, Callum found out the portal had taken them to the small clearing in Mondelac's forest, as it was supposed to. It was close enough that Viola had been able to drive the wagon through the gates to wait for him and Zara.

It was magic. Couldn't it have been more convenient? Less temperamental?

He grimaced. Jeffors had been adamant they needed to utilize the nocturnes living in Embury. Angus, Callum's father, had scoffed at stories of the nocturnes' abilities, claiming Emburian warriors never needed myths or magic to enhance their prowess on the battlefield.

Yet nocturne magic had played a pivotal role in the rebels' victory today. As a tool, little else could have enabled Callum and his crew to sneak into a castle on the eve of a royal wedding. Perhaps if Adrian hadn't interrupted them, they all could have escaped through the portal.

But then he'd have missed out on the experience of getting out with Zara. She was brave, serious—qualities he knew already, from her letters—but also surprisingly comely. She had turned out to be lovely. He remembered her as awkward and shy, with long black curls and big blue eyes. Most royal heirs were described in positive terms, their features immortalized in poems and songs with reverent praise. In person, despite the trappings of wealth, such princesses—and princes— rarely lived up to their reputations as beauties. Not that they were chosen for their looks. Jeffors had suggested Callum consider a political marriage to help take back the throne, but without a court authenticating his identity, he couldn't get very far in making such proposals.

Besides, he fought for his kingdom, and his revenge, and that took everything he had.

Zara was a woman who would be sought after for reasons beyond politics. The moment she'd walked into her chamber, his first thought had surprised him. *I want her for myself.* Callum the man, not the soldier, rebel, or even lost prince, wanted her. *Fiercely.* He had tried to tamp it down the second he recognized that hopeful throb somewhere near the center of his chest. But there it was. Another complication. He thought that organ had long since stopped beating. His life revolved around a mission of revenge and restoring his family's place and power.

She smells like lilacs.

He spied tiny silk butterflies woven into her hair, like a pixie. In another life, this soft-hearted, sweet-smelling princess would have been exactly the kind of woman he would have fallen for, title or no. Knowing he'd regret it later, he turned his face down and to the side, discretely nuzzling along the braid of her hair, and inhaled.

Like springtime.

Thankfully, Zara didn't appear to have noticed his fixation.

She'd given him a starry-eyed look when he stopped the wagon. She likely felt sorry for him.

By not marrying Torwyn, she'd dodged life tied to a heinous individual. Torwyn was wholly committed to Gracchus. He preferred violence first, despite his role as an unofficial ambassador. Torwyn led skirmishes with the rebels, gleefully and ruthlessly attacking his own countrymen and women. Torwyn was loyal to his father, but a selfish braggart. Marrying his son to a princess from a well-established royal line was savvy. Though L'Ortagia lacked a strong military force, Zara brought Torwyn, and thereby Gracchus, respectability and sovereignty.

Callum stopped himself and chuckled softly. He'd sought out her assistance for a similar reason. Everyone knew the rebels in Embury were desperate. If the L'Ortagians backed the rebels, perhaps they could turn the tide against the usurper.

Zara turned at the sound and looked at him questioningly. Strands of hair blew across her cheek, escaping the intricate braid that pulled most of her curls off her face.

"Just relief at our near escape, lass," he said softly in her ear. She stared at him for another few seconds and then turned back to face the road, a soft sigh escaping her.

Today he'd had magic when he needed it and a willing Zara.

Too good to be true.

As they turned at a fork in the road, an explosion sounded several miles back. Callum signaled to stop and the other riders pulled their horses around to look. Zara straightened and pulled against his hold.

On the horizon, a cloud of black smoke gusted into the night sky. Its placement along a high hill made the origin of the smoke undeniable: Mondelac Castle.

CHAPTER NINE

"We have to go back!" Zara cried. She leaned over the saddle. The sky was at its darkest point over Mondelac Castle, smoke billowing and obscuring the east tower. They were too far away to see the flames, but thick swells of smoke hung over the keep. It was her childhood home, and more than at any other time she could remember, it was filled with people.

"Zara, there's nothing we can do for them." Callum loosened his hold on her and adjusted the reins.

She gripped his thigh, her whole body tense as she strained to see. "My people could be hurt. Go back!"

"Princess, no. We can't." He signaled to the nearest rider. He clutched her closer and, unbelievably, turned the horse, heading away from the castle. He spoke at her ear. "Even if you rode into the bailey by yourself, they wouldn't let you help."

After one last look over his shoulder, she turned away from the sight and clutched his shirt. "How can you know that? The castle is overflowing with guests. There will be injuries. I can help!"

"Zara, we wouldn't make it back in time to do much good."

She tried to tamp down her fear, but it rose inside her, swirling across her vision until all she could see were her loved ones running through flames. A sob caught in her throat, but she wouldn't let it out.

The horse's gait made her head pound. Even when she was trying to protect them, something terrible happened. "Could the portal have caught fire? Or the candle?"

"The portal was closed and we blew out the candle." Callum squeezed her side. "I know you want to help. I know you want to be with your people during a crisis, but I can't take you back now. Zara, all that we've put into this will be lost."

"They need me." Her voice broke. "I thought I was doing the right thing."

"You are. If I take you back now, you'll marry Torwyn in the morning. You promised me you were willing to do anything to prevent that."

"I am. I didn't expect it to get tested within hours." She wanted to beat her fists against his chest. She was stuck tucked against him, his chest at her back, a warm presence against the cooling night air.

"And I can't get you back tonight without risking my crew." He spoke low and firm against her hair.

"I know." She put a hand over her eyes, squeezing at the tension along her temples. "We can't go back. I thought I'd already made the tough decision."

She'd have to watch the fire from the road or some other safe distance back at the castle anyway.

"I've learned that sometimes you have to leave." Callum's voice was gruff with feeling. His arms were tense around her, not tight, but as if he were steeling himself.

"Sometimes you do," she said softly. The air between them was thick with everything unspoken and unknown, but she got a sense of what he'd lost. Just a tiny bit, and she knew she had to push forward. She had to continue with their plan. Gracchus and Torwyn would bring her people to similar levels of misery if she let them. If she returned to the castle, it would be to a wedding in the morning. She'd worked too hard to avoid that.

The horses slowed, coming up on a curve in the road. "We'll make camp soon. I'll send word and find out what happened back at Mondelac. I swear it."

"Thank you." Zara closed her eyes for a long moment. She'd burned out her energy in worrying about the fire. She peered back over Callum's shoulder again. All she could see were clouds of smoke.

CHAPTER TEN

I t was well into the night by the time the rebels reached Embury. They found shelter at a farm on the outskirts of a small town sympathetic to the rebellion. The horses would rest in the barn, and they could make camp near an abandoned cottage next to it. Usually Callum stayed with his soldiers, but with their royal guest, they had to take different precautions. She couldn't be out in the open, even if they were only making camp for a few hours. They were too close to L'Ortagia to risk losing her.

Zara had drifted off in his arms on the horse an hour ago. He'd tucked her head under his chin and tried not to nuzzle her hair. She was still asleep when Callum handed her to Liam so he could dismount and help prepare the camp. They set up two pallets inside the cottage and posted guards outside the door. Callum took the first watch and met with Viola to go over her return trip from the castle earlier that day. He was about to ask her what had happened in the wagon when she was alone with Zara.

Liam entered after a brief knock. His eyes were wide. "Sire, you asked me to tell you when the princess woke up."

"Thank you, Liam." Callum gathered his pack and slung it over his shoulder. "Viola, thank you for everything today."

"Of course." Viola nodded and made her way to her pallet.

"I've got her, Liam. Get some rest."

Callum strode to the cottage to check on Zara. Liam was loyal and fearless in battle, but when it came to women, he was quite shy. One of the reasons Callum had chosen him for this mission was that he knew he could trust the soldier to follow orders, and he guessed Zara would not be afraid of the soft-spoken knight.

"Zara." Callum paused in the doorway of the small candlelit room. She sat with her knees pulled up to her chest and her chin resting on them. It was such a youthful pose, lacking fear, really. He'd been right to leave Liam with her.

"How long did I sleep? Are we leaving soon?"

"It's the middle of the night. You can go back to sleep." He set down his pack across from her and unrolled a blanket to sit on.

"Oh." She blinked, each touch of her lashes making her more awake, more aware, if the expression on her face was anything to judge. Her hair still kept its playful assortment of butterflies, but the pins that held it in place had begun slipping out. It sat like a cloud on her shoulders, her dishevelment stabbing him with guilt. Her brief rest had helped her shock wear off.

Zara was a gentlelady. She had likely never been on a midnight ride anywhere. She had probably never interacted with political dissidents of any kind. She'd certainly never had to witness an act of destruction against her people and been left wondering what happened.

Callum wished they could have met again under other circumstances. If his life had continued on the path it had been on before Gracchus murdered his parents and usurped the throne, he could have spent time with her in more usual ways. He would have been able to pull a handkerchief from somewhere on his jacket and offer it to her. She would be standing near a window looking out on a garden, or sitting in a salon conversing with artists and intellectuals, dressed in her finery. At present, she was dressed in fancier clothes than anything he'd owned in years, even if her clothes were a bit dusty and her coiffure loose.

"I appreciate the trust you've given me in coming with us," he said.

"We have mutual interests." Zara tilted her head, keeping her hands folded in her lap. "And given our families' history of goodwill, I assumed I'd be safe with you, or someone acting in your stead, as it were."

He sat across from her and held out a small flask in offering. The guards outside might hear much of their conversation but, by now, Callum was used to such lack of privacy.

There was no time to reflect on how they might've met again as neighboring royalty. There was only room for their present reality. From their letters, Callum knew Zara to be protective, and generally cautious.

"Do you think what happened at Mondelac was an accident?" he asked.

"No." She held the flask to her chest, her thumb running over the length of chain that held the lid. "It could be. But the timing is suspicious. I'm sure our guests will think the rebels did it."

"I imagine so," Callum said.

"I wish we'd been close enough to see what happened." She frowned. She patted her hair, sighing as she readjusted another hairpin that had come loose. "All the more reason to work together, and quickly."

"Today was to be your wedding day," he said.

"Thank you for helping me avoid that," she replied. She sat

up, smoothed the blanket over her lap and folded her hands carefully atop it. "How safe are we here?"

"Safe enough to spend the night."

The small candle reflected the deep blue of her eyes like a mirror. Callum saw fragility, perhaps for only this moment, and strength. Zara was rattled but trying not to show it.

"I don't think I can fall back asleep." She took a sip from the flask, wincing but sipping again. "Callum MacKinnon, would you tell me how you survived?"

CHAPTER ELEVEN

"It's not a nice story." Callum took the flask from her but didn't drink.

"How long have you gone by Ash? Are Duncan and Quinnah alive?"

"Gracchus and his men have tried to suppress my real identity from the people. Some of them think I took the name of one of the lost heirs to build up support for the rebellion." He leaned back and stared at the ceiling, his eyes dry. "I don't know where my brother and sister are."

Grief welled, never far from the surface, but he willed it back. The wooden beams above reminded him of the slats in the door to his parents' sitting room.

Zara touched his knee, the gentle pressure a reminder of where he was. "You're lucky to be alive."

"I know." He took a deep breath. "I can't... I don't know if they survived the assassination. I can't assume that they did."

"Callum, how horrible not to know. How did you survive? They buried five bodies, you know."

"Yes." He knew. On a raid one night, he'd visited his own grave on Blackthorne's grounds. Jeffors had fumed at him that it was bad luck, but he'd been unable not to. He'd run his hands over the stones that covered his family's bodies. One of the soldiers, Liam or Viola perhaps, had dragged him from the abbey before they were caught.

"Callum?" Zara's voice was gentle. "You don't have to tell me tonight. It must have been horrible."

He shrugged. "It's not the telling that's hard. I hid in an adjoining room but watched what happened to my parents. Sir Edmund, one of the outdoor royal guards, helped me escape." He stared at a point over her shoulder, the shadows of the room closing in on them. For a moment, it was if he weren't even there with her, but was pulled inward, staring at a hole in a wall, helpless as he heard his parents' screams.

"Duncan, Quinnah, and I were playing a game. We were scattered around the castle. A long-time family servant murdered my parents and searched for us. Felix had been working for Gracchus for years."

"And you saw it happen?" Zara's face was pale, her eyes wide.

"Yes. They may have found my siblings. I don't know. Edmund dragged me out and helped me get away. I wanted to pull the door off the hinges and charge in to save them, but he wouldn't let me. One of the royal heirs had to survive."

She wiped a tear from her cheek and reached for the flask again. "How did you?"

"I stayed in several safe houses, mostly relatives of Edmund's. We didn't know whom to trust. Things moved so quickly after the assassinations, nobles jockeying for power and influence, a trumped-up story of members of the royal guard gone rogue and therefore to blame. Nowhere was safe. Our allies were... quiet. I finally met with a group who opposed the king. We combined resources and for the last few years, have worked to overthrow him."

"I... I truly cannot imagine what you've been through." She

shook her head. "Surely, many were loyal to your family, grateful for what your father had done as their king?"

"Some helped. I think they appreciated the relative peace under my parents' reign." He swallowed through a hitch in his voice. "I learned that power will not protect you. It only goes so far."

She nodded. She had her own struggles with understanding how to use her influence, how to take a stand. He was the last person to fault her for running away.

"I will have my revenge for what Gracchus did. My family will return to the throne."

"I want to help you," she said simply. Her hand fluttered over her sternum. "For the past and for today."

"You are, Princess."

She gave him a half smile.

He reached for her hand, pulling gently until she extended her arm. He kissed the back of it, as a courtier would. It was a soft brush against her cool skin, a touch of relief and gratitude. "You honor us by being here. Thank you for trusting us to keep you safe."

Zara's fingers curled toward his hand, holding on for a brief moment. "I've trusted you with my life and my country's future. We have a lot of time to make up for."

He hesitated, needing to let her go but unwilling to sever the contact. They'd spent the day no more than a foot apart. He knew how she smelled, the texture of her hair against his cheek, the press of her hand on his thigh, and the softness of her body against him.

Callum reluctantly let go and rubbed a hand over his face. He propped his arm across his raised knee, needing a place to put it so he wouldn't reach for her again. Touching her brought a strange comfort and tension. He could relax with her but at the same time had to push away thoughts of tupping her.

"When I met you the first time, I thought you could slay dragons."

Zara made a sound between a laugh and a snort. "You didn't even notice me."

"That's not true. Granted, I followed my brother around constantly at that age, so I was preoccupied, but I noticed you. I saw you. You took command of the nursery. You got Quinnah to keep her shoes on the entirety of an event."

"—That was Sidony's doing." She smiled, clearly thinking of her sister. "Sidony has a way with children."

"Not entirely. You'd told Quinnah she had a responsibility to behave like a princess and she listened. She went back to her wild ways once you left, but she heard you that day."

"Getting a six-year-old to wear shoes is hardly slaying dragons. My own sister is forever taking off her shoes at inappropriate times." She rolled her eyes and gave him a sideways look. "You were impossibly handsome at twelve."

It was his turn to laugh. "Everything was either too big or too small for my body. Twelve is the furthest from handsome."

"The ladies at court swooned over you—I suppose they clarified once you'd matured—that you'd break hearts across a swath of kingdoms."

Callum rolled his eyes and shook his head.

Slowly, he lifted his hand and drew his fingers along her jaw. Zara blinked and leaned forward into his touch. All he wanted was a simple kiss, something to chase the terrible memories away, the future that stretched out in loneliness.

"Is this all right?" he asked.

"Yes," she said. Her gaze locked on his face. "When I close my eyes, I see such terrible things. I had nightmares for weeks about what this morning would be like until I got your letter."

"Hush."

His fingers coasted over her hair, tweaking one of the silk butterflies clasped in her curls. He cupped the nape of her neck, drawing her close until her mouth met his. At the last second, she closed her eyes. He brushed his lips over hers, learning the shape, the soft give of her mouth. She let him hold her for another moment before she kissed him back.

Callum's head swam. As Zara kissed him, she came alive, brushing her thumbs over the stubble on his cheeks and sliding her fingers into his hair. Her supple lips moved over his and her mouth opened, wetting the kiss. She moaned softly and tilted her head, drawing him in.

He lost his bearing, her passion so... unexpected.

He pulled away and placed a finger on her chin. He glanced at the guards in the doorway. Their backs were turned and they scanned the areas in front of them, their heads angled as if in conversation. He and Zara had some privacy, at least. Perhaps the guards hadn't witnessed their kiss.

The flame flickered, tiny streaks of light glimmering across her face. He should blow it out soon.

Her chest rose and fell on quick breaths.

"Zara."

She lifted her eyes to his, her expression still tinged with sympathy. Then her gaze dropped to his mouth. He wanted to kiss her again, this time carefully and quietly, yet he held himself back. He slowly slid his finger down her neck to her chest. Her light blue gown was relatively modest but still fashionably low-cut. He ran his finger along the neckline of her bodice, tracing the edge.

She shivered and leaned towards him. "What are we doing?" she asked.

He held her there for a moment, his finger skimming along the lace. The warmth from her skin made him want to bury his face in her neck, in those curls that hung over her shoulder. He was in over his head, and if it continued much longer, he wouldn't care that the guards were mere feet from them. The feeling of Zara almost in his arms, the slow breaths she took as she'd kissed him, the heat that raced along his cock as she'd sucked his lower lip was almost too much.

When he'd gone to her, Callum had no idea it would go this far, that she would fit against him, taste even, like she belonged there. He let go of the top of her dress before he pulled her into his lap. He dropped his head to her shoulder, needing that small bit of contact.

She brought her lips to his ear, whispering his name. Repeating it. He recognized what she was doing and shook his head.

A soft chuckle passed his lips and he whispered back to her, "Thank you, Princess."

"I'm glad you survived, glad you wrote me those letters."

He raised his face to her hair, inhaling her sweet lilac scent. She'd had no idea how much he needed her help.

He pulled away and stood before he made a promise he couldn't keep. As much as he longed for her, he was afraid his heart was buried too deep. "Get some rest. We'll leave early."

CHAPTER TWELVE

"Your Highness, how are you this morning? I was coming to wake you." Viola bustled about the cottage. She carried a jug of water, bread, and cheese as well as a small container of tooth powder. She set the items on the table where Zara sat, and lit a lantern. Zara took one last look out the window, a glow of pinks and oranges starting to brighten the sky.

"Better than I expected," Zara said. She quickly cleaned her teeth. "And you?"

"Me? I'm wanting to get back to camp." Viola brushed her hands together before folding up Zara's bedding. "We're leaving soon. There's still time to break your fast."

A light mist covered the farmland. Zara had managed to sleep again, waking briefly when Callum returned. He had tucked the blanket back around her before resting on his own pallet. He was gone when she woke up.

Viola took the pallets outside, presumably to the waiting horses. Zara took bites of her food, not really tasting anything. She'd made it out and was safely away from her odious bridegroom. Their wedding, and the alliance with Embury, was truly cancelled. Discovering Callum was alive only reinforced her desire to help the rebels.

Perhaps one day, her mother would see why she'd done what she had to prevent the wedding.

Without the trappings at court, her mother to guide her, and her sister as her confidante, who would she be? Was this boldness only something she had when she was desperate? Working hard and being a dutiful heir should have helped her earn the queen's respect, but it hadn't. What else did she have to offer?

She stared at the little row of hairpins she'd lined up on the table. If she concentrated, maybe she could tidy the pins in her hair using her powers. The pins bounced on the table before Zara gave up. How useless and silly. Some ally she was turning out to be this morning. She doubted a show of nocturne powers would aid the rebels. They needed resources, not tricks.

Viola came back and tidied Zara's hair, braiding it for her.

"Thank you, Viola. Is there anything you can't do?"

The soldier laughed. "I've learned to be resourceful."

"An admirable trait. Is there any word about Mondelac?" Zara asked.

"Not yet, Highness. Callum will find out, though."

Viola led Zara out to the horses. Zara stared at the soldiers, again impressed by how quickly they were able to clear the camp.

"Princess." Callum appeared at her side. "This way." He held out a hand and lifted her onto his horse.

"We need to talk," she whispered, acutely aware of all the people around them. She glanced at Callum, noting his face was clean-shaven, his eyes were bright, his movements swift. Gone was the man who'd rested on her shoulder in the middle of the night.

"Let's get out of here. Then we can talk all you like." He

checked their gear and mounted behind her. His familiarity with her wasn't unwelcome. She wasn't sure where things stood between them. She wanted him to kiss her again, but he'd made no move to do so.

Callum whistled, and they rode out of their makeshift camp, farther north, in a winding route that stayed clear of anything that resembled a main road.

Last night, she'd kissed him like she needed him to breathe. She'd kissed him for a thousand reasons. And, if given the chance, she'd do it again. Some of it was guilt for not helping him and his family until now. Some of it was out of a need to comfort him, to hold on and show him his survival mattered. There was gratitude too. But mostly, she kissed him because she wanted to. He was someone who understood her, at least the life she had, and she felt good just being around him. As if she was enough. Wanted.

After a few miles passed, he leaned forward and said close to her ear, "Zara, last night doesn't have to mean anything for today."

"What if it meant something to me?" she asked. Her hands twitched. Was she so easily dismissed?

"I don't take liberties with women." He lowered his voice, his tone resigned. "That has nothing to do with why you're here."

"Of course not." Zara's cheeks flamed. He didn't have to sound so... regretful. He'd genuinely liked kissing her. That much was obvious. "You hardly took. It was freely given," she said tartly.

"You are free from my attentions." Again, his voice had a faraway quality to it.

"What happened in the last few hours?" She wanted to see his face, but the movement of the horse made more than a quick glance difficult.

"Nothing," he said quickly. "I won't be making that mistake

again. Not even to keep you from marrying Torwyn. You are my guest."

What happened to the man who'd pulled her toward him, breathed against her neck and given her shivers? That was more than just kissing. Any two people could do that. She'd been kissed before, many times. But no man had made her want to forget the world around her.

Now she'd followed this man to Embury. And yet today, he was little more than a ghost.

For a moment, she wondered if Callum was scared. He was the face of a rebellion, but was his retreat from her fear of the unknown? Could she mean anything to him aside from an ally and an old friend?

She'd been too tired to sort through her feelings this morning. The shock of leaving, the fire at Mondelac, and then their kiss had her unsettled. Strangely, she'd felt... happy. With Callum's rejection, she had to face the idea that maybe their kiss had not meant the same thing to him. Perhaps it would only add another complication to his already fraught life.

Zara was so far outside of her normal that one more thing was nothing. Part of her wanted to reach for it—for *him*—with both hands. His gentlemanly regard for her comfort and not wanting her to feel put upon was appreciated, although assumed. But where was the Callum from last night? Had she only complicated her life all the more by kissing him?

CHAPTER THIRTEEN

Callum and his team made brief stops and exchanged horses twice throughout the day. Clouds hung low, making the air heavy, but the rain held off. They avoided the main roads, Zara assumed, in case they were being followed.

"When are we meeting with your possible backers?" Zara asked. They had stopped under a copse of trees. She sat on a rock, a small meal before her of an apple, crusty bread, and cheese. Viola brought her the food, along with a cup of wine.

In their letters, Ash had written he wanted her help persuading a group of nobles and several wealthy merchants to assist the rebellion. As the crown princess, she was the future of L'Ortagia and L'Ortagian interests. She hoped showing L'Ortagia's support for the rebels would influence Emburian sponsors.

"In a few days. I need to speak with Jeffors to finalize when and where we'll meet with them." He leaned one arm on the tree trunk above her.

"Jeffors is General M you mentioned?" Zara asked.

He nodded. "He's been with us for six years now."

"Good," She said, impressed. Callum had petitioned the queen for support. Her mother had ignored his requests. Zara had tried to persuade her mother to see the rebels' side, but she'd refused to listen.

Zara sipped at her wine. "Coming back to court with me would show my mother you're alive. You are the legitimate heir, unless Duncan survived."

"If she'd grant me an audience, which I highly doubt. We've heard rumors about Duncan, but when we follow them up, nothing comes of them."

"But if you escaped, maybe he did too. And Quinnah. You witnessed your parents' murder, not your siblings'."

"Zara, I only escaped because a soldier got me out through a secret door. Quinnah and Duncan were in the main part of the castle. There were no other ways out. They would have had to go through Felix and his compatriots, of which there were dozens."

"I'm sorry." She felt ill at dredging it up. "I only thought... the likelihood... since you survived..."

"There was no one left who could have helped them. The rest of the servants who stayed now work for Gracchus." With that, he walked over to the rest of his crew and grabbed another piece of bread, effectively ending their conversation.

An hour later, when they were back on the road, Zara brought up the other topic that churned around her mind.

"Did you send a rider back to Mondelac?" Hopefully a change of subject would get Callum to talk to her again. She hadn't meant to remind him that his siblings were likely gone. There was only so much they could discuss in their letters.

"Liam left before dawn." He adjusted his grip on the reins. "We should know what happened in the next few days."

"Thank you." His words had a calming effect. She took in the changing landscape. Embury was very green, the landscape somehow rougher, rockier, than the smoother L'Ortagian hills.

The sun was low in the sky, peaking out between the trees. Their general direction was north, but they'd again stayed to small trails.

"We are almost to camp," he said softly. His voice was low, with that lilt of a highborn Emburian, a slight rolling of his r's. She suppressed a shiver.

"Does the king watch the roads for you?" she asked.

"Not as much up here. He's close to taking two more towns in the south, completely blocking us from entering or leaving. We are more highly concentrated in the northern ends of the kingdom now."

Already, without him telling her much, she had confirmation of her fears about Gracchus and Torwyn. The king had stolen a throne, assassinated a family, and used violence against his own people to retain control. Marrying his heir would have only emboldened him and his aim to quash the rebellion. She had to keep her country safe from him.

She'd left Sidony behind. There hadn't been a choice to bring her, though Zara doubted Sidony would have left with her. If Gracchus tried to marry Torwyn to Sidony in Zara's absence, he'd face delays, given her and Torwyn's contracts had already been written up. He'd likely want more concessions, since her absence would humiliate him.

She had worried over this for weeks, so she'd decided not to leave a note. In her absence, the courts of Embury and L'Ortagia would assume she'd been kidnapped. She trusted Torwyn would wait for the wife he wanted, the crown princess. Sidony would be safe from him.

Zara regretted causing everyone at Mondelac to worry over her and search for her. But she could not marry Torwyn.

Sidony would keep her secret. Though she seemed to have a fondness for Prince Adrian, whom they'd met a few weeks ago as part of the betrothal negotiations. The prince had come to live with his uncle during the assassinations and Adrian had been his heir for a few years. Sidony had stolen glances at Adrian, flashes of yearning in her gaze. Though Adrian was nothing like his cousin, his reputation as the king's spy didn't endear him to Zara in the least. Hopefully Sidony would move on from her fascination with the prince. At the very least, Zara trusted her sister wouldn't betray her.

Zara leaned back into Callum's arms, accepting how safe she felt with him. It was hard to tell if his prickliness was due to them discussing his family or if he didn't quite trust her.

She really had no choice but to trust him. She'd thrown her lot in with the rebels, and gladly. She was there to see what she could do for them, out of gratitude and necessity.

They crossed a river at a narrow point and then traveled alongside it for another two hours. The river got wider and wider as they made their way, continuing after the sun set. Fires glowed in the distance and what looked to be the edge of another forest. She'd studied Embury's geography, both for her wedding and her escape, but seeing was different than reading a map.

"Is this the Blue Flax?" She pointed to the river. They crossed a low bridge, the span three wagons long, over the flow of water. Callum tightened his arm around her as they trundled over it. She shivered again, mentally cursing herself for her silly reaction to him. Thankfully, the darkness would conceal her blush.

"It is. Don't catch a chill." He rubbed his arm over her back as if to warm her.

Though it was dark, she made out lines of tents and campfires. The camp was larger than she'd expected. If they were camped by the Blue Flax, that would put them on the eastern side of Embury.

"How many camps do the rebels have?" she asked.

"A few like this," Callum said vaguely. "Some are static and some are only for a short time."

Two boys came out to greet them, their excited voices bringing several other soldiers out of their tents. The soldiers' expressions were solemn but alert. Once they spotted her, they smiled.

Zara turned her face toward Callum. "They knew we were here."

"I sent a rider ahead. Your arrival is big news, Princess."

CALLUM SCANNED THE SOLDIERS' faces for Jeffors once they dismounted and handed off their reins to the camp children. He tossed a bundle of fresh plums to one of the children, his usual habit of bringing back a small treat or token.

He wanted to give Zara a moment to get settled before he introduced her to the rest of the camp. Her regal air gave her away despite her disheveled appearance from traveling. She looked more wood nymph than crown princess after the last two days she'd had.

He needed to clear his head as well. He regretted his abruptness with her, but he hoped by putting a wall between them, he could staunch his reaction to her. He glanced over his shoulder and quickly shook his head. She remained lovely.

It was damned inconvenient.

"Welcome back!" Jeffors grabbed him in a bear hug. "Looks like it went well. Ranulf gave me a brief report."

Callum grinned. "We got Zara out. It'll be a long time before I let you talk me into another spell."

"I think you managed well enough," Zara said.

"Your Royal Highness, this is General Jeffors Millerton." Callum completed their introductions, amused by the relief that flashed over Jeffors's face. He didn't fault him for his reaction because he thought the same thing. Zara's agreement to help them could shift the tide of everything they'd worked for.

To a weary soldier, she was the embodiment of hope for better days. To Callum, she could be, perhaps, something more, but he made himself quash such thoughts.

He had awakened curled next to her, his limbs more relaxed than he could remember. He'd scrambled away from her in shock. His life, his purpose, was for one goal. He didn't have it in him to care for someone new. He'd had enough grief for one lifetime.

Even though he couldn't remember his last full night of sleep, it had surely never been with another woman. He hadn't had time for such luxuries beyond mutual gratification. His lovers had understood.

Zara's time with the rebels was not for a tryst, no matter how much he desired her.

All his energy must be focused on revenge. He owed his family that. He'd failed them, with their dying breaths and these eight years past. His time with the princess had to be focused on service to his goal, to that greater purpose. Not for his selfish heart. That greedy organ had sped to life the moment she'd stepped into her rooms at Mondelac. So foolish.

Was she possessed, like he was, with more bravery than sense? Or merely desperate, and lonely at the thought of what stretched out before her? It had taken every ounce of his control not to fall at her feet or swing her around in celebration when he'd first seen her.

But he had to keep some distance.

She was a means to an end.

Callum rubbed a hand across his eyes, trying to erase the image of Zara leaning into him, her skin glowing in the candlelight, seeking out his kiss. So unexpected. Wholly mistimed. He had to stop wanting it to happen again.

With a streak of gallantry, Jeffors kissed Zara's hand and made an elegant bow. She blushed and tipped her head.

Despite her courage, she was truly sheltered. If Gracchus

got his hands on her, he would chew her up and spit her out. Being from an old royal line and wedding Torwyn, Zara would have helped Gracchus tighten his grip on the Embury crown. Callum longed to tear it off his head. He'd been protective of her in the abstract. Truly, no woman deserved to wed into that branch of the MacKinnon line. After spending time with her, it hit him anew how in danger she'd been. There was a deep satisfaction in keeping Torwyn's bride from him.

He had to be careful about wanting her for himself.

Jeffors addressed the group. "The cooks have warm meals for everyone." To Callum and Zara, he said, "Come and tell me how you escaped."

Callum looked over his shoulder at Viola, who had held back, waiting for his signal, and nodded.

"It was quite thrilling, actually," Zara said.

"Your Highness," Jeffors said. "I hope it wasn't too frightening. I'm sure you were very brave." He offered her his arm and she took it. "We want to make your stay comfortable. We'll have a light supper and then you can get settled."

She looked around the tents. "Where will I be staying?"

"Callum has offered his tent for you. He'll be staying close by. You'll have guards to keep you safe."

They made their way toward Callum's tent. Weariness from the mission made his bags feel heavier as they crossed the camp. Viola nudged his arm as they trailed behind Jeffors and Zara.

"Will there be a repeat of last night?" The soldier pursed her lips and fluttered her eyelashes.

"Of course not," he answered quickly. He reminded himself that he'd stopped partly due to their lack of privacy. "That was a celebratory kiss. It meant nothing."

Viola chuckled before leveling him a look. "Don't be too quick to ignore what fate dropped in your lap. She may walk around like she's never set a dainty slipper on a dirt floor, but she hasn't complained once."

"Well, that's because—"

"I heard all about how the both of you are so appreciative of each other." Viola rolled her eyes. They stopped at Jeffors' tent. Viola clutched her satchel to her chest. "Don't deny yourself something out of fear. That is how the usurper wins. He gets you to give up because he's already taken so much from you."

She walked away and Callum stared across the space into his own tent. Zara had gone inside but one of the flaps was tied open. She leaned against a camp chair seated around the table where they reviewed maps and made plans for the rebellion. The glow from the torches and a lantern from within the tent illuminated her face, leaving her free from shadows. She stared back at him, her expression unreadable, her posture straight, horribly lovely and vulnerable.

A means to an end. He would protect her but he wouldn't let her in.

CHAPTER FOURTEEN

Zara sat on the daybed, half-heartedly listening to Callum and Jeffors discuss the ride from Mondelac. They argued over the portal spell, with Callum unsure if he'd use it again. Jeffors was pragmatic about aid from nocturnes, while Callum was skeptical.

She felt similarly torn. Until her powers were under control, she'd keep them a secret.

Her magic was rusty, aside from bursts of it when she was alone. She'd stopped using her powers as a child. Their mother had scolded and shamed Zara the day she discovered them. She'd been putting on a puppet show for her father, controlling the puppets through her telekinesis.

Zara shook off the memory. She could practice her powers *here*. There were no such prohibitions against nocturnes using their powers in Embury. She'd make sure Callum didn't observe her.

There was a stack of books a few feet away from the edge of the tent. She scanned the pile and selected a small tome, no bigger than her hand, with a red leather cover. Zara pictured the cover flipping to reveal the first page. The book flopped open to somewhere in the middle, landing with a soft thud on the pile.

Zara jumped up to right it on the pile. Now was not the time to polish up her nocturne skills. She'd only call attention to herself.

She stood at the table, glad she'd familiarized herself with Embury to be able to identify several landmarks. "When do we meet with your possible supporters?"

Jeffors rubbed his hands together. "How about tomorrow? I've arranged a meeting in Vespertine."

"Will Byrne be there?" Callum asked. He frowned at the maps.

"Who is Byrne? You'll have to fill me in on those I'm unfamiliar with."

A look passed between Jeffors and Callum. "The Duke of Byrne is the noble whose support we want the most. He's ambitious and wealthy and has thus far not gone all in with the king."

"He sounds promising."

Callum crossed his arms over his chest. "He's elusive to the point I'm concerned he's secretly working with the king."

"You are overly suspicious, sire," Jeffors added. "He hasn't said whether he will attend. I've had confirmation from the rest, though."

Callum went over to a small table and poured himself a glass of wine. "Then we need to strategize tonight."

CALLUM STEPPED out and bathed in the Blue Flax while Viola checked on Zara. The icy river waters were always a shock, but it felt good to get off the grime from his swordfight and the road. Another bed was set up in Jeffors's tent, which stood only a few feet away. When he returned from bathing, he found a note on his bedroll. Zara wished to speak with him.

He hesitated.

He twisted his intaglio ring. Viola had given it back this morning after he'd stormed off from Zara.

Callum nodded to the guard and went into her tent.

Zara had left one of the lamps burning but had fallen asleep waiting. He went to turn down the lantern and was struck by the little changes she'd already made to the sleeping quarters of his tent. Her stockings lay across a trunk, embroidered butterflies dotting the silk. He'd caught flashes of them for days as she'd sat ahead of him on his horse. There was something vulnerable and intimate about her undergarments in his space. Her shoes were lined up in front of the trunk, her gown, now dusty and torn at the hem, draped over a low chest. Her petticoats and stays rested on a chair in a neat pile. Even a bracelet she'd worn was on his bedside table, another ring beside it. She'd even stacked the piles of books he kept between the chair and the trunk.

His limbs thrummed with a quiet energy, warming to her presence in his space.

He blew out a breath, exhausted at fighting his reaction to her. He'd tuck her in and go back to his new bed, and remind himself of all the reasons he needed to give her a wide berth.

Zara slept on her left side, a glossy dark curl laying across her face and flowing down past her arm. Gently he smoothed it behind her ear, pressing a soft kiss to her cheek. He was about to leave when Zara caught him. Her fingers stroked across his wrist, freezing him in place, his traitorous hand still in her coil of hair.

Her midnight-blue eyes cracked open. They were nearly black in the low light of the lantern, but he'd already memorized their color on their escape from her castle, almost against his will.

"You found my note," she said softly, her blurry gaze moving over his chest. He wore a loose shirt that seemed thin under the glow of light. "Sorry, I fell asleep." Her hand moved down to pet across his muscles, her fingers skating along the ridges. He sucked in a breath. How did she know where to touch that could make him shiver in want?

"I didn't mean to wake you." He hesitated, tracing a curl with his finger before pulling away. He would never take advantage of her, would never hurt her. She was dependent on him and he wouldn't abuse that.

"I wish you'd stay here."

"Lass, I'm sleeping in another tent for your protection."

Disappointment crossed her face, and she moved her hand back to the pillow.

"I can keep my hands to myself." He thought he heard her mutter "barely," but he couldn't be sure. "Stay and talk to me?"

He pulled over a chair from the table in the front room of the tent. "Only for a little while."

She smiled and sat up, pulling to covers to her chest. She was wearing some type of chemise, the material nearly transparent. He wasn't sure how long he'd be able to resist her.

"I see that Viola gave you back your ring." Zara nodded to the intaglio ring on his left hand.

Callum twisted it and gave her a half smile. "Yes. She, ah, threw it at me this morning and told me to be more polite to our guest. I do apologize for that."

Zara blinked. "Thank you. It seems that it's good to have Viola on my side."

He laughed. "She's an impressive, if opinionated, soldier."

"Is there anything I need to know about tomorrow?"

He blinked at her. "Is that what you wanted to talk to me about?"

She frowned. "Yes."

"We can go over it on the way to Vespertine. These people

are skeptical, so we need to go in being confident and lay out a plan for how they can help."

"Is that all? Be convincing." She yawned.

"You'll be great." He stood to leave, as if waiting for a sign from her. "Get some rest."

"You didn't have to leave your tent. I don't need to be in this one." She nodded at the corner where she'd strewn her belongings.

The way her hair spread across her shoulders, she was a temptation just sitting and talking with him.

"Goodnight, Princess." He walked out before she convinced him to spend the night.

CHAPTER FIFTEEN

The meeting in Vespertine was at the Corinthos Bank, half a day's ride away. Zara had blinked at Jeffors when he'd told her the agreed upon location.

"A bank?" Zara had asked.

"It is safe for such a meeting, and the guests' presence would not be remarkable. The other option would be the Opera House but that wasn't possible." Jeffors had added, "Do not inquire."

It took some persuading, but she arranged to sit with Callum in the middle of the table. Various Emburian nobles and merchants took up the rest of the seats. The room was longer than it was wide, located on the second floor of the bank. She and Callum had entered through a back entrance, with Viola and Ranulf accompanying them. Jeffors stayed at the Blue Flax camp, as he and Callum rarely traveled together when not on a raid.

The plan was simple: present their argument in favor of helping the rebels, show unification from both royal families, and make specific requests.

"Are you going to show them your ring?" Zara asked Callum before the other guests arrived.

"I'll do my best to convince them of my identity. With what Gracchus has done in his years of ruling, unseating him should be an easy argument to make."

"Tyrants are hard to remove from power," she said. "My mother would remind me of that. She favors a ruling style of compromise to avoid greater conflict. At least with diplomats."

"Not with her daughter," he added.

"No," Zara said. "Not in my case."

THE MEETING STARTED off well enough. In all, four merchants and three members of the Emburian nobility showed up. The Duke of Byrne, however, was not in attendance. Callum delayed the meeting just to see if he would arrive.

"Byrne's not coming," the Earl of Bamwich said. He eyed Zara, his ice-blue eyes taking her measure. "He's a cagey one."

Zara nodded. She needed to convince a roomful of people who were somewhat amiable to her proposition to take the next step and back the rebels.

"I'm glad you are all here. We'll make this brief. I've met with you, most of you that is, or corresponded with you as Ash, the rebel leader. I want to confirm that I am Prince Callum MacKinnon." Callum made sure to imbue his words with an extra sincerity since the men and one woman in this room were not known for their loyalty to his late father. It wouldn't help his cause to remind them of that. "I've pursued my family's claim through the courts and been denied."

A few shifted in their seats. Zara refolded her hands in her lap.

"And that is why we have sought your assistance. My family's claim is legitimate, and a usurper sits on the throne. The monarchists have formed a small army, but we are outnumbered by the kingdom's forces." He outlined their victories against Gracchus, as well as the king's failings, which were mostly a drain on the royal coffers for his expensive renovations of Blackthorne Castle, now Palace, as well as his policies of suspicion and paranoia.

"Good sirs and madam, my presence here cannot be known," Zara said.

"You were supposed to be married by now," Mr. Rufus Plume said. He was the owner of the Corinthos Bank. Jeffors had served with one of his brothers

"It was a delicate negotiation that did not end in matrimony," she said. A corner of her mouth hitched up. "I needed to come to Embury myself to confirm L'Ortagia's support for Prince Callum."

"Is that so?" Lady Willoughby asked. The countess was from an old family. Her mother had been close to Callum's before she'd been married. Lady Willoughby had married a much older earl, but she managed most of their public appearances by herself. She was known as an eccentric woman, but he thought of her as modern. "It seems that you are here in defiance of your queen."

"Yes." A slight flush rose on Zara's cheeks. "She and I have differing views. The prince and I have much in common, a mutual understanding of the risks the king poses to our countries. It only made sense to help."

"Your mother betrothed you to Torwyn, yet here you are," Lady Willoughby continued. She waved a hand airily. "It would seem you and the queen are at cross purposes. How could we count on her support?"

"We both want what's best for L'Ortagia." Zara hesitated and looked at Callum, but he didn't think it was for assistance. "Marrying a man under the will of a false king would, ultimately, be disastrous. The queen refused an audience with

Callum, but I did not. He is the true prince. He wears his family's signet ring as proof. He needs your help. It is in L'Ortagia's best interests to make sure the rightful family is on the throne."

Callum waited, ready to answer more objections and questions. Instead, the room was silent for a long minute.

Again, Zara met his gaze, her features composed and earnest. He wanted to reach for her hand. She was so brave, so trusting. He hoped he wouldn't let her down.

Lady Willoughby placed her hands on the table as if seeking balance from it. "What I am looking for is what would be the path forward? If you survived, did anyone else?"

"We are pursuing leads on both Duncan and Quinnah," Callum said quickly.

"But you don't know for certain if either survived," Mr. Plume said. "So, it is your claim to the throne that is at question."

Callum nodded. He'd know if his siblings were truly gone. Sometimes his hope vacillated with the day. His only certainty was that if he'd survived, there was a chance they could have too.

"Too much of this is unsettled and unsupported, Your Highness, or Ash," Lady Willoughby said drily. "A good jeweler could create such a ring."

"Lady Willoughby, I knew Callum when we were children. After spending time with him, I can assure you that he's the prince."

Lady W nodded at Zara, likely unmoved. "With what the king has demanded in taxes, we are squeezed. I need more to go on to invest in a rebel group than what I've seen today." Her gaze cut to Callum. "The queen and I were close before my marriage. I loved her like a sister. You were... wherever you were, but I was there, at those funerals."

"Did you see the bodies?" Callum asked.

"I helped bury them." Her spine straightened. "You bear a

strong family resemblance. You could very well be Maeve's middle child. But what you don't know, and can't appreciate, is the amount of effort that went into putting the royal family into the ground. We need more to go on if we are to go against the king. I'm sorry."

The countess' words sounded a death knell on their meeting. Chairs slid back and their guests waited until Zara stood before standing.

Lord Bamwich cleared his throat and addressed Zara. "I would have to concur with Lady W. You are convinced, but I do not believe that your mother is convinced. You may have lost her ear in not going through with the wedding, my dear."

Zara paled. Callum wanted to step in but knew he needed to let Bamwich voice his objections.

"I would need greater proof that Isabeau has any interest in supporting the prince."

"She does!" Zara insisted.

"You wouldn't be here if she did," Lord Bamwich said. "Every day that goes by, where you hide from her, hide from your responsibilities, lowers your usefulness to any cause, my dear."

CHAPTER SIXTEEN

"I've made your situation worse." Zara paced the room, skirts swirling, careful to stay away from the window.

"It was already terrible." Callum sat at the table, his chair half turned to face her. They had the room for a few more minutes before they'd need to leave. The guests' reactions to Zara had surprised him. "I assumed the two of us together would make a bigger difference to them."

The meeting had ended after Bamwich's words, though Lady Willoughby had paused at the door, her gaze on Zara. Callum had said goodbye to all of them, Zara at his side, glassy-eyed and stiff.

"Perhaps you should send me back to L'Ortagia. Bamwich was right. I should never have left like that. It was childish to run away."

"Zara, you're here now." He fought a familiar sinking feeling. Grief, like a tide pool, welled up and pulled him down. He focused on the woman before him. "We just got you out and safe. If you returned now, she'd marry you to Torwyn."

"What if she's right? What if marriage would soften the prince? Maybe I could lessen his... Somehow keep him on a better path?" She stopped and lowered her head. "I'd do it if I thought it would work."

He went to her, standing close but just out of reach. "A man should be worthy of you, not you lowering yourself to him, balancing him out."

She shook her head. "If the prince is truly like his father, then he's past influence, but I would try."

"Let me remind you who your betrothed is. Torwyn has ordered the torture of innocents because he believes they plot against his father. He's burned their fields as punishment. He participates in his father's disgusting rituals involving the blood sacrifice of animals. Those are not acts of his faith, but purely ambition. Whatever it takes to please the king."

She shuddered. "I know. I believe you. He's repellent and vile."

"A pompous ass, as well," he added. He reached for Zara's elbows, gently holding her. She still wouldn't look at him. "He would destroy you and your country. Maybe you could slow him down, but he'd do it eventually."

She tipped her chin up, her gaze finally meeting his. He'd imagined tears swimming in her eyes, but the princess looked lost. "How do you do it? I feel so helpless. This is like trying to push the ocean away from the shore."

He wanted to pull her into his arms and offer reassurance, promises that tomorrow would be a better day. Charm her with sweet kisses to turn her thoughts. But that wasn't in him anymore. It leeched out year after year. "All I know is that I survived and I have to try to make it right."

"You will." She touched his cheek with a simple brush of her fingers. "*We* will."

"Today went badly, but I need you here. You are the future of L'Ortagia." He pulled her closer, until her hands fell against his chest. "Your letters convinced me to trust you. We have to try again."

"Ah, so you do trust me?" She tilted her head.

"You doubt this? I brought you to one of the most important meetings we've ever had. Zara, if I'm cautious, it's only because I can start to see a future for Embury and I want it desperately."

"Very well." She narrowed her eyes, fingers tapping. "Then we'll have to try again."

Ranulf opened the door. "It's time."

Callum dropped his arms, but Zara reached for his hand. He led her from the room, her hand clutched in his.

THEIR HORSES WAITED a few blocks away. Zara had kept her head down and seen only a quick glimpse of the street when they'd arrived. She couldn't draw attention to herself—her borrowed cloak once again shrouding her figure and hair—but she stole glimpses here and there of the people of Vespertine. Perhaps if she better understood their lives, she could convince them to help Callum's cause.

They passed a pub near the end of the block, the sign overhead calling it the Rowdy Librarian. As they waited to cross, a whistle broke the sound of horses and carriages. Callum stiffened and tucked her behind him.

"In here," he said, as he retreated into the tavern with her.

It was dark as the curtains were pulled shut by a person dashing in behind them. "Royal Guard on patrol!" A short man in a green jacket brushed past them to the back of the tavern, adjusting his cap and grabbing an ale.

"Back here." Callum led her to a table, keeping her back to the door. He sat so he could see the front and back entrances, signaling to one of the barmaids for a dram. "It'll be quick. We're safer inside."

Ranulf stayed with them, sitting at the next table.

"Where's Viola?" Zara asked.

"She's making sure the horses will be ready to leave."

Their entrance must have attracted attention because the couple seated at the next table was whispering to each other and shooting them looks. Zara glanced at the other patrons. Several tables of people, perhaps a dozen in total, stared before turning to a man who sat in the corner.

"Do they know who you are?" She asked.

Callum shrugged. "Likely."

"Aren't you worried they'll tell the guard you're here?"

His lips pressed together. "I doubt it."

She frowned. "What are you not telling me?" She kept her gaze on him, but the energy in the room had shifted. Their barmaid brought two tankards, winking at both of them before hustling toward another table.

The man from the corner pulled up a chair, sat at their table, and tilted it back. His clothing was modest, if a bit eccentric. At least four timepieces hung from his waistcoat. His dark hair was pulled back, it and his short beard both liberally sprinkled with shocks of white. "Have you come to ask for my help, Ash?"

Callum took a deep drink. "Not after the last time, Varro. The spell was unreliable. I can't waste coin on that."

Varro hitched a thumb in her direction, shooting her a quick grin. "It was reliable enough to bring her here." He dipped his head. "Byrne didn't show? That got you all bent?"

"Who are you?" Zara asked, because Callum wasn't going to fill her in.

"I'm just a thorn in the lordling's side, if you ask him. Ungrateful wretch."

She gasped. Why didn't Callum didn't say anything?

"Are you going to drink this?" Varro asked. She shrugged, and he downed it in one gulp.

"Varro, I don't have time for this."

He pushed the tankard around, drawing circles on the table. He shot a disgusted look at Callum.

Then the entire tavern went silent. Callum froze, his lips half open as if he was finally going to speak to Varro.

"Too late, lordling." Varro turned to her. "Hopefully you'll be more open to what I have to say. We have three minutes before my power runs out and everyone can move again, so I'll be brief. Your prince dragged you into a nocturne bar. I don't think it was an accident. When he's desperate, he'll ask for our help. Otherwise he stubbornly continues on his own. We want to help. At least, some of us do. The king has made offers to many of us in... exchange for certain things. I won't be persuaded by *that man*, but many of the nocturnes are. He offers safety, at least for now. To come out of the shadows and be appreciated for our gifts."

"Wait. What did you do? How is it that I can move and they cannot?" Zara asked. She scanned the tavern. Everyone had frozen in place, their expressions unchanged. Not even the fire crackled in the hearth across from her.

"I can freeze time, now and again, in bursts. A useful power, no?" Varro tapped Callum on the nose.

"Obviously." Callum never mentioned he knew a nocturne who could do this. "What has Ash offered?" She had an idea of the answer, but she wanted to be clear.

"He's an improvement over his father, at least. The lordling thinks some of us helped that man kill his family. He only trusts us so far. He's offered nothing but small jobs, which he then grumbles about."

"So what do you want?"

"I want him to align with us, openly." Varro stared at her, unblinking. His words came from the heart, likely, of every nocturne in the tavern and beyond. "We are just as much a part of the rebellion as he is. As *you* are." He crossed his arms.

Could he know she was one of them too? She fiddled with

Callum's tankard, twisting it ever so slightly on the table. Varro handed it to her and she took a sip, wincing at the bitterness.

She slid the mug back to Callum using her powers. "I'll talk to him."

"Wonderful. In so many ways." Varro stood, grinning. "Congratulations on your unmarried status, Your Highness."

"Thank you for the role you must have played in it." Zara grinned back, relief at sharing her secret with someone in Embury filling her. "How do I contact you?"

"He knows how." Varro snapped his fingers and the bustle of the tavern resumed.

CHAPTER SEVENTEEN

"Did you take me there to meet with Varro? Why didn't you say anything to him?" Zara's barrage of questions about the nocturne leader started the moment they began their journey back to the Blue Flax camp.

"I went into the bar because we needed a place to hide. However...fraught my dealings with Varro might be, I trust them not to give me up."

Zara shot him an incredulous look. "Why is it fraught? It seems like you both want the same thing."

"Not entirely true," Callum bit out. His feelings about the nocturnes were ambivalent. He didn't know what they wanted. "I don't know how far I can trust them because of their past associations. Because Varro has his own battles to fight."

"Everyone has their own battles. If they were that disloyal they all would have joined with Gracchus years ago. Some may have, but most have not."

"They could still change their minds. They could play both sides." She didn't understand. She didn't know how far people could be pushed. That self-interest—or survival—could drive someone into desperation.

"Then give them reasons to choose your side. Give them the belonging they crave. You resist an alliance with them out of stubbornness." Zara's voice softened, her next words for his ears alone. "They are right here, Callum, asking for your help, offering theirs. They're Emburians."

"I know." She could cut through to the heart of a problem, even while respecting the complexities. He'd consider her entreaty. "I appreciate your counsel. I need to discuss it with Jeffors."

Zara nodded and silence fell between them the rest of the journey.

As they rode into camp, Zara asked, "When will we return to Vespertine?"

"Perhaps a week," he said. "Gracchus is scouring the countryside for you. We'll go back once it's safe. In the meantime we'll meet the nobles and merchants somewhere else. Since they haven't committed to our cause, I don't want to lead them to our safe houses and camps."

"Very well," she said. "Will you dine with me tonight?"

He wanted to.

In the days they'd spent together, his fondness for her had only grown. Despite the meeting ending badly, he could imagine many such times when it would be the two of them, side by side.

He needed to stay away for her own good. No matter his past, his present was unworthy of her. The best he could offer was a life at camp, and even his identity was tenuous with his own people.

"Not tonight. I'll send Viola to you."

"Viola, is there any word of Mondelac?" Zara had again woken up to nightmares of the fire engulfing the castle, helpless to act.

Days after they'd returned from Vespertine with no word from home, they were waiting to establish another meeting. Zara would have paced the camp if Callum had let her. Viola kindly served as a distraction.

"Hopefully soon." Viola ran her finger around a spot on the table where they played whist, tracing a knot in the wood. "Liam should have been back days ago. There's fear he was captured."

Zara gasped.

"Maybe not, though. Gracchus sometimes tortures those he captures." Her voice was low, so unlike the calm, steely soldier Zara had gotten to know.

Zara flinched in sympathy. Softly, so as to match Viola's tone, she spoke again. "Have you been captured by him?"

Viola nodded and a dark strand of hair slipped from her braid. Her hand shook and she flattened it on the table. Zara checked an urge to cover Viola's hand with hers. She heard stories every day at camp about the king, each one outlining his terribly cruelty. It was as if the well had no bottom.

"Gracchus had me for nearly a week before Callum got me out." Viola stared at her hand.

"Callum's good at that." Zara added more wine to Viola's glass, and hers as well, and they both drank. "I can listen if you are up for telling me the story."

Viola tilted her head, her deep brown eyes intent with purpose. "Your former betrothed was involved, which is why I volunteered for the mission to help you escape. I don't know where he came from, but that bastard is soulless."

Zara took a deep drink of her wine. "You are reaffirming all my fears. Please, continue."

"As you may know, the usurper ordered extensive work on the castle. My guess is he wanted to know how at least one of the children escaped Blackthorne. He walled up the staircase Callum left through. He also reopened the dungeon, closing off a few cells as his private holding pen. I was captured on a raid of one of the buildings on the castle grounds—I'd stayed too long trying to fill another wagon with anything that would help us—and his guards surrounded me."

"They took me to one of the cells. Only the barest sliver of sunlight showed at midday. Torwyn visited me. They tortured me for information about the rebels. I sent them on fool's quests, anything to buy time. On the fifth day... I broke. I told them things I shouldn't have. Jeffors said it never came to anything. I'm not sure why. But that night, Torwyn came to me again. I thought he would kill me. He gagged me and bound my wrists, put a sack over my head, and took me to another room —I don't know where it was but we were outside for several paces so I don't think it was in Blackthorne."

Zara swallowed the bile in her throat. Viola paled, her eyes glazed. "Where did he take you?"

"He took me to watch a ceremony. It was in another grim corner of the place, with hooded, robed men, torchlight lining the walls. I don't know what he'd intended. I watched them sacrifice a doe—though the poor thing was nearly dead anyway —in some ritual. They slit its throat and painted themselves in blood."

Zara recoiled in her chair. "Did you see who was there?"

"The king and what looked like most of his guard. I don't know them all and it was hard to see their faces. Prince Adrian stood by. He didn't say anything. It seemed like he was being made to watch too. Maybe that was his initiation. Torwyn was obsessed with showing him up."

"What? How?" She'd never heard of a rivalry between the cousins. Adrian had represented Torwyn this spring, but hadn't hinted at any strife with him, not that she would have expected him to.

"The king sat at the head of the dais. The offering was for him. Torwyn was excited because he'd arranged the sacrifice of the doe. He said Adrian hated it and he was the only one committed to his father's cause. Something about being a nocturne. I assumed he meant Adrian."

Adrian's nocturne status was well known across both kingdoms.

"The sacrifice had to do with nocturnes?"

"More like a blessing towards their magic," Viola said. "I didn't understand it all. Once it was over and I was certain they weren't going to sacrifice me, Torwyn carted me back. Somewhere along the way, Callum attacked him and freed me."

"He couldn't leave you behind," Zara said.

Viola nodded slowly. "I raged at him that he should have killed the prince when he had the chance."

"Do you know why he didn't?" Zara asked, her mind swirling with everything Viola had told her. It only strengthened her resolve. She'd make her mother listen to the stories, all of them, until she brought her to the rebels' side.

"You'll have to ask him yourself." Viola sipped at her wine and rolled her eyes. "We don't agree on that point. I grew up a simple girl from a small village. Even I know if you catch the thief who's been picking off your herd, you don't set him free."

Zara would have to hear Callum's side, though she had a feeling she'd understand his point of view. It was clear that despite their disagreement, Viola and Callum were close. He'd trusted her to recite the spell to close the portal at Mondelac. He also charged Viola, despite there being many other women at the Blue Flax camp, with her care and protection.

A part of her envied their closeness. Other than the first night of her escape and the night they returned from Vespertine, Callum avoided her efforts to draw him into more personal conversation. And yet, hearing Viola's story, she admired him all the more.

"Tell me about growing up in Summerly. Is that right?"

Viola laughed. "Yes, Highness. It's in the northwest, close to some of the highest peaks of the mountain range." As Viola talked about her small village, her eyes lit up and a smile flickered across her face. Some of what Viola fought for was a return to her peaceful village, to the time before the current king.

"Of the young people in my village, almost all serve in the king's army or the rebellion's."

"Had you wanted to be a soldier? Was that something your family planned for you?" Zara asked.

"Maybe part of me. When the time came, there really wasn't a choice. There were no more eligible men in the village to marry—none who weren't older than my father. And my two older brothers had been killed in the prince's raids."

"I'm so sorry." Zara could only offer sympathy and a promise. "I will do all that I can to get him off the throne and turn the tide."

Viola dashed the tears from her cheeks. "For a minute there, when you jumped out of the portal, I was worried you'd changed your mind. A lot of us doubted you would stay once you got here."

Zara flushed. She'd had an idea of what to expect, but the reality was worse. The rebels were all kind to her, but the pace was frenetic and the accommodations... not what she was used to. This time with them was something she had needed. "In case it hadn't worked and I ended up staying for the wedding, I didn't want Adrian to know I'd plotted with Callum. My sister is clearly the one with better acting skills."

Viola huffed out a laugh and shuffled the cards. "I'd wondered if, at the moment you were about to leave, you doubted yourself."

"Perhaps a bit." Zara's fingers grew damp against the cards. "Leaving with all of you is unlike anything I've ever done. Panic set in."

"Only natural."

"Abandoning my wedding seemed so impulsive."

"As I was preparing to leave for this camp, years ago, saying goodbye to my parents, my hands started shaking. They wouldn't stop. I thought I'd stop breathing, as I couldn't draw a deep enough breath. My mother sat me down and said that sometimes the body has old fears, and tells you as much, even when you know in your heart what you need to do."

"Did it help?" Zara asked.

"Aside from certain memories, yes. My hands don't shake before a raid anymore." Viola drew a card. "I trust that I've set myself on the path I need to be on."

"Me too," Zara said softly, shuffling the cards.

CHAPTER EIGHTEEN

One week later, the camp arose early to ready for another trip into Vespertine. Zara was ready when Callum went to fetch her. She'd unrolled one of the maps he stored in his tent and was studying it. Just her presence soothed him, as if, given enough time, she could solve all the problems they faced. The lantern's rays washed her skin with a hint of gold.

He'd expected to feel a certain affinity for her. They had similar childhoods and status, mutual goals and a common enemy. But this attraction to her, this pull and need to be near her took him by surprise.

"Vespertine and the forest along the edge of the Blue Flax are the boundary between the rebels' land and the king's?" Zara traced the path of the river, following it west to where it edged a few miles from Blackthorne Palace.

"Yes. One of a few such places." Callum's gaze caught on the locations of their camps. "A few years ago we were scattered across Embury. With a couple exceptions, Gracchus has pushed us farther north."

"It's as if he'd push you into the sea," she said in a low voice.

Her fingers coasted over the different regions of Embury. L'Ortagia had mostly valleys and hills while Embury's topography had more variation.

"He'd like nothing better." They'd been over this before. She knew how the rebels had fought the usurper. How, in his darker moments, Callum feared they'd lose to Gracchus. "What do you see?"

"I see a city that is persuadable." Zara pinched her temples. "And I'm imagining what Gracchus would do to L'Ortagia, wondering where the faithful would be if Torwyn became their king."

"There's some extra motivation for our meeting. We need to leave." Callum rolled up the map, storing it carefully. "Torwyn has returned to Embury and met with Gracchus. They're searching for you."

Her gaze met his. There were only so many places she could hide. "Sooner or later, they'll come here, won't they?"

He didn't want to scare her but he wouldn't shield her from the truth. "He knows where to look."

The camp was in danger, and Callum didn't know how long he and Zara could stay there. They left before dawn. Today, they were meeting with the Duke of Byrne on the outskirts of Vespertine in his observatory. Upon his marriage, the duke had purchased buildings that belonged to the old college. The observatory on the hill was rumored to be his favorite.

Thankfully, Zara shared Callum's sense of resolve. All week, she'd been going over what she wanted to say and how she would convince the Emburians of her country's commitment to them. She'd practiced with Viola and Jeffors, learning what type of objections she'd have to overcome.

"This one will be different, Callum." She paced the antechamber of the observatory where they waited. Her dark hair was pulled up, with loose, long curls trailing down her back. Her gown was a simpler style than the one she'd fled

L'Ortagia in. It helped her disguise, from a distance. Up close, her regal bearing was undeniable.

Callum had had time to reflect on what went wrong at their last meeting in Vespertine. He'd make sure they wouldn't make those mistakes again.

The door opened and a footman led them into a room with a soaring ceiling. A row of tables took up one side, various bottles and jars filling shelves along the wall at the end of the room. The huge telescope had been dismantled and sold to a different school. The aperture closed. A small deck where the telescope had stood was a few steps down from the main room. The footman led them to the top of the stairs and bowed, leaving them with the duke.

"My errant royals, welcome," the duke called, waving them down. He was younger than Callum's parents. Lines etched his forehead and bracketed his mouth. His red hair was lighter along his temples, the rest pulled back into a queue. He was a handsome man, his features even, but there was something, perhaps a smirk to his mouth or an arched brow, that Callum watched for.

Callum held Zara's hand as she descended. Ranulf stayed behind at the top of the stairs, discretely out of sight but close enough should the prince need him.

Byrne stood, offering them seats across from where he'd sat. He'd assembled a makeshift library in the half-circle of space, shelves and stacks of books pushed to the edges but arranged neatly, meticulously. A row of stoppered vials was lined up on a tray to his left.

Callum did the introductions, using their titles.

"Of course. My apologies for not being at Corinthos last week. I was called away." The duke smiled. "I'm sure you know how that is, madam."

Zara stared at him. That he began their meeting by mocking one of the most perilous events of her life was not a good start. "Another comment like that and we will leave. We carried on just fine without you last week."

"My apologies. I meant to make light of what was surely a stressful situation. A bad habit of mine, truly."

"As you are aware, we have continued to have such stresses. If you are less than serious about hearing what we have to say, please speak up." She sat straighter in her chair and paused. "Good. Callum, why don't you begin?"

Callum laid out his request. Byrne had heard it before, but not in person. This time, as he went over the events of his family's assassination as well as how he came to be with the rebels, he tried to home in on what a man of ambition would want to hear. Despite Callum's birthright, he focused on his father's works and legacy. "And, as you are aware, should my brother be returned to the throne, we would need a new court, composed of loyalists."

"Without doubt," Byrne said. He leaned forward. "May I ask, why aren't you seeking the crown for yourself? You could remove the usurper and *then* look for your brother."

ZARA HAD WONDERED the same thing. It was as if Callum lacked the desire for himself. Perhaps it was because he'd spent most of his life knowing his brother would be the future king.

"I want to believe my brother is alive. My sister too," Callum said simply.

"May the fates have willed it so," Byrne said softly. "Madam, what is your take on all of this? It appears that Callum's marriage to you would solve Embury's problems. Our prince should use his time wisely while you are here with us. Wed you and beget heirs. That would ensure a more lasting connection between our countries."

The words stuck in Zara's throat. His manner was less

polished than her mother's but had a similar cutting edge. In coming to Byrne instead of her mother, had she traded one strategist for another? One Emburian prince for another? Was marriage all she had to offer?

"Prince Callum and I have an understanding. I am his guest and ally while I'm here. That is all you need to know. My marital status is my business alone."

"You can't be serious." Byrne laughed. "Who you marry has everything to do with your future and that of L'Ortagia's. Your power rests in that." He held up a hand, bowing his head, his mockery still stinging. "Pardon, my dear, but wanting something different doesn't make this less true. You'd do well to be married to a man of your choosing before you return to the queen or she'll choose *again* for you. Naiveté doesn't become you."

"Byrne, that's enough," Callum said. "She's risking her future to help us."

"Until the two of you understand what you could do together, you are wasting our time. Plume told me how you hadn't convinced them to finance the rebellion."

"The rebellion is the only group putting up any resistance to Gracchus," Zara said. "He has an army, the seat of the kingdom, and the courts. Without the rebels putting a drain on his resources, he would have squeezed the rest of the nobility dry. He will use you all for his purposes. Not only did he lay waste to the royal family, but he will do so with the kingdom. It's appalling that you take convincing at all."

Byrne winced.

"We are aware, dear Zara, that you are the future of L'Ortagia. Do all that you can in your time with our prince. This cannot merely be a summer holiday for you. As I understand it, our Callum, the only current and rightful heir, rescued you from marriage to Gracchus' cruel, sycophantic dolt of a son.

Once you go back, you'll no longer have any ties to us, nor any loyalty."

"That's entirely untrue. I'll forever be grateful to Callum for helping me. L'Ortagians will be grateful when they are not held under Torwyn's rule. The ties between our countries will remain strong. My mother will recognize Callum as the true heir."

"And where will the rest of us in Embury be? You are asking for us to put our titles, land, and monies on the line for our rebel prince. And then you'll walk away, a free woman. A marriage between you and Callum would ensure your loyalty, L'Ortagia's loyalty to *us*."

"Byrne, I assure you that a marriage isn't necessary," Zara said. Her cheeks heated. She felt like a length of iron in the smithy's, hammered until she came out a blade.

With a raised brow, Byrne said, "What else have you been approved by the queen to negotiate?"

Zara had no answer for him.

"Unless you are willing to play the cards you hold, you should go back to your mother and beg her forgiveness."

Her last engagement ended mere days ago. She'd freed herself from one man, only to be tethered to a different one. It was maddening. All her preparation, and she was back to where they'd been in Vespertine. Her word, her presence and promises would never be enough for them.

Zara stood, and both men joined her. She approached Byrne, her stays tight against her chest, her breaths shallow and fast. Her hands were steady as she stood before him, fingers steepled. She wanted to shout at him that she wasn't his to order about, nor did she need any more marital advice, or yet another man to question her loyalty. But after her time with the rebels, and hearing Viola's stories and more like them, she had to persuade the duke to their side.

"If I agree to marry Callum, what is your offer? Your true

king's army lies scattered, and you sit in your nursery room playing at being an apothecary. Make us your best offer, make good on it, and then we'll be back to talk again, about your legacy with the MacKinnons in Angus's line."

Byrne tilted his head, his expression intrigued. "Well done, my dear. My offer is to fulfill your request." Then he swallowed and crossed to a shelf, pulling off a set of portable writing implements. He scrawled a short note and sealed it. "Take this to Plume. Your funds should be available in two days' time. Please accept my congratulations."

CHAPTER NINETEEN

A carriage took them from the observatory to the next meeting point. Ranulf and Viola played coachmen. Callum sat across from Zara, his excitement nearly bubbling over. He wanted to shout for joy, call it out into the valley below.

"Zara, that was amazing! Now that we have Byrne, it's only a matter of time before Bamwich and Willoughby come around. You were glorious!"

She put her fingers to her temples and gave him a wan smile. "That bastard. I think he planned that all along."

"Very likely." He had fought too long and hard to equivocate over the details. The win was what mattered. "He'd never give without getting something in return."

She stared at him. "I didn't leave my own wedding only to be forced into another!"

"We don't have to do anything right away," he said quickly. "If we make our betrothal official, that might be enough for now."

"I don't want to be forced into this," she said. "Byrne does not order me to do anything!"

"What did you expect? Did you bring any monies with you? You are here on borrowed time if you wish to go back to L'Ortagia. We have to use what we are given, Zara."

"I know that." She stared out the window. "We don't even know if we would suit."

"Aside from today, we've shown an enormous capacity for that. We've known each other since childhood."

"Loosely." Her gaze shot to him. Was that doubt in her expression? "And that is not a good reason."

He frowned at her. "Zara, your parents nearly chose me for you anyway. You'd be doing what they already intended."

"That is not better. Can't you understand wanting to choose a man for myself? My parents were miserable together. They loathed each other. All Sidony and I could count on was the two of us."

Callum shot her a look. "You can grow to love someone."

"Or hate them. If my father liked something I did, she hated it. He ignored what she showed attention to. It was horrible. I didn't know who I was supposed to be. It was one person for her and another for him, all until he died."

"How old were you?"

"Ten. My mother hasn't spoken a kind word about him since."

"Zara, I had no idea." He held out his hand and she placed hers in his. "I would never be so cruel to you or to our children. I would do everything I could to make them feel adored."

Zara sighed and sagged against the back of the carriage. "I need some time to adjust to this."

"Of course." He lifted her hand to his mouth and kissed the back of it.

"You're only doing that because of Byrne." She pulled her hand back, fire in her gaze again.

"Not true. I've been wanting to do that for days." He had nothing to lose by admitting that. He'd avoided her in order not to form more of a connection to her. But now, that would be unavoidable. Byrne had cleared a way for the rebels and for Callum to have the monies he needed to search for his siblings.

"You left me alone nearly the entire week." She stared at him incredulously. "And right now, you'd say anything to make me amenable."

"Can't it be both? Can't I see the wisdom of this plan *and* want you?"

Her mouth fell open. "We had all this time. I've practically thrown myself at you and you've done nothing. How would I trust your affections? They could be different next week."

"Zara, please. You don't understand." He wanted to tell her of his fears, that he couldn't stand the thought of losing another person. "I've been focused on my survival and the rebellion. I'm in no position to woo a woman, much less for marriage."

"And?" She waved her hands, tilting her head at him.

"Give me a moment, Zara. I wrote to you out of desperation and then here you are, with your hair and your stockings and the way you smell. You are here under my protection. What would you be thinking of me if I pressed my suit with you that first night?"

"I don't know," she said weakly. "I didn't know you had a suit."

Callum put his head in his hands, the thread of things he couldn't tell her slipping away from him, leaving a bare truth. "Any man with a heart beating in his chest would pursue you. Zara"

The carriage stopped before she could answer him.

CHAPTER TWENTY

When they returned to Blue Flax camp, Zara requested a hot bath. It had been offered since the first night she'd arrived, but she understood the effort it took to make one. She'd made due by bathing in the river. Tonight, she needed a bath.

She replayed their visit with Byrne, going over any other options she could have taken to avoid the outcome. Eventually, she wore herself out. Agreeing to the marriage was the only sensible option. She almost fell asleep in the tub before Viola called her to get ready for dinner.

Zara had dinner with Callum, Jeffors, Viola, and Ranulf. The entire camp celebrated the news of Byrne's patronage. Zara forbade Callum from telling anyone other than Jeffors the terms they'd agreed to.

The general was pleased. He made several toasts throughout the evening, as did Callum. Zara stood and made a short one.

"To Viola, for protecting me and keeping me company while I'm away from home. I am blessed to know you all, and especially this brave soldier."

Viola, who blushed at nothing, flushed at the praise.

As their festivities wound down, Callum escorted Zara back to his tent. "Zara, may I speak with you?"

"Of course." She'd caught him watching her tonight. After their carriage ride, she'd needed to sort through her thoughts.

She greeted the guard, watching as Callum closed the tent flap behind him. "Let me pour the wine."

He took the glass she offered but didn't drink. "Zara, I—"

"Remember our first night in the cottage? Why did you kiss me that night? Why haven't you kissed me again?"

"I thought I went over this in the carriage."

"You mostly told me that you'd been reluctant to pursue me for marriage because you didn't want to put undue pressure on me. Somewhere in there you told me that you wanted me." She felt foolish, but she knew she couldn't sleep if she didn't get clarity.

He set down his glass. "I want to kiss you most days I'm around you."

She sighed, angry with herself for going down this path with him. "You don't have to say that."

"I clearly should have said something to you." He indicated the tent and the broader camp beyond. "This wasn't the place. I've also never courted a woman. What would that look like: a midnight raid and then we enjoy looking at the stars?"

That sounded wonderful.

"You don't even know that much about me. But now, after today, you are ready for marriage?"

"Princess, nothing's been decided. I want to give you all the time you need." His voice softened, sinking into her. If he had any idea of what he did to her, she'd lose her advantage. Her mother would be appalled. She steeled herself against his attempts to soothe her.

"Stop saying that. Stop being so calm about this." Her voice rose. She wasn't sure what she wanted to convince him of, but he was so reasonable about all of it that it grated. Would he be this accepting when he found out he was bound by marriage to a nocturne? Would he make her hide her powers too? All week she'd practiced them. She done silly things with them like making her bed or cutting her meat if she ate alone. But they were tasks that took several steps and after a week she could do them without tiring too quickly, all with her powers.

She backed away, setting down her half-empty glass of wine. "You kissed me a couple times and now you're ready for marriage."

Callum stepped toward her, his amber eyes haunted. "There is death all around me. I would do close to anything to make it stop."

"Then kiss me like you mean it."

He closed the distance and, cupping her jaw, kissed her softly.

She wanted to hold herself back, as if she hadn't tracked his movements, watched his mouth when he spoke, but she couldn't. His touch awakened something within her, a tenderness and a heat she hadn't felt in a long time. She kissed Callum like she'd wanted to when he came out of the shadows of her room at Mondelac.

It started gently, but as his lips moved over hers, he responded to her too. She clutched his shoulder, anchoring herself as she rose up on her toes. Their breaths mingled between kisses, lips sliding together like they'd done this dozens of times before.

One of the guards outside her tent coughed, and they drew apart.

"Zara, I didn't mean..."

She put a finger to his lips. "Not just yet."

She took his hand, leading him farther into the tent, past the table to another set of curtains that were drawn back, and next to the bed.

~

CALLUM WANTED to tell Zara she was beautiful, like a fairy queen, with her dark hair that tumbled over her shoulders and deep blue eyes that saw so much. Her lips were reddened from kissing, her cheeks flushed a soft pink.

He'd left his coat in Jeffors's tent, had rolled up his sleeves long before dinner. He untied the laces at his neck and pulled off his shirt.

She reached behind her back, loosening something in her gown. The skirt gave way and she let the dress fall to her ankles. She was a vision of soft curves and long legs.

He scooped her up and lifted her to the bed, following her down. He lay beside her and kissed her neck until she turned her head.

She brushed a strand of hair that had fallen across his brow. She rolled toward him, hitching a leg over his hip, and kissed him again.

Heat traveled up his spine and he resisted the urge to clutch her closer. She surprised him over and over today. But this, this swirling tension, that tightened and curled each time she touched him surprised him the most.

She wasn't supposed to kiss like that.

They should have had a simple sweet kiss, something that sealed the arrangement they'd made with Byrne.

Instead, Zara kissed him back with what felt like pent-up emotion. She kissed him like she knew how she wanted to be kissed. It didn't surprise him, given what he knew about her, that she was more experienced than he'd first thought. Though she would contemplate and weigh her options, Zara was a woman who, once she had an idea about what she wanted, went after it full force.

It was devastating. He was supposed to be demonstrating his attraction, but instead, he got it back from her tenfold.

Their limbs tangled on the bed, her shift bunched at her hips, her stays loose and tossed onto the floor. His heart thundered in his ears when she dragged her nails up the back of his neck.

Callum pulled away, gaze roaming her face while he caught his breath. "What are we doing? I only meant to kiss you."

She blinked up at him. "Well, I liked it. Quite a bit."

He laughed, dropping a quick kiss on her collarbone. "I should go."

"Not yet." She ran her hands down his sides, firmly enough not to tickle. "You feel so good."

So did she.

He cupped her face again. "I won't do anything that would put a babe in you, but let me give you pleasure."

She narrowed her eyes a fraction at him. "Is this you proving something to me?"

"No." His thumb smoothed her brow. "Not everything is transactional. This is because I want to."

"If you want to, then yes," she said.

He wanted to ask about her experience but stopped himself. It didn't matter and they could talk later.

She pulled his head down and he kissed her again, lost in the way she fit against him. He groaned and rotated his hips. She clutched him to her, arching up for more. If he kept this up, he might spend against her leg.

Callum pulled back and slid down. He hooked his thumbs into the straps of her chemise and tugged them lower, loosening the neckline for more give. Her nipples were already drawn into tight points beneath the sheer fabric.

He was a lucky man. "Zara, you humble me."

He cupped her breasts, squeezing just a bit, and she laughed. She tweaked a lock of his hair, still giggling.

He mouthed her nipples through her shift, licking the peaks until they grew damp. He blew on one and she shuddered, releasing a breath on a moan.

He pushed up her shift, impatient with the fabric between them. His fingers trailed a path down her belly, over soft skin that glowed like honey. He found her maidenhair and parted her curls, slipping down to the bud of her sex.

She arched again, her breasts in his face and her legs falling open. He sucked at her nipples, his fingers dipping into her sex and sliding over her clitoris.

"Callum," she said, her voice tight.

Her hands were in his hair, at his neck, trailing over his shoulders. Her breath came in quick pants and soft moans.

"Zara, let go." He rubbed over her tight bud, his fingers sliding. She grew wetter and hotter. He ground his answering hardness into her hip. He'd loosened his breeches enough to adjust himself.

Touching her made him instantly hard.

He moved his mouth to where her neck met her shoulder. As he licked and sucked at her, she gasped. Her body tightened around him, the finger he worked inside her held still by her grip as pleasure seized her.

"Yes, yes," she cried out.

He kept up the strokes, wanting her climax to last.

She curled up against him, tiny quivers squeezing his finger.

He kissed her mouth once she fell limp. Then he rose from the bed and brought her a damp cloth from the washstand in the corner.

His cock pounded for attention and he ignored it. He pulled Zara against him, her back to his front, and tucked his nose into her hair. She smelled of the lilacs she'd somehow found in their camp. She curled back against him and clutched his hip.

Shouts sounded outside.

Jeffors burst into his tent. "Milord! We are under attack!"

CHAPTER TWENTY-ONE

Zara pushed at Callum's hand and tried to squirm away. Jeffors spun on his heel and directed his words to the other side of the tent.

"Gracchus sent men to raid the camp."

Callum climbed off the bed, pulling a blanket over her to hide her near nakedness. She sat up and looked around for where her stays had landed on the floor.

"Callum, you have to leave," Jeffors said. "Leave and take her with you."

"What? No! Put extra guards with the princess. I'm suiting up and protecting our camp."

"No, sire, please. You must leave."

Zara located her stays and dress. She snapped out of her sensual fog and hurriedly dressed.

"Zara, help him see reason." Jeffors' calm in the face of the attack and their state of undress was impressive.

"Jeffors, I have no intention of staying here," Zara said.

Callum spun around from strapping on his battle gear to glare at her. "I'm not taking you out into a battle." He collected his weapons and she thought she heard him mutter, "I won't lose you now."

"How many attacked the camp?" She smoothed her hair, pulling it over her shoulder to braid.

"Nearly a dozen. A small raid, given the size of Gracchus's army." Jeffors's gaze darted between Zara and Callum.

"It was only a matter of time before he found us." Fully dressed and armored up, Callum paused, brows drawn. "I need Zara protected."

"That's what I'm trying to do."

Callum let out an exasperated breath. "We don't have time for this. Have they set fire to the camp?"

"Yes!" Jeffors turned back around. His tone was commanding. "You need to leave. Go to the keep. You'll be safe there."

"We are safer here with our small army."

Zara donned her scratchy cloak, vowing to sew a liner into it when she next had the chance.

Jeffors got louder. "They know where our camps are. Go to another, and they'll raid it until they find her."

"Fine." Callum reached for Zara's hand. "We're leaving."

THE SMOKE WAS thick but helped in their escape. Callum relieved the guard who'd been at the back of the tent. He gave him a swift pat and pulled Zara along the back path, staying low and running as best they could. They reached the last line of tents when a soldier in black armor came out from behind a tent, sword raised. Callum dodged his first swing, then his hand shot out, using the hilt end to knock into the soldier's temple. He fell to the ground. Zara stepped over him and they kept going.

"We are going into the trees, Princess. Can you remember which one opens up to a small path?"

"I think so." Viola had showed her the path the first few days she was at Blue Flax.

"Start making your way to the clearing. We're heading that way."

"Aren't you coming with me?"

"I'll be right behind you. I have to make sure we aren't being followed."

"Very well."

Keeping low to the ground, they made it through the trees a few feet then stopped behind a fallen tree trunk. Callum scanned the way they'd come for Gracchus's soldiers.

"We can't stay to help?" She must have spotted the tents, several of which were burning. Soldiers threw buckets of water on the blaze and the air was thick with smoke.

He met her gaze. "No."

She squeezed his hand and turned, gathering her skirts and making her way toward the path in the forest.

He waited until she moved farther into the forest before he continued along the line of trees, advancing closer to the skirmish. Two of Gracchus's men stood near the perimeter of the camp. He snuck up behind one and slit his throat.

He cleaned off his knife on a bed of clover and made to stand. The second soldier pointed a sword at his neck. Slowly, Callum edged his fingers into his boot, grabbing hold of the dagger he kept there.

"Where are they?"

It was dark behind the tents, with just enough light to make out shapes but not see details distinctly. In case he was more recognized than he'd thought, he lowered his voice to respond.

"Who?" he asked gruffly.

"The princess and your leader." The soldier pressed the sword point closer, using the flat edge to lift Callum's chin. There was a warm trickle where the blade cut into his neck.

Callum kept his voice low. "I don't know."

"But you do. Your man Liam told us they were both here. Take me to them." The soldier moved his weight to his back foot, presumably waiting for Callum to stand. He slowly got up on his knees, the dagger hidden in his right hand, and then shifted to the side to place a foot on the ground, preparing to stand. The soldier moved the sword back, allowing Callum to turn. The moment he leaned forward, Callum feinted left, dodging the sword that swung in that direction. He charged right, knocking the pommel of his dagger into the soldier's temple. The soldier dropped his sword and fell next to his comrade. Callum shook his head and tied their hands together.

There wasn't time to look for Jeffors to let him know that Gracchus's men had captured Liam, their scout. His heart squeezed in his chest at the thought of one of his men under Gracchus's control. He'd have to find a way to get him a message so they could free Liam. Seeing that the side closest to the forest was empty now, he ran back into the trees after Zara, Hopefully she'd made it to the fountain.

The fight had taken his mind off what had been happening in his tent before they were interrupted. He was reasonably certain he could take the soldiers, but there was nothing like a sword point at one's neck to finally drain the blood from his erection. He adjusted himself and loped after the princess.

CHAPTER TWENTY-TWO

A half-moon lit the night sky, but it was enough to make out the tents and temporary dwellings of the rebel camp. Not that Gracchus needed the scant light to locate them along the Blue Flax. The rebels had been at this spot near the river for several months now. It was a decently defensible position. Gracchus couldn't lead a large army to defeat them without alerting them. He didn't want to use any more of his military power than was absolutely necessary. Their resistance was a drain on his rule.

Gracchus looked back at the young soldier, gagged and lying tied to a tree. His face was barely recognizable and already starting to swell. It had taken longer than he would have guessed, but Torwyn's men had broken him. Callum would feel the pain of this one in particular.

The king spat in the dirt. The torture had been unnecessary, because he knew where most of the rebel camps were. To save time, he'd needed confirmation that Callum had the princess at Blue Flax. His search party had happened upon their scout. Gracchus had wanted to be present when his men returned Zara and captured Callum, bringing them both to him.

When flames shot up in the night sky, he smacked his lips, pleased to see the raid beginning.

Gracchus had magnanimously had one of the squires take water to their prisoner. He wasn't ready to give it to him yet, but placing it within eyeshot should be enough of a reward.

The scout gave a muffled groan. The fact that he still seemed to react to the water showed Gracchus the young soldier wasn't broken quite yet, a fact that was most pleasing, for it had been a while since he'd been able to do his own torturing.

Sounds of the raid carried even from this distance. He chuckled. Gracchus planned to return them all to Mondelac Castle to resume the wedding plans. He should have insisted the wedding be held in Embury, but he had gone along with the L'Ortagian queen's demands. He was quite pleased with the match for his son and would have willingly had the wedding in the middle of a lake if that was what was needed to make it happen.

As the days had dragged on and his men were not able to track down Zara's whereabouts, he'd begun making alternate plans. He kept Adrian at Mondelac to be his eyes and ears, but he was already considering other possibilities, ones that would help validate his rule and endear his people to him.

He snapped his fingers at the squire again and indicated that the scout could be allowed a drink. He tamped down his disgust at the gurgling. Thankfully riders finally came up the hill.

Torwyn approached with knights from his guard.

"You dare approach me without them?" Gracchus asked.

"They were gone. We searched the tent he'd been keeping her in and it was empty."

"What? How could you let this happen?"

"They must have known we were coming. I don't know."

"Did you take any prisoners?"

Torwyn's normally stoic expression faltered, and he paused, his gaze skittering along the ground. "No, the rebels fought us and drove us back. They captured three of our men."

"In hopes of converting more to their side?" His voice rose in fury. "Kill. Them. Bring Ash and Zara to me. Unless all you are capable of is failure."

"The mission was a raid, sire. We didn't get the target this time."

"You didn't get anything," Gracchus said. "An utter failure."

"They were gone." Torwyn held up his hands. "What more could I have done?"

"Now they have another head start. Again. At least we have one of theirs. He's no longer of use to us. Dispatch him." Gracchus strode off to his horse, readying to leave before he slapped his son. He mounted his horse and waved at the burning tents in the distance. "Burn the whole camp down."

Torwyn turned to the scout tethered to the tree and sliced his throat. His foot slipped in the blood at his feet and he staggered to keep from falling.

As Gracchus turned his horse, he called out, "Torwyn, to me."

Torwyn wiped his knife on the grass and approached the king. "Father."

"I am leaving half my guard with you. Destroy the camp. Get the princess back. Then return to me when you have her."

CHAPTER TWENTY-THREE

Zara ran along the path through the woods, using her powers to clear the larger pieces of debris. She slid several branches and sticks aside so she wouldn't trip, but left the leaves and fallen pieces of bark where they were, covering the trail.

She was out of breath and drained from using her powers in so many small bursts, but she made it to the fountain in the middle of a small clearing and sat on its edge. The air was thick with smoke. Clouds only gave glimpses of the night sky. She hated running away. It was yet another fire, people were in danger, and she was leaving. Someday she would figure out how best to stay and help.

"Zara, I'm here. Are you all right?" Callum ran over to her. Drops of blood dotted his shirt.

"What happened? Is it yours?"

"It's fine. Bleeding's stopped," he said.

"Where are we going?"

"I have an estate farther north that's abandoned. We'll go there and wait for word from Jeffors. Come on."

He held out a hand and she took it, squeezing in relief.

"We're far enough from camp to use this." He held up a lantern.

He drew flint from the bag over his shoulder and lit the wick.

"There, now. One more thing." Reaching for her with the other hand, he pulled her to him for a swift kiss. His lips were sure and strong, almost taking her breath. Her body throbbed, swamped with too many sensations, and she clutched his waist, holding on for more contact.

He rested his forehead against hers. "I'm glad you're safe."

"You look like you put up a good fight," she said.

He hesitated. "Every time I have to... fight one of his soldiers it takes something out of me. They're my father's people."

She put a finger to his lips. "It doesn't have to make sense. You're trying to survive, as they are."

Callum closed his eyes. "I wish it got easier."

THEY WALKED through the forest for hours. Zara stumbled every few steps, but she didn't complain.

"Can you make it a little longer, Princess?"

She yawned and pulled her cloak closer. "Yes."

When she swayed on her feet, Callum called for them to stop.

He blew out the lantern and hooked it to his belt. He walked over to her and swung her up in his arms, fitting her head against his shoulder.

"I can make it."

"I know. We're almost there."

She settled in, arms around his neck. Her breathing quickly turned even, and he got little chills every time she exhaled, the air tickling across his neck.

A bolt of protectiveness hit him, along with relief that they'd escaped the camp.

Around a turn in the path was the large rock that marked this entrance to the forest. He spotted the estate house, a curl of smoke rising out of the main chimney. He strode across the back lawn and was greeted by two greyhounds that occasionally ran along the back hills.

Once his feet hit the crushed gravel of the back path, he wasn't surprised to see Omara standing in the window watching his approach. He nodded and she left the window.

Callum passed the gardens and the back staircase, weariness sinking in. They'd be safe for another few hours, perhaps even a day, then they'd have to move again.

"Is that who I think it is?" Omara asked.

Callum stopped and resettled Zara in his arms. "It is."

"You'll be needing a carriage as well?"

"If it wouldn't be too much trouble."

"Come inside, then. You can stay in the south wing. She can be put next to my chamber."

"She stays with me."

"Oh, that's how it is, then?"

He grimaced. "One day, then we'll leave."

"You still owe me for the last time. You're lucky I was so partial to your father. Good king, he was."

"I am in your debt."

Omara turned and preceded them into the grand house. "The servants will be awake soon. I'll keep them from disturbing you too early. They can bring up a meal in a few hours."

"And a bath for her?"

"Greedy scamp." She shook her head, curls swaying. "I'll have a bath sent up this evening. You've tripled your debt to me."

"What is it you want this time?"

"The same as always, Prince Callum. Information."

Callum followed her up the staircase, down the hall, and past another doorway to a guest suite. He sighed in satisfaction when he spotted the large, lush bed. It had been a long time since he'd slept in something so soft.

"It's almost too much, Omara."

"With me it always is. Get settled and rest. Food will be up in a few hours."

CHAPTER TWENTY-FOUR

"Is everything to your liking?" Callum asked from where he sat across from Zara.

She sipped her tea and raised a brow. The tea service was formal and ornate, including an array of foods on the intimate table they shared. She was reasonably certain she'd slept most of the day, but she had awakened to the smell of freshly brewed tea. She adjusted her robe, wishing for a change of clothes.

From the ornate moldings to the lushly canopied bedding, Zara found the setting to be so out of place from the past couple weeks that she had trouble believing it was real.

"Yes. I think. Where are we?"

"We're in the home of... a friend."

"You don't sound very convincing."

"Mostly a friend. She'll help us get provisioned for the journey to the keep."

"I'm sure she'll be good at that." She waved her hand to indicate the room. "Who is she?"

"An old friend who is sometimes more trouble than she's

worth." He buttered another roll and took a bite. "You slept well."

It was an understatement in the extreme. Zara had slept like the dead, waking to find Callum wrapped around her, his body warm and heavy where it rested against her. It brought back memories of the night before, which she had tried to block out in order to focus on their escape. He brought out her lusty side.

"So did you."

He nodded.

As she'd lain in bed next to him, she'd run her hand along the length of his thigh, amazed at how hard it felt. His hand had gripped her waist, his fingers splayed across her ribcage, and she didn't know how she'd ever slept without him. How they'd managed to keep from touching for days, she didn't know. She wasn't going back to that. This felt too good not to enjoy it.

A knock sounded at the door and a woman entered. She walked with the bearing of a ballerina. Her gaze was warm, with a touch of steel behind it, reminding Zara of the way Callum had hesitated to call her a friend. She was dressed in a sumptuous yellow silk gown. Several servants trailed her, carrying gowns of a similar style.

He stood and went over to greet her.

"Madam." He kissed her hand. The woman watched him closely. He turned to Zara. "Princess Zara, let me introduce our hostess. This is Lady Omara."

Zara smiled back and nodded. "Thank you for your hospitality."

"You are quite welcome. I hope you are feeling more rested. You arrived looking quite exhausted. I've had my maids bring you fresh clothing."

Lady Omara made the comment without a change of expression, but Zara still felt the sting. She had never really thought about her own clothes, letting her ladies-in-waiting make many of her wardrobe choices if she was busy with something else that morning. But sitting in the chair, tired and probably disheveled, she missed her intricate gowns, and she missed Juna, who styled her hair. It was one thing to be a pixie queen living in a tent, but it was quite another to be a pixie queen with wild hair in a formal salon. It shouldn't matter to her, but it did.

"Thank you."

"It's nothing. Callum, I'm assuming you already bathed after your harrowing journey?"

He nodded.

"Good. I'll need you to come with me, and we can discuss... terms. Are you ready, then?" She held out her arm, as if waiting to be escorted out of the room.

"I need a moment with Zara," Callum said as he tried to usher Omara and her servants out of the room. He and Omara had a nonverbal showdown, and she finally caved, hissing under her breath that she would expect him downstairs soon.

The maids had laid out several dresses for Zara, and her bath was imminent.

"Promise me something." He took a seat on the settee next to her.

"What is it?"

"It's important that Omara not know where we are going."

"Not a friend, then?"

"Not with this." He stood and brushed her cheek with his thumb. "She's too amenable to bribes."

"Then we should leave. Gracchus is just across the woods."

"We'll leave tomorrow. I'm waiting for a message." He smiled ruefully and walked to the door. "Omara will keep us safe for today."

The moment Callum left, Omara's maid brigade returned. Zara was bathed, coifed, and dressed in a different style than she was used to but quickly came to appreciate. The tighter fit and lowered bodice were attractive. *Less sweet, more... tart.* She liked it.

～

SHE PEEKED her head into the salon, spotting Omara and a young man. She hesitated, watching their heated discussion.

"Ah! Princess Zara! Please, come meet my nephew Matteo."

Zara smiled at the dark-haired man as he bowed to her. Omara's earlier venom was missing. Perhaps it was being with her nephew? How much time had Omara spent at court, because she had the temperament to fit right in.

"Matteo, be a dear and tell Cook we would like a light supper served on the back balcony."

"Yes, Aunt. It is an honor to make your acquaintance, Your Majesty."

Zara nodded. "Your aunt is a gracious hostess. I'm sure you enjoy visiting with her."

"I do, ma'am." Matteo left after another quick bow.

"Would you please sit with me?" Omara asked. "There's something I wish to ask you."

She led Zara to a pair of tufted green chairs that overlooked the back gardens.

"I've known Callum for a long time," Omara said.

"So have I."

Omara raised a brow then snapped open a fan. "He seems... protective of you."

"He's helped me quite a lot. I hope to return the favor." Zara resisted her natural urge to disclose, instead trusting that if she waited, Omara would eventually reveal what she wanted to know.

Omara fluttered her fan. "What are your intentions?"

"Pardon?"

"Let's not be too subtle, dear. What are your intentions

when it comes to the prince? He may have grown up at court, but he hasn't mingled with the aristocracy since the usurper took the throne."

"What are you telling me?" Zara didn't trust this woman, but there was something noble about how she was—possibly—concerned about Callum.

"I'm saying that he is a good man. But, in many ways, he has not forgotten the day his family died. I believe his heart is not his own to give."

A tiny burst of jealousy stabbed at Zara. "Do you know this from experience?"

"Ha! Callum and I don't have that kind of relationship. What I'm saying is, be careful. Unless you commit your hand to him, you are on borrowed time here."

"I won't discuss my relationship with you."

"I know what I saw when I walked in the room this afternoon. He can only play at love with you."

"You don't know what you're talking about."

Omara gave her a rueful smile. "But I do. And I know Callum. It is you who doesn't know your own power. He needs to reunite this country and find his family. That is all he has room for, and you, my dear, are a distraction to that."

"Quite the contrary. My presence here is to assist with his goals."

"You shared a bed last night. I doubt that's the type of diplomacy to which you were referring."

"What if it were both?" Zara raised her voice slightly. Each time she dodged one of Omara's concerns, she would bring up a new complaint.

"It might be for now." Omara inclined her head, as if conceding the point. "Callum would do anything to advance the cause. For now, you are useful to him."

"I believe Callum can speak for himself."

Perhaps Omara was hitting on issues she hadn't considered.

Was there only a physical attraction between them? Could Callum ever see past his grief and love again? They'd agreed to wed, at least with Byrne. Would it be a marriage like her parents' had been? Eventually distant and hostile?

"I'm merely want you to be prepared to walk away." Her fan snapped closed. The corners of her mouth tilted up, perhaps with compassion. "Finding his family has consumed him. I worry there's nothing left. You would be tying yourself to a shell of a man."

Would her suitors only be bad choices?

"I appreciate your honesty," Zara said simply. She didn't trust her enough to disclose the inner workings of her heart and mind and loyalty. She appreciated that Omara seemed to be warning her about something no one else would bother with. Her sister Sidony would, but likely, no one else.

Callum likely valued Omara's frankness.

"Come now. Let's have some tea, and you can tell me about the L'Ortagian court. It's been a long while since I visited. I fear I would not know who was whom."

The rest of Zara's anger diffused. She was back on familiar territory. "Lady Omara, I doubt you would make any missteps in the L'Ortagian court."

Omara poured their tea and sat back. "You are too kind. But please, tell me about the D'Arles. You come from lively stock, Your Highness."

Zara sipped her tea. "Oh, yes. Quite."

The change of subject enabled Zara to relax and open up about her homeland. Omara showed a sincere interest and told Zara a few stories of her mother she'd never heard.

CHAPTER TWENTY-FIVE

Omara had invited Zara to promenade in the garden with her before dinner. As the day was getting chilly, she went back up to her suite to find a wrap. It was a frivolous thing to do, especially since they had been fleeing the embattled camp last night, but she wanted to feel like herself again, if only briefly. She stepped behind the screen to select a shawl just as the door opened.

"Tell me what you've found." Zara froze at the sound of Callum's voice. Two sets of boots walked across the floor. Naked curiosity kept her behind the screen. The chance to listen and observe him when he didn't know she was there also held a certain appeal since she had been highly observed when she was moving about the camp.

"Here. Read this." The second voice was Matteo's. There was the pop of a broken seal and then papers shuffling. The silence on the other side of the screen stretched Zara's nerves, but she held still, fascinated.

"Where did you get this?" Callum asked.

"Marenburg. I made a transfer of information before heading back to Embury."

"How long have you had this?"

"A few days. I arrived at my aunt's hours before you did. After returning to Embury, I had to return to her with everything that has been happening." Zara assumed that meant her "kidnapping."

"Do you know what is in this letter?"

"No," Matteo said. "But the courier was familiar with the kind of information we sought."

"Have we had any confirmed visual sightings?"

"Two. Both say it is him."

It had to be Duncan.

"Reliable?" Callum's voice broke.

A cough. Matteo then said, "One, yes. The other, not always, although he was insistent."

"Thank you."

Zara was riveted.

The chair at the escritoire scraped across the floor. More paper shuffling and then the scratch of a pen across the page. She assumed Callum's letter would be sealed as well. The unmistakable drips of wax confirmed it.

"Get this to Jeffors. I need you to deliver it personally."

"My aunt—"

"She cannot know this. I won't risk him. You can leave with us then double back."

"I accepted a position as a tutor."

"Why?"

Matteo cleared his throat. "I can't only be a courier. It's too suspicious. I'll get your letter to Jeffors. That was my last trip to Marenburg."

"Thank you." Footsteps came closer to her, but they went to the sideboard along the wall. She was still hidden from view. If one of the men had approached the washbasin, they would discover her. Someone poured a glass, presumably of scotch, since that was what was in the decanter in the suite. "Do you?" Callum asked, likely offering a glass to Matteo.

They needed to finish up and leave. Omara wasn't waiting on her, but someone might notice that all three guests were absent from the main rooms of the house.

"Yes, please." More footsteps across the floor.

"So, your position as tutor? I thought Omara provided for you."

"I am her heir, yes, but I am free to choose my pursuits, and I have to make my own fortune."

"No one made a fortune by being a tutor."

"That depends on who they work for." Matteo chuckled. "She has an eccentric father."

"Is he considering your suit?"

"Not in the slightest." The men laughed again, and Zara rolled her eyes.

She needed Matteo to leave. More clinking glasses.

In a quieter voice, Matteo said, "You honor me."

"Ah, lad. Now, go." Footfalls landed on the soft rug and bedroom door opened and shut.

"How long were you going to stay back there?" Callum strolled behind the screen, arms crossed.

Zara startled. "I was in here first."

He raised an eyebrow. "You could have come out at any time."

"I was here for my shawl. Good news?"

A knock interrupted them. "Miss? The mistress would like to know if you need any assistance?" One of the ladies' maids inquired politely from the other side of the door. Zara scooted around Callum to answer it. Callum stayed behind the screen, leaning against the wall.

They needed to talk.

"Hello, Rosalie." Zara yawned, feeling only a smidgeon of

guilt. "Please tell Lady Omara I've decided to rest and won't be joining her."

"Yes, ma'am." Rosalie bobbed her head and left.

Zara shut the door behind her. "What happened with Matteo?"

"There's an account—two, actually—of Duncan spotted in Marenburg. In Casparre."

"What's the plan?" Zara squeezed his shoulders, excited at the news.

"I need to confer with Jeffors."

"Certainly. Matteo is doing that?"

"Yes. And we leave in the morning."

"For Casparre?" she asked.

Callum hesitated the tiniest bit. "I'm not sure I can take you with me."

"What? Why?"

Zara wished she could have brought some of her own people with her. Though, really, the only person who would have left with her would have been Sidony. The rebels outnumbered her. Having to stick to their timetables and resources, meant she had to go so much more slowly. It was humbling to see how much she'd taken for granted in L'Ortagia. Yes, the queen dictated many of her tasks and duties, but once Zara decided on something, she could go after it.

"I know you had a life, that you risked your future by helping us." Callum lifted one of her hands where it clutched at her skirts. "I have to make sure I can keep you safe before taking you with me. There are too many unknowns right now to promise you."

Zara was floundering. Was this what Omara had hinted at? That he would pull away from her?

"For now, we have this." He pulled her toward him.

CHAPTER TWENTY-SIX

"Y ou're trying to distract me with kisses," she accused. She tilted her head, giving him access to her neck.

He leaned down, brushing his lips across a place just below her ear. "You like my kisses."

"Let me help you find your brother." She recognized that flush in his cheeks. After last night, she was keen to experience more with him. Would he truly leave her behind?

"You are helping me by being in Embury."

"Are you talking marriage? Do you mean to keep me?"

"Zara, be patient. I thought you wanted time to consider that." He drew his finger along a curl that tumbled over her shoulder, winding it around. He dragged it back and forth across her cleavage, brushing the curl over the tops of her breasts. Now he was the one changing the subject.

"I'm terrible at patience. We are so close to having what you wanted—to what I left home to do. Why make me wait behind?" She'd opened up her heart to him. He'd been on many such searches for his brother. If he said they weren't safe, she should listen. "I can't explain it, maybe it's something Omara said. I just have this feeling that if you leave without me, that you won't come back."

In the past, she'd had confidantes and lovers, but never really in the same person. It scared her how easily she and Callum fell into that with each other.

She wanted to keep her head out of it, merely engaging her body, but something about him wouldn't let her. He was hard to resist, with his easy charm and noble heart. Other lovers had been content with what she offered: her attentions and her willing body. Callum, and she didn't even think he was aware of it, made her give more. She was starting to crave that from him, and she worried the more she gave, the less she'd be able to do without. And until she decided what she would do about her future, she risked a lot to be with him.

He ran a finger down her neck, and chills raced across her skin. "I might not come back. This could all be a trap, and yet I have to find out if this time it's him. I owe him that. And Quinnah."

Zara blinked up at him, not letting the tears fall. "I know. I wish you'd let me protect you."

Callum chuckled at her words, pulling her close. "If you could, you'd encircle us all, save us from harm."

"Yes!" It felt good to be so understood, but infuriating that he kept her at a distance. She would have to make sure she had something left of herself, so she could let him go when she needed to. "Would that be so bad?"

Zara reached behind her back, grasping for the ties to her gown. Was she going about this the wrong way with him?

"Only because I don't deserve you," he said softly.

Callum let her fumble for a moment before he spun her around and unlaced her dress. She made herself stand still, but all she wanted was to press back against him and beg him to finish what they had begun the night before.

It seemed like another lifetime that they had lain together in his tent. What she had been prepared to give so freely last night, however, gave Zara pause. Callum had protected her at every turn, something she'd rarely experienced, certainly not from the men in her life. She didn't know how to handle it.

Her dress and stays loosened. She balanced herself against the back of the settee and stepped out of her dress, quickly setting it back behind the screen for a maid to hang up or pack away. She took off another set of small hoops underneath her gown, relieved to be free of the contraption and her corset.

"Leave your shoes on," Callum said as she bent to remove her slippered heels. She straightened and walked slowly back to where he leaned against the wall. He'd been busy while she tended to her wardrobe. His jacket was slung over the back of a chair, and his shirttails hung free.

"Are you planning on taking that off?" she asked, eying his shirt.

"I could be accommodating." He grinned. "I don't want to test your patience."

Her heart sped up as he grabbed the hem and pulled it over his head. The late afternoon sun cast a soft glow through the room that unerringly found Callum. His golden, sun-kissed skin had her mouth watering. She again had the sensation of being pulled into his orbit, not by anything he did deliberately but more from an allure he couldn't dim. She drank in his long, lean, muscular frame, her steps bringing her closer.

She sighed, hands itching to touch him. She put her palms on his chest, unable to resist, and raised up on her toes to kiss him. Again, it was sweetness melting into something hotter as he pulled her close. She kissed him, caught in the swirling passion, uncaring about the world around them for long moments, held tight to him against the wall.

But she pulled back, needing to keep her head. "Callum?"

"Zara?" He kissed her neck, and she held on to his shoulders to keep from dissolving against him.

She needed to maintain her equilibrium and not get so caught up, she couldn't see a way out. The ease with which they moved together was tempting and terrifying. Bringing her hands forward against his chest again, she pushed him back against the wall.

"Stay."

He gave her a quizzical look but tightened his hold on her waist for a brief moment.

She kissed the place on his neck where his throat met his chest. "I need," she said between kisses, "to do this."

It was old-fashioned in a sense, but Zara wanted to keep her head clear for a moment, otherwise she'd get swept away by the undertow. And in her experience, what she planned to do would be enjoyable, but let her keep the focus on him.

Her hands coasted along his sides, feeling the strength of his finely honed muscles, dipping into the ridges between and along his abdomen. She could study him for hours, he was so finely made. Just touching him made her wet. She cupped him through his pants and smiled as he groaned.

Her mouth stayed at his chest while her hands worked to undo the buttons of his buckskin breeches.

"Lass?" He reached for her, pushing the straps of her chemise off her shoulders.

She opened the placket of his pants and slipped her hand inside, rubbing against his lower abdomen while she sought his turgid length. He sucked in a breath when she squeezed him. She worked her hand along his length for a few moments, resting her forehead against the plane of his chest. Her breaths came out in small pants as she touched him, so pleased by how hard he was and how he filled her hand. Again, she felt herself spinning out, especially as his hand cupped the back of her head, holding her to him so he could lean down and bury his nose in her hair. It was all too much. Too much sweetness from him.

She twisted her head out from under him, breaking away, and sank to her knees. She leaned forward to kiss his lower abdomen as she yanked his pants lower. Her hand swept along his length, turning at the end to catch the head of his cock. Her lips took the same path. Callum groaned and pressed his hands against the wall behind him.

"Zara, you don't have to—" he bit out in a rush. One hand cupped her face.

Keeping her hand on his cock, she looked up at him. He held himself still, his hands gentle on her, but she could see that it cost him to pull her back. His cheeks were flushed and his pupils dilated.

"I want to."

He nodded, his hand fisting in her hair for a brief second.

Zara set back in, this time running her tongue around the head of his cock. She sucked along his shaft, while her hand stroked the base. Callum moaned when she finally brought her lips around him, lapping at the tip before sliding a few inches into her mouth. She did it again, adding suction to her ministrations. As she set in, working her mouth along his shaft, she expected to numb out, her enjoyment focused entirely on his reactions to what she was doing to him. But as she gripped his base and ran her hand up to meet her mouth, her own arousal was painfully peaked.

One of Callum's hands slid into her hair, rubbing along her skull, and all Zara could think was him touching between her legs with those strong fingers. She moaned around his shaft and gripped him harder, determined to make him come before she lost herself in mutual pleasure.

His cock grew harder. His taste was addicting, and his moans of appreciation confirmed that she was bringing him closer to completion. She glanced up, wanting to see his face. His eyes met hers, burning into hers for a long moment before he closed them on a groan. Her glance slid down his body, noting his quickened breaths, light sheen of sweat, and the way he held himself still for her. She ran her fingers up his abdomen, enjoying his quickly drawn-in clench, and she determined to have him on his knees for her. The longer she pleasured him, however, the more she was drawn into his thrall, her own arousal sharpening. She paused, pulling him out of her mouth, and willed herself to stay calm, to keep her own feelings in check.

"Don't you dare stop."

Her hand worked, and she gave Callum a wicked grin. "Tell me."

He shook his head to clear it. "What. Do. You. Want? Anything."

"Ah, Callum. I don't want anything. This one's for you. All I want is for you to enjoy it."

"Then stop teasing me and get on with it." She saw what she wanted to see: a man lost to sensation. In their previous interactions, he'd been nothing but gentle and sweet with her, and she didn't want that, couldn't take that from him. She knew having that from Callum would be addicting.

In something she had previously done willingly, if not with the same utmost enthusiasm she was showing him, she set herself to give him a taste of what he'd given her the night before. She gripped his upper thigh to steady herself and resumed sucking and stroking his cock. Each time she pulled up, she swirled her tongue under the tip of his shaft, her hand following her movements.

"Oh, yes."

There was something about seeing him so out of control. Her underclothes, which had felt naughty to reveal to him, only seemed to constrain her. Her breasts pushed against her chemise in a chafing way. Her nipples were so hard, she thought she could poke holes through the thin linen. She toed off her shoes for a semblance of relief, but longed to be naked before him.

"Don't stop." Callum was right there with her. He held her curls in his grip. It was loose enough to allow her enough room to move over him, but his fingers flexed again and again in her hair.

His cock was so hard and smooth in her mouth. She moaned at the feel of him sliding past her lips and across her tongue. She twisted her hand against his base, pulling down as her mouth went up on his erection.

Callum sucked in a breath, and his muscles tightened against her hand.

"Zara?" She knew what he was asking, and she answered by running her hand up his front and curling her nails into his lower abdomen. This was where she had wanted to take him. Victory over her unruly emotions was so close. They were safer tucked away.

"Mm, yes." She kept up a steady rhythm, sucking and swirling as he climaxed in her mouth. She hummed, gentling her strokes, and rested her cheek on his thigh.

He pulled away from her with a hand on the wall, eyes closed, chest heaving.

Zara sat back on her heels to catch her breath. Tendrils of dark hair hung around his face, giving him a rougher, rakish appearance. His eyes snapped open, and he reached for her, pulling her up before swinging her into his arms.

He held her like that for a long moment, his head tipped to hers. Zara vitals buzzed, excited and aroused. She'd kept her head, but her body would ultimately win the battle.

"While that was amazing," a word he punctuated with a kiss on her lips, he continued, "this is not happening without you."

Zara nodded, joy washing over her. She relaxed in his arms. The distance she had sought for herself was elusive. It was like she'd stood on a shore, apart from the water, but the longer she stayed, the closer it got.

Callum slid an arm under her knees, and Zara almost begged him to take her right there. She had gotten her distance and made him lose control, but she hadn't counted on what seeing him and being with him like this would do to her. She couldn't remain an observer as she was sucked right in to what he was feeling and what her body now demanded.

Her hands coasted over Callum's back, half soothing and half out of a restless ache. Since she hadn't been able to back away in the past few minutes, she had no chance of doing so now. From the determined set of his jaw, he had some plans for her.

With a quick toss, Callum set her on the other side of the settee. She bounced once and then got back up to face him as he bounded over. He cupped her face and kissed her again, pulling her up against him.

Zara realized the waves were only coming closer. She could no longer remain detached, in control, or in charge. Her limbs shook with desire.

CALLUM DEBATED GOING to the bed across the suite but changed his mind. He pulled away from Zara, grabbed her a glass of water from the sideboard, and sat down to remove his boots. She sat next to him, gloriously half-dressed, her lips blurry from kisses and her devil-sent skills. She sat back and, in a move that mirrored his actions with his feet, although was decidedly more feminine, held up a leg and untied and unrolled her stockings. He almost stopped her, but the sight of her bare skin and obvious delight in stripping off her garments made him hold his tongue.

Once she was done, he pulled her across his lap so she straddled him. She looped her arms around his neck.

"You make me wild for you," he said.

She smiled and arched a brow. "So I saw."

He ran kisses down her neck, squeezing her close as he pulled their hips together. The instant her core touched his cock had them both moaning.

"Callum, don't make me wait too long."

"Never."

Zara rocked her hips, a gentle grinding that made his already engorged cock swell painfully harder. His head spun with how quickly he could want her again.

He buried his face in her breasts, tonguing her through her shift, and Zara moaned. She tugged her neckline down for him.

"More."

He chuckled and set back in to sucking her nipples. She writhed again, and Callum moved his mouth to the sensitive underside of her breasts, licking and kissing her perfect globes. When her hold seemed to break, he set her back from him and turned her to face the back of the settee.

"Callum?"

"Need you now," he said in entreaty, setting a knee behind her. Zara bent forward slightly, and he pulled her right knee up, placing her foot flat on the cushion. He notched his erection against her gate. He entered a few inches and stopped. She was tight and hot. He brought a hand forward and dipped into her curls, finding her nub at the top of her sex and rolling it. She pushed back against him, driving him even farther. With his other hand, he tilted her hips, arching her, all while rubbing along her sex, adjusting his movements to what made her moan.

"More," she cried out. "In me. More."

Happy to oblige, he worked in a few more inches, clenched in her heat. Zara shuddered against him.

It was all Callum needed. He began using short thrusts, timed with his fingers against her clitoris, getting deeper with every downstroke.

Zara bent forward so her head rested against the back of the settee.

He stopped pumping into her and held himself deep. He leaned over her and kissed the back of her neck. She gasped. He cupped her breast and held her nipple in a firm grip. Not quite a pinch, but enough pressure that she would feel it. He moved his fingers against her sex, sliding in her wetness. Zara moaned, "Oh, yes. Please!"

She was unraveling, right where he'd been moments before, at his mercy and happy to be there.

"Do you want more of my cock?" he whispered at her ear.

She answered with a breathy, "Yes, please," and he moved against her in short, hard thrusts.

That did it as she arched against him, moaning her pleasure. Her pussy clenched hard on his cock, and he bit his lip in order to keep from coming. She kept moving her hips back so Callum accommodated her, steadily increasing his speed, finally gaining her depths.

She leaned back and turned her head, and he kissed her mouth, continuing to plunge into her, loving the feel of her ass as he pressed against it. Their lips moved wetly against each other, the glide and suck resembling, almost, their lower bodies. He kept his fingers on her pleasure nub, rubbing fast, and she cried out, clenching on his hardness and driving his own arousal to unknown heights.

He spoke at her temple, keeping their lower bodies locked together. "Zara, you enrapture me. I could come to need this."

Something he'd said had hit a nerve with her, and she kissed him hard then turned forward, slinging her hips back and riding along his shaft. Callum's eyes almost rolled back in his head at the sensation. They slid against each other, gripping and clutching and writhing on the settee.

Callum was truly lost. He looked down at where their bodies were joined, and the sight sent him over, a deep tension release rolling through his limbs. Zara leaned farther forward, slamming their bodies together, and moaned louder, twitching her ass against him. Callum felt her spasms and realized she had peaked again. He pulled out of her, so much pleasure, so much relief, as he spent his seed against her thigh. He rested on her back for a moment before pulling away and wiping her leg with a handkerchief.

Callum cleaned up at a washstand in the room and returned, wrapping her in a robe. He carried her across the suite to the bed. Zara lay pliant in his arms, quiet and introspective, not quite meeting his eyes. He set her down, kissing the top of her head. He tucked her into the sheet and sat at the edge of the bed.

He rolled the tension out of his shoulders and went over to the sideboard to pour them each a glass of wine. Crossing back to her, he held out her glass.

"Here. Unless you'd like me to ring for tea?" His voice sounded gruff, even to his own ears.

She met his eyes, shook her head, and took a drink. She held the robe close at the center of her chest, but she still looked quite tousled. She was utterly unlike any woman he'd ever known, and what they had just done had shaken him. It was so easy with her.

She was a sensual woman, but something about the way she had wrung his orgasm from him convinced him he'd never meet another like her. It rattled him and aroused him beyond measure.

He ran a hand through his hair, gripping the ends.

"Princess, that was… You don't … I …" he started. "Ah, hell." He stopped in front of her, leaned down, and kissed her hard on the mouth, softening after the first contact, and opening his mouth to claim hers. She gasped, and he took advantage, sweeping his tongue against hers.

"I'm sorry." He ran his hand over his face. "I'm not over what we did."

Her lips quirked. "To kiss me like that, you must be." Two spots of color rose on her cheeks.

Callum couldn't help it. He blurted out, "There's no shame in what we did. I'd kiss you anywhere."

She blushed even darker. Callum realized that her other lovers must have somehow had qualms about kissing the woman who had just brought them such pleasure.

"You, ah…made that clear." She raised her glass to him and finished the contents, setting it on the table next to her.

He couldn't stop himself from noticing her gaping neckline and how it revealed her gorgeous breasts. He pulled back, wanting to reestablish something with her before giving in to his baser needs and properly, or not, tupping her again.

"That's been at the top of my list since last night."

"Me too," she said softly. She turned on the bed, angling her body toward him, and he swallowed, again, struck by her beauty.

How was this happening between them? They were allies, old friends, perhaps, but now, lovers and maybe something more. It was happening so fast, at both the best and the worst time, and he wasn't sure he would be able to follow through on where his feelings for her would lead.

He finished his drink, seeking the false courage for what he wanted to say.

In the end, it was the sweetness, the sheer domestic comfort he felt with her that was too much. What he wanted was within his grasp—toppling the usurper, finding his family—and yet to do it, he'd tie himself to someone he wasn't enough for.

He could give Zara his body and his sword, but his heart had stopped beating long ago, back in a tower room.

He dashed about for his clothes, clutching his shirt to his chest once his pants and boots were on. "I have to go. We leave on the morrow. Write a letter to your family to assure them of your health. Omara will make sure they get it."

CHAPTER TWENTY-SEVEN

"Explain why you continue to fail me," Gracchus said. He twisted the heavy sapphire on his pinky finger.

"Father, they must have had help." Torwyn, stood before him, head bowed.

"Obviously." Gracchus wouldn't hide his disgust. "They knew we were coming and were able to get away." Gracchus leaned forward in the throne, in a small antechamber he used for private meetings. His son hated the room, convinced there were spies everywhere, which was true. Gracchus could manage both spies and his unruly heir.

"We believe they've gone north." Torwyn was always so eager to be back in his good graces.

"They could be anywhere. All of this is taking too long." His tenuous alliance with L'Ortagia was at stake. He was so close to what he wanted, would be able to achieve. He wouldn't let another MacKinnon brat take it away.

"Ash is making a fool of you, Your Majesty," Marlowe said from the shadows of the chamber. He was irritatingly late, but at least he stuck to using the false name Callum went by. He wouldn't tolerate hearing Callum's birth name, unless it was to discuss his death.

Torwyn jerked around, a hand on his sword hilt. Marlowe, Lord Sullivan, one of Gracchus's advisors, stepped forward to stand at the edge of the long runner.

"Marlowe, quit lurking about. And you're late, which is unlike you. You are, however, quite right. The situation cannot continue." Gracchus glared at Torwyn. "That is why I've decided you need assistance."

"What we need is to launch an all-out war against the rebels," Torwyn added.

"Silence! We are not going to start a civil war to quell some upstarts."

"He does have a point, Your Majesty," Marlowe said. "Those upstarts have seriously thwarted your plans."

Gracchus preferred aggression in all things, but it was a tactic to be used sparingly. He had to do something else, something to hold onto a bride for his kingdom.

"Perhaps I'm looking at this in the wrong way. Perhaps there is an advantage to be gained by losing the princess, for now," he said.

"Sire?" both men asked.

Gracchus took a sip of wine from a heavy, jewel-encrusted goblet. He set it down on the arm of the throne and turned it, the metal against metal a grinding, discordant noise.

"There are other ways to unite Embury and to solidify alliances. I'm sending you both back to Queen Isabeau." He sipped again. "We are requesting a replacement."

Torwyn rolled his eyes. "Another? Which one is it to be this time?"

"We'll let your cousin handle this. I've heard he's grown fond of the younger sister. Let Adrian and Sidony unite us."

"What are you planning to do about Zara?" Marlowe asked.

"We must retrieve her. Then, I'll decide how to handle her. How convinced are you that they went north?"

"Reasonably certain," Torwyn said. A tic started at his right cheek. It didn't necessarily mean he was lying, only that he was perhaps hiding the whole truth.

"Eventually, she will have to come back to L'Ortagia."

"Do you want me to take a search party?" his son asked.

"I want you to create a blockade," Gracchus said. "Post soldiers along the routes between holdings in the north and roadways that lead south."

"That will take scores of men," Marlowe said. The baron could be counted on to note the human cost. It was his main weakness. With further guidance, he could be rid of such a fixation.

"I will have Princess Zara in my custody. We are merely creating a net to catch her."

"Yes, Father. I'll prepare the maps and gather the men. We will bring her to you." Torwyn paused, a hand on the dagger at his belt. "Do you still want the princess captured alive?"

"I suppose. If you kill her, we'll blame it on the rebels. Sidony will do for the alliance. How fortunate that our neighbors have so many daughters."

Torwyn and Marlowe bowed, waiting to be dismissed.

"You do know where to find Master Felix, don't you, son? He's been itching to return to a more challenging service. "

"Yes, Father."

CHAPTER TWENTY-EIGHT

Zara stared at the ceiling. They had arrived at Ballyreine, the abandoned keep, in the middle of the night, after several long days of travel. Callum had them leave Omara's estate in the wee hours of early morning, in order to have fewer eyes witness the path they took. They rode at a hard pace, and she appreciated Callum's extra precautions in case they were followed.

The route to the keep was circuitous; she could not have led anyone there by herself. All she'd been able to see when Callum had dragged her off her horse were high, flat walls, a round tower at each end, and a dark, but spacious dining hall.

Zara could have slept for days. The room she was in was dimly lit, but birdsong carried through the narrow windows. It was the most peaceful place she had been in for weeks. Perhaps that was one of the reasons Callum chose to bring her here.

While the comfort level was rough, Ballyreine hadn't been totally abandoned. The rebels kept some supplies there, and someone cleaned the living quarters. The morning light showed both the cracks in the walls and the dust and cobwebs in the hall, but it also hinted at how gorgeous the keep had once been.

When they stopped for supplies and fresh horses, Callum had told her a little about the keep. It had been damaged by canon fire over a hundred years ago, and the duke who owned it lost his lands and title once he surrendered to Callum's great grandfather. Despite a plan to repair and refurbish the dwelling, the king kept it as a northern stronghold, making improvements over time. When King Angus had acquired it, he'd brought the living quarters up to more livable standards. Since the assassinations, it had fallen again into neglect, though it was held by the rebels. And without staff and guards, they were well and truly alone at Ballyreine.

Their privacy may have kept them safe but Callum hadn't touched her since Omara's. He'd been close to her, kind to her, hospitable, but nothing in the realm of a heated kiss or glance.

Zara used her powers to unpack and went about her morning routine. She'd been managing without servants for weeks and enjoyed being able to do things for herself—aside from her hair. She did not enjoy her newfound independence with her unruly locks. She added some braids to tame the wilder pieces and then let the rest go. It managed to escape whatever she tried to do with it anyway.

She made her way downstairs and looked for Callum. He'd put together a small meal for her near the great hearth. She carried it with her as she followed the sound of splitting wood coming from the courtyard.

"I see you found breakfast." Callum wiped his brow and indicated a bench that lined one wall of the courtyard.

Zara sat, glad the bench offered a good view of Callum chopping wood.

"You don't have to keep that on for my sake." Zara waved at Callum's loose shirt.

"I didn't want to be presumptuous." With that, Callum

whipped off his shirt and wiped his face and chest with it. This time, her sigh escaped as she ran her gaze over his taut torso. She looked away from the riveting sight of his brawny arms when her stomach grumbled. Food first.

"How long have you known about this place?"

"My whole life, really. My father always loved Ballyreine. He visited it when he was a boy. He said he regretted that the uprising couldn't have been handled differently, as he was sad when his grandfather waged war against such a lovely pile of stones."

"It seems your great-grandfather was the victor. And your father, perhaps an architect as well?"

"Quite possibly. He added to Blackthorne regularly too."

Ballyreine had held up remarkably well, considering it had had modest repairs over the last three generations of owners.

"Was there a wall over there?" Although the four towers still stood, along with most of the main, exterior walls, the architecture of the inner bailey was difficult to determine. There was a large space between two towers, providing a view of the countryside.

"I think so. It faced a moat. The other side is nearly intact."

"How do you know we'll be safe from Gracchus here?"

"The nearest city is Parthe, and he barely holds it." Callum grinned.

"Does he keep troops nearby?"

"Generally, no, not year-round. We keep him busy in other parts of the kingdom. And this is in a remote region."

"How would you hold it if you needed to?" Zara asked.

"Aside from having the people's loyalty?" He smiled. "During the warmer months, Parthe operates a small port by the sea. I'd open a larger trade route."

"We're close to the sea?" Zara went to the closest window, hoping for a view.

"You might be able to see it from up there." He pointed to

another section of the keep. "Come on, I'll show you, and you can see the outside walls."

He took her hand and led her across the small bailey. It had become cluttered with small, gnarled fruit trees along the section that used to have a wall. As they walked through it, Zara noted the even spaces between the trunks.

"Who planted the orchard?"

Callum looked back over his shoulder at her and shrugged. "Me and my siblings."

Zara raised a brow. She couldn't imagine that royal children would ever be allowed to play in the dirt, much less to help plant trees.

"My mother's family's holdings are nearby. We convinced our cousins to help. We may have had my father's gardeners doing most of the work, but we helped."

"In the bailey?"

"They get plenty of sunshine. It was only temporary, as a fix to the wall. We did it the summer before they were all…" He looked away.

"I'm sorry." Zara touched his shoulder. "This place must be full of memories."

"Yes." He cleared his throat and started again. "It's gotten overgrown."

"Yes, well. You plugged the wall effectively." They had made their way through the trees and reached the outer walls of the bailey. Callum walked around to where another section of wall still stood. The ledge was perhaps wide enough for a horse, but then dropped off sharply into the moat below.

"Careful. Look out there."

"Oh! I see it!" The water was still a ways from the keep, but in the distance, the dark waters of the Catarine Sea sparkled in the morning light, little whitecaps winking in the breeze. It made for a lovely view. She leaned against the wall next to Callum as they looked out across the low valley toward the water. She patted the stone behind her, reminded of her favorite sections of Mondelac.

"I see why your family kept this place. It has such a sense of permanence. It seems like it withstood many attacks over the years."

"It's nearly four hundred years old. That's probably why my father was interested in its condition once he became king."

"Do you feel close to your father here?"

Callum's features tightened. "I've never thought about it, but yes. He used to tell me stories about how it was defended and what other armies had tried to do to get past its walls."

"What finally worked?" Zara asked.

"My great-grandfather's army found a weakness and kept launching cannonballs at it."

"Ah, persistence. Must be a family trait."

Callum laughed. "My mother used to call it stubbornness."

Zara peeked over to catch him smiling at her. She smiled back, and their gazes caught. She leaned toward him, hoping he'd reach for her, but he didn't.

"You don't seem stubborn when it comes to Jeffors," she said.

"What do you mean?"

Zara dug deep for her mother's sense of diplomacy, not wanting to offend, although given what she already knew of Callum, he wasn't someone who took offense easily.

"You allow him to disagree with you. Outwardly."

"He's supposed to do that. He's the person I trust the most in this army."

Zara bit the inside of her cheek. "It seems like more than that."

"What? Just tell me."

She sighed. "He openly challenges you in front of others. That's not something we'd allow."

"You or your mother?"

Zara stayed silent for a moment, considering. "Her, I suppose. I like hearing others' opinions. They tell me things I haven't thought of."

"That's what Jeffors does for me. And I need him to do that. We don't have the time or resources for him to wait for me to come to a conclusion he's already reached."

"How do you know to let him do that?"

"It's something I'd decided to do differently. My father led with confidence and a single-mindedness. I believe he had some idea that Gracchus planned to overthrow him."

"What?"

Callum's voice was quiet. "I think he'd heard what Gracchus planned and had spies among my father's men, but he carried on, stubbornly, thinking he could overpower anyone who tried to take his throne."

"That his arrogance could keep him safe?"

"Yes. And that he knew best. He should have trusted his advisors, let them do their jobs for him. That's what I strive to do with Jeffors. Besides, he lead a resistance to the usurper before I found him."

Zara didn't know what to say. She felt hollow, an aching pit of loss for Callum's family. But she also admired the man who pushed himself to do differently, to learn from past mistakes. She laced their fingers together. "Jeffors cares. Viola cares too. I can see them doing their best for you."

"They do. I only hope I'm worthy of their efforts." He squeezed her hand and rested his head against the wall next to hers. "You must have some family traits too."

"More my father's than my mother's. I'm quite the disappointment." In the moat below, wildflowers that grew along the banks were reflected in the water. She wiggled the fingers of her free hand, debating tapping into her magic while they talked.

"What could she possibly find to be disappointed in?" Callum's assurance warmed her.

"Many, many things." Zara concentrated on the flower closest to the water.

"Like what?"

Picking the whole flower would be too much, so she settled for plucking the petals off and having them fall into the water, similar to what a breeze could do. "Too soft-hearted, not shrewd, fraternizes with the servants, not punctual, and she never liked how I played with my dolls." She plucked off the petals with her magic as she spoke, one for each detrimental trait. Each one had been hours of lectures and lessons.

"Ridiculous," Callum said softly. "I rather like those sides of you. Maybe I wouldn't if I saw you with your dolls." He shuddered playfully.

Zara nudged his shoulder with hers. "You have no idea." There was something soothing about the image of the petals floating along the dark water. Like those old hurts could fade away.

"Aside from a glaring exception, you're an admirable daughter."

"Thank you. Desperate times." For good measure, she plucked the petals off one more flower, but this time had them float longer in the air before falling into the moat. Callum stared down into the moat as well. She fluttered her fingers, letting the petals float, as if on a breeze.

For a moment, she considered telling him she was a nocturne.

"Callum, there's something I want to—"

"Can it wait?" He frowned at her. "We should go back. It's breezy back here."

"Never mind." Zara pushed down a hint of guilt at hiding her magic from him. She couldn't think why she performed it in front of him either, other than that his acceptance of her made her feel more free to be herself. Her magic was the part of her she'd kept to herself for so long, she wasn't sure how to reveal it. Perhaps she'd wanted to gauge his reaction. Inwardly, she cringed, ashamed she hadn't just shown him more deliberately. It was her mother's habit to test those around her. Now, she'd resorted to doing it too.

Callum led her through the orchard. At the courtyard steps, he said, "You're quiet this morning."

"Just thinking of our next steps." She waved, indicating the trees. "Thank you for showing me the lovely view."

He tilted his head, eyes narrowing on her face. "I think I lost you out there."

CHAPTER TWENTY-NINE

"Is there nothing you can't talk me into? Are you sure you don't have any servants out here?" Zara was half kidding but she was surprised that he'd had her come along to hunt for rabbits for their dinner.

"Shhhh," Callum chided.

Zara quieted and then walked slowly, stopping here and there so Callum could check a trap he'd left earlier that morning. He held up a hand, drew back an arrow, and loosed it, hitting a rabbit several yards away. Moving quickly, he got another one, and he walked over to bag his kills.

"Dinner."

"I hope you know what to do with that. I have no skills in the kitchens. I can plan banquets and name foreign heads of state, but cooking, no."

"I'll take care of it. But you are helping me with dinner. We're gathering."

"Is that what this basket is for? I've been putting flowers in it."

"You can leave them. Come over here. There are raspberry bushes along this side."

"You're quite the farmer, you know."

Callum laughed. "I've had to expand my education so I wouldn't starve."

"Of course. I'm sorry. I didn't mean…"

"I know. I lived a sheltered life for most of my years. I learned to appreciate what I used to take for granted."

"That has been an unexpected side of this time together." She patted her hair, recalling the long dinners in heavy gowns and heavier headpieces. Her wild braids certainly were freeing.

They hiked through tall hillocks of grass. As they came around to little patches of bushes, Callum took the basket from her and began filling it with berries.

She snatched it back. "I can do this."

"But you don't have to."

"You aren't doing anything with me!" Zara realized she'd switched topics.

"Now, that's not true. There are several things I want to do with you." Callum stepped closer, a heated look in his eyes.

Zara lowered the basket, eager to see what he'd do. It had been so long. They'd enjoyed each other at Omara's. But this… this nothing hurt. How many times could she open herself to him, only to have him push her away?

Callum touched her cheek. "Did I go too far last time, Princess? I stayed away the last few days because I was afraid I'd never want to leave your bed."

"And yet…" She couldn't resist. His lack of affection stung.

"And yet I managed to make a mess of it anyway." He kissed her, sweet and solemn. "I'm sorry."

She smoothed the hair across his forehead. "I worried I'd done something wrong."

He closed his eyes and put a hand over his heart. "Never."

The ache in her chest eased the tiniest bit.

"All right, then." Callum turned and picked a few berries, dispelling the tension between them. "Before I tumble you on this hill, you were going to tell me all the ideas you had about our next steps."

"Yes. We need to write to your sponsors, encourage more loyalists to support the rebellion. Reconsider utilizing the courts for your claim."

"The king has the courts in his pocket."

"All of them?" she asked.

"The magistrates that could make any difference." He dropped a handful of berries into the basket.

"You need better finances in order to take back your crown. Obviously, Byrne is helping with that. If it's too dangerous to meet with any of the judges, we can't just give up. We have to contact them."

"That's difficult when the person in power has all of the advantages."

"You have two major advantages, political advantages, that Gracchus cannot come close to taking away, but you aren't even using them."

Callum pressed his lips into a thin line. "What do you suggest?"

"You need to make an official claim to the throne."

"Gracchus would deny that, if he even let me live long enough to venture into Blackthorne Palace and make a petition."

"You need to petition your *allies* to recognize you as the sovereign ruler of Embury."

Callum stared at her for a long moment. "Go on."

"Obviously Gracchus won't grant you a formal, public appeal. Officially, you've been declared dead."

"Correct. At least as much as we've been able to determine."

Zara waved that away. "We'll get back to that. Anyway, you and your family have allies, within and outside the kingdom. It worked with me."

"You didn't know it was me when I contacted you."

"No, but I do now. With L'Ortagia's support, you could reach out to more and have them recognize you as the surviving heir."

"Perhaps one of two surviving heirs." He looked down. "You said the queen doubted your shrewdness. Clearly she is ill-informed."

Zara flushed with happiness at his praise. "I think she believes it's her role to teach me."

"Then you've learned quite a bit from her." He offered his arm, as if they were about to enter a ballroom, and not standing in the middle of a field. He tucked her hand against his side and turned, so they could walk back to the keep. "It's something we have considered, seeking foreign acknowledgment and support."

Zara nodded in encouragement.

"The concern was in being captured by Gracchus or his allies before being able to make such petitions."

"You've eluded him so far."

"Had lots of practice."

"Well, you have, once you knew what kind of man you were dealing with. Have you ever been captured by him?"

"Close, but no. Fine. What else would you suggest?"

"Ask them to help you take back your crown, either through financing your army or using theirs."

"There have been pretenders. The lost princes have made several appearances in several royal courts across the continent."

"So they were false princes, right? You are the real one. Prove it to them. Gracchus could never do that."

"I think they're past listening."

"You proved it to me." A shadow crossed his face, and Zara reached out to touch his arm. He captured her hand and brought her fingers to his lips, kissing the tips.

Zara smiled at him, feeling an ache in her heart. "You're persuasive man, you know."

He pulled her toward him with a gentle tug on her fingers. "You are quite bold, you know."

Zara placed her hands on his shoulders and tilted her head. "You bring that out in me."

Dropping the basket, he put his arms around her and bent toward her, brushing a kiss at the corner of her mouth. "You are bolder than you think, Princess." He kissed her, and Zara softened at the pressure of his mouth on hers.

Callum moved to kiss her chin, then made his way down the side of her throat, brushing lightly against her. "I'm bold with you."

At her words, he brought his face up to hers again. He looked at her, his eyes crinkling in the corners. "You are more than I ever thought you'd be. I've done nothing to deserve what you offer me."

"Are you ready to discuss terms?" she asked. "We have to decide what to do about Byrne's agreement. I've had time to consider my options."

"I don't think we need to decide just yet." He gazed at the pasture below. "Let's start with getting you fed."

As he led her back to the keep, it hit her that she had no idea how much time they'd have together. The palace intrigue of her life had kept her from realizing the danger in their world. They needed to hear from Jeffors soon, so they could look for Duncan in Casparre.

She and Callum were in a delicate dance. Eventually, she would have to go back to L'Ortagia. She had more to do for her own people. She wanted to establish ties with Callum, for some sort of future for them. Would he even want a future with her? If he knew she was a nocturne would it change how he felt about her? What they'd promised to Byrne?

CHAPTER THIRTY

"It's rabbit," Callum said carefully.

"Yes, I know." Zara stared at her fork. "There are so many on Ballyreine's grounds that I feel... odd eating one."

They sat together in front of the hearth in the great hall. It was light enough that the early evening's rays warmed the stone floor.

"They were expedient."

"You called it 'roasted hare' earlier. That sounded appetizing." She sniffed at the meat and grumbled before taking a bite. "Oh. Well, that's quite tasty."

"Thank you," he said. "The berries are... tart."

She smiled. "Have some more wine. That helps to wash them down."

He raised his cup to her.

"Once we hear from Jeffors, I think we should discuss when you'll go back."

He'd meant his words to her earlier that she was beyond his reach, despite their similar upbringings and status. The latter was why Jeffors wanted Callum to woo her and marry her himself. Callum wasn't sure Zara was in any place to agree to a marriage. It was one thing to offer her his body. It was another to consider a future together when he had very little to give her in the present and would, in essence, be at someone else's behest. She'd told him how important it was to her to choose for herself.

They'd told Byrne they were engaged. Callum had wanted their fake engagement to be true, had hoped their circumstances would change to make it so.

He also knew that, if this lead fell through, he would keep searching for his siblings. He wasn't fit to be a husband. Until he got answers about his siblings, he wouldn't be able to let someone else in, couldn't be a good husband to anyone.

"Why then?" Zara asked. "I think we wait until you get Duncan back."

"That could be weeks or even months from now. It's a risk taking resources away from the rebellion on what could be another fool's errand. This would be the sixth sighting of my brother. None of the previous five proved to be him." Callum sipped his wine. "The longer we keep you with us, any chance of your mother's understanding and future support dwindles."

"She could still have me marry Torwyn upon my return."

Silence fell between them.

"Zara, I...It's doubtful he'd want to go through with it."

"But not completely out of the question." She glanced at the fire then back at him. "When Sidony and I were much younger, she promised us we could choose our husbands. I realized this spring that her hasty promise might have had more to do with her own miserable marriage and wanting to protect us from that. Once the time came and we were of age, she reneged."

Their agreement with Byrne hung in the air between them. It was yet another time someone had coerced Zara into agreeing to an arranged marriage. Her fear of Torwyn was evident.

"I hate taking away your choice."

"Byrne did," she said softly. She rested her hands on the table, palms flat. "Another option is that I don't go back. I can help you in Casparre. I could be your escort into the city."

It hit Callum in that moment that Zara could conceivably continue offering to help until he refused. She'd stay with him in this limbo and risk her own crown. He couldn't let her do that.

"Zara, what would make you ready to go back?" he asked.

"Once you no longer need me. Once Gracchus is defeated and your family returned to the throne." She gave him a puzzled look. "Isn't that what we agreed on? What we're working toward?"

"Yes, but…" He trailed off and rubbed a hand over his face. He stood from the table and went to the hearth. He grabbed an iron and poked at the fire that kept the evening's chill from reaching their table.

He faced her again before he spoke his next words. "All of that could take years. And in the meantime, you'd be living with me indefinitely as… a guest? My betrothed? I couldn't do that to you. Besides, L'Ortagia needs you. You've helped us tremendously. And even again today, you had more ideas for ways to turn the tide. I owe you so much."

Zara flushed and lowered her gaze. "This feels like a different kind of goodbye. I know my time is limited here. But there is a solution. If we were to draw up a contract for marriage, that would fix all of this."

"Zara, I want that with you. But I'm not ready."

ZARA REFILLED her cup of wine and sipped, amazed that an abandoned wine cellar could house something so fragile.

"When were you going to tell me that? What have you gotten me into, Callum?"

He had the good grace to look sheepish. "Plenty, I'm afraid."

He leaned back against the wall by the hearth. The firelight danced over his features. Did regret reside in that ridge between his brows?

Zara stared into her cup. "I left with you to avoid marriage, not stumble into another one. True. But I'm not quite ready for marriage—now—*or* to return home just yet."

"I've made a hash of it, Princess. I'm sorry."

"There's nothing to apologize for. You've kept me alive and free. You're likely the only person who could have done all that."

"Doubtful." He set his cup on the mantle.

She stood and straightened her skirts, a tiny part of her lamenting that her actions were pointless since the skirt had never been ironed in the first place. She set her shoulders back and waited until she had his attention.

She took a step toward him and put her arms behind her back, clasping her hands together. She watched as his eyes left her face and traveled down the front of her gown, pausing where it was pulled across her breasts. She walked closer.

"I'll give you an answer in the morning. Didn't we talk about you doing something for me earlier?"

"What did you have in mind?" His voice was like a caress, husky and deep. Everything about him was so appealing.

Part of her could see herself marrying Callum. It would be easy. If she focused on this time with him, she'd easily say yes. But with all the ramifications of marrying him before her mother acknowledged him as a true MacKinnon, she might lose her crown. She also hated that Byrne thought he could order her to make such a life-changing decision, even if they had agreed to it in the moment.

She tucked such concerns away, needing the heat of his

gaze and the press of his body. She felt wanted, and for tonight, that was enough.

He moved his hand back down to his side, and she couldn't help but peek into the collar of his shirt, noting the strong tendons in his neck, wanting to bury her nose in the slope where it met his chest.

She stood close enough that her skirts brushed his legs. Callum kept still, leaning against the wall, but his attention was all on her.

Swallowing her pride, she asked, "Have you ever wondered what it would have been like if we'd been able to choose each other?" She stepped closer, pressing against him, his warmth rivaling the fire at her side.

Promise hung in the air, the fire crackling in the hearth echoing her shallow breaths.

Callum stared at her, brows drawn. He finally grasped her waist, his thumbs brushing down her sides. He was quiet for so long, she didn't think he'd reply.

In a low voice, each word laid out like a promise, he said, "Zara, I would choose you."

She kissed him before he could take the words back, as if to seal something between them as precious and final.

"Thank you for that."

Pulling at his shirt, she made a decision. She was getting what she wanted, tonight at least.

Thankfully he helped her relieve him of the offending garment, laughing at her efforts, and when it hit the floor, that ignited something in him. He reached for her, and Zara, with her hands on the ties of her gown, stumbled.

"I've got you." He caught her elbow, stopping her wobbling.

She kissed him fiercely, needing to push away a burning in the back of her throat, the first sting of tears. "Here," she managed to get out between kisses. "Take me here."

Callum loosened her gown and turned, setting her back against the wall where he'd been.

"Princess, we can—"

"Right here," she said.

He pushed the straps of her chemise down her arms as if the time for words was over. He gazed hungrily at her barely covered breasts. She pushed her insecurity away as she slid the neckline lower, revealing one tawny nipple.

He stepped back and leaned down to her, his mouth on her breast. Zara fell back against the wall, dizzy with relief at his touch. She clutched his shoulder, lifting herself up to him as he suckled her.

"You taste sweet."

He reached between their bodies and freed his cock from his breeches. She pushed his pants lower and brought her hand down to cup his hardness. He sucked in a breath. She squeezed, working her hand along his length, thrilling at his size. She squirmed, anxious to have him inside her.

Callum had made his way across to her other breast and was suckling her nipple, licking along the underside. His fierceness and hunger for her made her head spin.

"Callum, now." She pulled on his cock, long past wanting to tease and play.

He kissed her neck and flipped her underskirts up. Setting his fingers against her, he parted her folds, testing her wetness.

"Come for me first." He kissed the jut of her chin and then her mouth, giving her his tongue.

"Now," she begged. She slid her knee against his side, her soft stocking catching at his hip.

He pushed two fingers inside her, working back and forth until they were fully embedded in her sheath. She moaned encouragement but he wouldn't be moved.

"Let me give this to you." He pulled back to look at her and brushed a braid off her face. "It will make it better." His fingers found her again, working the spot between her legs that brought her so much joy.

The pull of her arousal built and tightened as he touched her intimately. She let go of his cock and held on to his shoulder, setting her face against his neck, almost panting with want. Callum rubbed circles over her clitoris until her breath hitched. She moaned as the spiral swept her up, heat rushing across her body before she arched back in a release, crying out.

Before she could fully catch her breath, he picked her up against the wall and spread her legs. Her skirts were tucked about her waist. All she wanted was to be filled with his erection. He held himself at her entrance and rubbed her again, swiftly wringing another orgasm from her. Once the waves ebbed, he entered her, seating himself fully against her and pulling her legs around his waist.

She was at his mercy against the wall. She touched his neck. "You won't... finish inside me, right?"

He kissed her cheek, his hot breath coasting over her ear. "No. I promise."

She moaned again, relaxing and pulling him close.

Callum worked her as he pounded into her, one hand clutching her shoulder, the other holding her hip as he churned their sexes together. She stared at him, watching as he thrust into her body, and the sight was nearly too much.

"I've got you," he said, punctuating the words with his thrusts. She went over again, tightening around him. The hall echoed with the noise of their lovemaking, the shadows longer now, the corners dark.

She gazed at him, his chest heaving, his torso glistening with sweat, and wondered if she had ever seen a body more beautiful. He cocked an eyebrow up as if he could read her thoughts. Pushing into her, he wrapped a hand behind her neck and pulled her to him for a swift, hard kiss. His lower body rocked against her, rubbing along her sensitive nub, and she gasped.

She held him as he fucked her against the wall, the slap of their bodies an intimate, earthy sound. She needed this pleasure with him and she told him so, whispering words in his ear about all the things she'd wanted to do to him in the nights he'd left her alone. She was rewarded with his groan, his thrusts speeding up again.

"Ah, Zara, *yes.*" He pushed hard into her, tensing, then pulled out, spending on her stomach. He gusted out a sigh and collapsed against her, pinning her tightly.

Zara stared up at the ceiling, into the shadows the light couldn't reach. He pressed a kiss against her shoulder and squeezed her hip, murmuring against her, sweet words of praise and affection. She closed her eyes, trying to hold onto the moment, clutching him close and running a hand down his back.

A whisper of fear, however, worked its way into her heart, telling her that she only had a finite number of such moments left with him.

CHAPTER THIRTY-ONE

A week went by as they stayed at the estate. Callum taught her how to skin and roast a hare. Zara found a wooden chess set that had most of its pieces. Every night they shared a bed but stopped speaking of the future.

Callum met the rider at the front gate. He'd been watching for the past three days. He took the parcel, scanning the contents quickly, and sent the rider off with provisions and a short note back in response. He sat in the apple orchard to read the letter from the person he trusted most in the world.

Jeffors, with his strategically placed spies, had been able to make another confirmation as to the identity of the prisoner in Casparre. The glimmer of hope Callum had felt when Matteo delivered the news burst into a shining ray, bittersweet, but nonetheless real, that his older brother was identified, and therefore alive.

He grabbed one of the apples that had fallen and clutched it. His brother was alive and in Casparre. Jeffors, ever dependable, had a plan.

Tears blurred his vision as he stared down at the piece of fruit in his hand, likely planted, with a little help, by his brother and sister. He had a chance to bring Duncan back to Embury, and hopefully together, they could overthrow Gracchus and restore the throne to their family. The tears fell, and Callum sucked in a breath, the tightness in his chest easing for the first time in a long time. His parents were gone, his dear sister was presumed dead too. But he had Duncan within his grasp and there was nothing he wouldn't do to get him back.

He thought of this morning and waking up with Zara in his arms, held close, her hair tangled across his chest. She'd become his good luck charm, turning events in his favor and changing the course of a long battle.

He bit into the apple, wincing at its mild tartness. When he closed his eyes, he heard the sounds of his siblings chasing each other through the newly planted orchard, racing around the castle, and talking in hushed tones at formal ceremonies. He was so close to having a family again.

Gracchus would pay for the lives stolen and years lost.

But there was no reason Zara's life needed to be put on hold anymore.

CHAPTER THIRTY-TWO

Zara walked through the keep, holding Callum's hand as he led her out into the bailey. "I have something I need you to see."

They passed the spot where on her first morning at Ballyreine she'd watched him chopping wood, and they kept going, down into the greater courtyard.

"Close your eyes."

"Isn't the sun going down soon?"

"Close them. Just a little farther."

She closed them and kept walking, tightening her hold on his hand as they stepped onto an uneven section of ground.

"Here. I've got you. I won't let you fall."

She made her way several paces farther, and then he turned her and said, "Open your eyes."

Out in the orchard he had managed to string a row of lanterns, made from empty wine bottles, between two trees. In front of the lights was an oaken barrel set with two cups and another candle.

"This is all so lovely! Where did you find everything?"

"I had a busy afternoon."

She smiled at him. She knew he had things he worked on during the day, and she made d0, keeping herself occupied, getting fairly good at scaring up berries. In longer moments she was alone, she snuck into the crumbling library and selected a weather-beaten tome. She'd used her powers to dust and sweep the room first, checking over her shoulder in case Callum came to see what she was doing.

Today had been a day she spent nearly entirely alone, apart from their luncheon together. And now she knew why.

He led her over to a small table he'd set up in the middle of the orchard. He pulled out a chair, a stump, really, and helped her sit. Once he took a spot beside her, he handed her a cup.

"What are we drinking to?" Zara asked.

He looked sheepish. "I spent so much time making it look right, I didn't decide what I was going to say."

Zara was suspicious but tried not to show it. "Tell me."

"I wanted to thank you for all that you've done for me. With your help, we were able to get the resources we needed to look for my brother and provision the army for at least another two years. We also have gained the support we needed from the group in Vespertine."

"Jeffors's letter came?" she asked.

"It did. He sent the good news." Callum smiled. "I never dreamed such a desperate plan would bring me to this moment."

The bottom dropped out of Zara's stomach, and she began to wonder what he was gearing up for. The moonlight, the orchard, the candles, the wine...it was all so romantic, she wasn't sure what to think. But being at this place with him, over what had been an idyllic week, her feelings had grown. She'd been raised to think such sweet gestures were only a means to an end, but with Callum, she was looking forward to what he might be proposing. Er, suggesting.

She looked at him hopefully, sighing as a wave of tension

left her. Maybe tonight, if it all went well, she would show him what her magic could do.

"I was saying that this might be one of our last nights together. A messenger arrived this morning, and I need to go to Casparre."

Several seconds passed as she let his words sink in. She'd known this was coming. She'd hoped to come to more of a resolution for herself. It was a proposal. Just not the kind she had been—foolishly—hoping for. Hurt and regret washed over her.

"Are you sending me home?"

"I need to leave in a couple of days. Zara, I'm sorry. The timing is critical."

"Why won't you take me with you to get Duncan?"

"I won't put you in any more danger." Callum glanced away and lowered his voice. "We'd need to make things more permanent between us, and I don't think either of us wants that."

Zara let the wave of shock go through her before she responded. "I don't see why we have to decide tonight. You know I can help you in Casparre."

"You can, but you don't belong with me like this. Your mother could choose to make Sidony her heir. I won't have you lose the crown while you help me. Zara, it could be *years*. And the longer we're together, the more apparent it would be that we'd need to marry."

"Then just ask me yourself," she said in a heated tone.

A long silence stretched between them. The bottles bobbed in the evening's breeze.

"I can't take a wife like this. I won't have you live like this with me."

"Let me determine how I want to live." Zara swallowed. She still had reservations about a royal marriage, but with Callum, she'd begun to hope that the ease they had between them could continue, perhaps for years to come.

"I'm not fit for marriage like this, Princess. Surely you want more." He crossed his arms over his chest, his expression flat. "All I'm good for is revenge and raids and sweeping damsels up on my horse. There's nothing left inside of me anymore. I'd make a rotten husband like this."

"Damn you, Callum."

"You know I'm right. I haven't made you promises because I don't know that I have a future for you. I don't know how to make that real anymore."

"I could teach you," she said in a broken voice.

"Zara, I can't."

She finished her wine, wiping a rivulet that ran down her chin. "You won't."

He placed his hands flat on the table and leaned forward. "Look. I needed you not to marry Torwyn. And you helped us immensely. I can't risk your mother's displeasure any more than I have, by keeping you with me indefinitely."

"I guess if I wanted to stay, I should have taken Byrne up on his request when he made it. Weren't you giving me time? It seems that instead, you were deciding for me." She turned and strode down the middle of the orchard.

"Good night, Callum."

Indignation fueled her steps back into the keep. When she opened the door to the bedchamber using her magic, she ignored a stab of guilt at not telling him about it.

She was angry with both of them. Callum's grief ran deep. Maybe it was so deep he didn't have room for her.

CHAPTER THIRTY-THREE

Zara stood on the beach, waiting for the sun to rise. She clutched the blanket tighter around her shoulders. They were leaving today: Callum to Casparre, and Ranulf would accompany her home to L'Ortagia.

She loved rising early to catch a sunrise. The view from Mondelac Castle's towers was stunning, but she'd miss this one terribly. The water looked cold and dark, even in summer. But then the sky would turn pink and orange, casting warmth over everything. It was stark and serene at once. Standing in that tender glow, she stopped fighting the inevitable.

She took off her shoes, determined to experience the day for all it had to offer. She dropped the blanket next and quickly set to work on her stockings. She walked to the edge of the water and let the tiny waves splash her toes. She gasped and froze, wiggling her feet. Clutching the hem of her gown, she stepped in, going up to her knees. She raised her face to the sky and blew out a breath.

There were so many things she would leave here in Embury. That felt both terrifying and oh so freeing.

She stayed until her lower legs were numb, then bundled

back to shore. She walked up the steps to the keep, past the orchard in the bailey, and into the room she'd shared with Callum for two weeks.

He fastened the strap on his bag as she walked in the door.

"I packed this morning," she said, leaning against the doorframe.

"I saw that. Ranulf is ready." He faced her, his expression pensive. "Did you sleep well?"

"As well as could be expected." She wanted to go to him and brush his hair off his forehead. Or tell him he couldn't spend his whole life closed off to the people still left around him. "When do you leave?"

"Just after you. We're meeting a small contingent to escort us to Dorven, where we'll board."

"So, it's all planned?"

He paused before answering her, weighing his words. "I have to get my brother back. Our best chance for success is with him."

"It is." The gulf between them widened again and she wasn't sure what she could do to prevent it.

"I meant to give you this." Callum reached into his bag. "A letter arrived for you, from your mother. Here. I'll let you read it alone."

He went over to the bed and grabbed her bags, slinging them over his shoulder, and went out the door.

Zara took the letter and broke the seal.

The letter read:

Dearest Zara,

We hope this finds you in good health as we are overcome with concern. If by chance this letter reaches you, please know that we love you and miss you and are praying for your swift return. King Gracchus assures us that he will find and punish the rebels who took you from your home. As more time goes by and you are not returned to us,

we can only hope you have not let them sway you to their side of the
conflict. You have such a gentle heart. Be strong in spirit, daughter.

Isabeau, Your Queen

ZARA LAUGHED. Of all the things to write to her missing daughter, her mother chided her for her disposition. How like her.

Her mother did sound concerned.

She would be strong, though. She couldn't return the same person she was when she left. She'd be right back where she started, a pawn to be used for the crown's gain. From now on, she would set her own course.

"Zara." Callum returned to the room. "I have something else for you."

His amber eyes burned bright, his cheeks high with color. He held out his intaglio ring, the one she'd used to identify him that first night. He worn it ever since. "I want you to have this."

She took it, holding it in her palm. "Why?"

"It's all I can give you right now, in thanks." He stepped close and cupped her face, his gaze roaming her features. "I hate doing this without you, but it's the only way. I can't let my family down. Not again."

She frowned, feeling mixed up in too many emotions between them. Maybe the separation would be for the best. Maybe she could get some perspective and plan for her future without being surrounded by all the excitement he brought. Maybe there'd be another man someday who could compare.

She kissed him before she could talk herself out of it.

He wrapped his arms around her like he'd never let her go, and for a moment she believed they could have a future, that it was truly in him to give and that she was ready for marriage.

They broke apart, breaths heaving. Callum touched her cheek. "I won't ask you to wait for me. I don't deserve that."

Zara let two tears fall before she pulled herself together. "What about Byrne?"

"We'll tell him the betrothal is still on, that you returned home to discuss it with the queen."

"For how long?"

He cupped her cheek, running his thumb over her bottom lip. "As long as we can."

"I know you have to see if it's truly Duncan this time, but at some point, you have to live your own life. I want you to be happy, Callum. To have joy. I can only imagine how it feels to have lost your whole family, but you are still here."

His hand fell away. That haunted look in his eyes returned.

"I'm here. I only wonder what it would be like if you fought for *us*. If you had it in you to try."

She spun on her heel and left, racing down the stairs, and out the door to Ranulf, who waited with their horses. "Let's go."

CHAPTER THIRTY-FOUR

Ranulf kept close to the edge of the forest. They'd traveled for four days. Zara was no longer completely certain of the direction she was going. They hadn't seen a road in two days.

No one had come after them from Ballyreine. From Ranulf, she learned the direction of Parthe, the port city Callum would be going to, which was nowhere near the direction they traveled. She'd left him a note of introduction into the city of Casparre, capital of Marenburg, via L'Ortagia's ambassador. She couldn't bear to have him risk getting captured, and she wanted him to be able to reunite with his brother.

She focused on getting home and what she would say to the queen about her absence. She had to convince Isabeau of what she knew of Gracchus. Her betrothal to Torwyn was surely ended. The gossip she'd heard during her time in Embury was that it was. She heard that her sister was betrothed to Prince Adrian. She and her mother would have to discuss any further connections to Embury. Zara wouldn't let L'Ortagians—especially her sister—be used to legitimize Gracchus or what he'd done to his people.

Some of the times she'd shared with Callum were the best weeks she'd had in her life. She refused to regret her reasons for leaving, or the time she'd spent with the prince and the rebels. She would convince the queen to help them.

The nights were the hardest. Ranulf found homesteads where they could stay. Hearing stories of Callum's bravery—truly the man was fawned over—only made her more heartsick. Other than her sister, no one else made her feel as loveable as he did.

Then she would recall the way he let her go, telling her he would rather sit in his grief than move forward with her.

Her emotions ran in cycles. Currently, she missed him, hard. On the heels of missing him, she usually plunged into self loathing, doubt at her ability to read people, and then sheer loneliness. For he, even if he was a charming scoundrel, had utterly ruined her for other men. She wanted what she'd had with him, the intensity, the sweetness, or she didn't want it at all. He'd said it could take years to return his family to the throne. She was swamped with guilt at what she would be doing to her country if she tried to wait that long to marry.

The other thing making her feel guilty was the way she had abandoned her people. She'd left no note, no explanation, and waited weeks before she confirmed she was alive. Granted, her personal guard needed a complete redesign, but she still had chosen to leave, and chosen to stay away, and while she'd been gone, she'd learned things she needed to share with her queen and the small council.

Animals scurried around the forest floor and birds called from the trees. Zara and Ranulf kept going, sustaining scratches here and there, but as another day passed, she grew more sure of her decision to return home. She was needed there.

Lost in her thoughts, it took her a while to realize the sounds in the forest had stopped. She looked to the right, along the tree line, hoping she was getting closer to the road. She almost fell when she spotted two knights dressed in black armor, their chest plates dull and menacing, marking them as Gracchus's men. They approached the wood line and stood perhaps thirty feet away.

Ranulf motioned for her to go farther into the forest.

She ducked around the closest tree, hoping they would move on to search another section of forest. As she scrambled to hide, a branch caught the hood of her cloak and slid it partially off her head. She held still, while the swinging branch dislodged her cloak, giving away her location.

She panicked, hearing footsteps move closer. Then nothing. No sound from Ranulf.

"I'm heading back. She couldn't have made it this far yet."

"You go on. I'm going to take another look."

Zara clasped her hands and said a quick prayer. She heard a thud and a curse from Ranulf and flinched. One curl swept over her forehead, loosened by her nervous jump. She reached out and held it, heart pounding.

Wind blew through the branches overhead, seeping through her gown, making her shiver.

A hand grabbed her arm and swung her away from the tree, pulling her off her horse.

"There you are, you stupid bitch. I knew you were out here." One of Gracchus's knights, a frightful looking man with a cruel mouth, pulled her arms behind her and bound her wrists.

She kicked and screamed, reaching out with her powers to loosen the knots. It was detailed work. Tugging with her powers had only made them tighter. She felt along a different part of the knot until it went slack. She worked each section, straining her shoulders and twisting her wrists until she got her arms free. She ran in the opposite direction, shrieking when she nearly tripped over a fallen branch. She succeeded in frightening her horse. The animal bound past her.

The second knight caught her and cuffed her on the fore-head. In a daze, she fought him, but he bound her more quickly than the first. The second man stuffed a rag in her mouth and gagged her. He used a length of rope tied to her bound hands to pull her along after him. She struggled, trying to work the knot loose with her powers again. If she got free, he'd just hit her again, maybe harder. Her head throbbed. She kept the knots loose and stumbled ahead.

Zara stared into the forest as he led her away, her long curls blowing across her face and into her eyes.

CHAPTER THIRTY-FIVE

A serving wench emerged from a doorway, carrying a huge tray laden with cuts of meat, tureens of stew, and several loaves of crusty bread. Short and scrawny, she walked up the stairs of the dais and set the tray at the end of the trestle table. Zara's eyes followed her movements. All she'd had to eat in the last two days was watered down stew and stale ends of bread.

She had spent two nights in a tiny, dingy, dark room. Zara thought of it as the "upstairs dungeon" because it had two narrow windows near the top of the wall that barely let in any light. She'd tried working the window loose but it was sealed shut. She's fidgeted with the lock but hadn't made progress on that either. No one visited her or spoke to her, besides bringing her food once a day. She was given two pails, one filled with brackish water. The other was empty.

Tonight she'd been surprised when a guard arrived to take her to the dining hall, saying only that Sir Felix requested her presence. She assumed he would ransom her, either to her mother or to Gracchus. She'd considered trying to escape, but once she got out of the manor house, she wouldn't have known where to go. Traveling by herself across Embury seemed like a good way to wind up where she was now.

Her stomach growled as she watched hoping one of the loaves would fall off the tray and bounce to the floor. If they were busy enough, she could use her powers to hide the roll under her dress to eat when she returned to her tiny room. Others before her had gone longer without food, but she had never skipped a meal.

The serving girl lifted each dish off her tray carefully and set them before the man seated at the center of the table. As she scrambled away, a taster ambled over and snagged his bites and sips then gestured to his master that the food was fine to eat.

The tall, thin man seated at the center of the table barely acknowledged his servant. He stared at Zara seated across the room from him and turned the stem of a heavy goblet in his right hand. When her stomach had growled, he had taken a sip and toasted to her. She stared dispassionately back.

"Girl!"

The serving wench returned, taking two steps into the room.

"Make a plate for our guest."

The girl did as she was told, carrying a small plate toward Zara.

"Milord? Where do I put it?"

"On the floor by her feet."

Zara sat on a hard, low stool, her hands bound behind her, but the gag had been taken out of her mouth. Her lips were cracked and her mouth felt like dust. She had been sitting on the stool for what felt like hours, her left leg going numb from the position.

The plate clattered when it hit the stone floor, the bread rolling off and hitting her foot.

"What do you want with me?" Zara asked.

"Oh, pretty bird, be patient. All in due time."

"Who are you?"

"An old nightmare, you could say. Put back into service." He tore off a piece of meat, part of it slapping his chin as he chewed. She was still in Embury, though she hadn't seen Ranulf.

"Do I know you?" He didn't look familiar to her, but he seemed to know something about her.

"You will know me very well." He choked and slurped some wine, nearly slamming down the goblet. He shrugged. "As my guest. I was granted a knighthood for my service to the crown."

Choking down her bile, Zara made herself speak. "Ah. So you're Sir...?"

"Felix Roux." He burped. "At your service. You can call me Felix." He gave her a mock salute.

"Sir Felix, what do you want from me?"

He rolled his eyes at her. "What he always wants. Information. Retribution. Then maybe I'll get a little fun."

"I think there's been some mistake. I'm Princess Zara of L'Ortagia. My family is looking for me. You'll get a handsome reward for returning me." He narrowed his eyes at her, and she hastily added, "*Unharmed.*"

"I already have everything I need. I don't care who you are. You can stay quiet until I bid you to speak."

Zara said nothing as she watched him eat. His manners were rough, as if he did not dine with formal guests very often. But she supposed she wasn't really a guest, so she didn't know if manners applied. She didn't know what rules applied at all anymore. A bubble of hysterical laughter escaped before she could stop it.

Felix scowled and nodded to one of the guards at the back of the hall. He came up behind her and pulled the braid that held her hair hard, yanking her head back and tipping the stool onto the back peg. "That's enough out of you."

Zara recognized the guard as the one who had pulled her

off her horse and brought her here. She peered at him in silence, refusing to show her pain.

"Felix?" A tall man entered the hall. "How long has she been here?"

The man she recognized as Marlowe strode up to Felix and cuffed him on the ear.

Felix smacked his lips. "If the princess bitch can keep her mouth shut, she won't need to be gagged. What'll it be?"

"I'd like some lunch," Zara said. Marlowe watched her closely, his expression stern. She refused to give him any satisfaction either. She was already humiliated by having been captured. The man had obviously come to collect her for the king. "I'll be quiet."

Felix pointed at her with a piece of bread. "Much better."

Marlowe righted her on the stool and tore off a piece of bread for her. She ate it out of his hand, disgusted but hungry. He stepped back from her, but stood just behind her. Zara tested her bonds again, wiggling her fingers. The rope was tight. Hope flared that her bonds weren't iron, but she knew it would take more than releasing those ties to escape.

Felix took a deep drink of ale and pushed back from the table. "Now, then. Tell me about your time with dear little Callum?"

It clicked into place who, exactly, was holding her prisoner, and for a moment she couldn't speak. This was the traitor who Viola had alluded to and Callum had talked about. It had to be. A wave of hysteria rose in Zara and she fought to stay calm. But her palms grew sweaty, her heart beating thunderously in her chest, and a chill rushed over her skin.

"What's the matter? Don't feel like talking? Do you need Marlowe to remind you how this is going to work?"

Although he was intimidating to look at, Marlowe hadn't hurt her. Still, she did not want to see what he was capable of. Panicking, feeling like she would break before they even tried to ask her anything, Zara unfocused her eyes in front of her, seeking a brief escape.

The slap across her face brought her back to reality. Felix had come down from the dais and wiped his hand on his leg. Marlowe stood immobile behind her, so she guessed it had been the smaller man who had struck her. Either way, she needed to think of something. She blinked back into focus and tried to concentrate. Her cheek stung.

"Let's try this again. I asked you about Callum."

"What about him?"

"Come, now, prissy. Tell me everything. Where did they keep you?"

She wasn't sure what to say. She decided to stick as close to the truth as she could. "Embury."

Felix rolled his eyes. "I figured as much. Almost got you when you were in the Blue Flax River."

Zara tried something else since it seemed that he was unpredictable.

"If you want to hear much more, you'll have to feed me. I've barely eaten." She pressed her lips together and waited.

Felix grabbed her chin, squeezing hard. "Oh, forgive me. That's right." He let her go and turned to the side to yell, "Girl! See that our guest is fed."

The serving wench quickly reentered the hall and kneeled before Zara. She picked up the plate and began holding out morsels of food. Zara leaned forward, taking a bite.

"Ale or wine," Felix called. "Which will it be, little bird?"

"Anything," Zara said weakly. "Thank you."

Zara again drank from a cup provided to her and suffered through the indignity of wine dribbling down her chin when the cup was removed too quickly. Strangely, Marlowe offered a handkerchief to mop her chin. The sheer lunacy of the scene struck Zara, but this time she tamped down her reactions.

"Now that you've been fed, tell me what you know of Callum's plans."

"I don't know anything." Zara kept her voice flat and looked Felix in the eye, careful not to seem too challenging.

"Do you take me for an idiot? I know you were with him for weeks! I bet you even spread your legs for him. What do you know of the rebels' plans?" This time Felix's voice boomed into her face and she flinched.

"No. No. I only heard bits and pieces. Nothing, really."

"Tell me the bits and pieces then." Felix sneered at her.

Her mind raced, trying to recall small details, anything that she could use to lead him off the trails Callum had left.

"He spoke of correspondence between the camps. He took me to one by the Blue Flax River." Felix already knew of the camp they'd stayed in.

"Just how does he seek to destroy Gracchus?"

"I don't know," Zara said, already exhausted. "We were chased by the royal guard."

"Who is helping him?"

"I don't know. You mean the rebels?"

"I mean the money. He would have talked to you about helping him." It was so close to the many discussions she'd had with Callum she wasn't sure what to say.

"I don't know for sure. L'Ortagia hasn't aided the rebels."

Felix's brows rose. "Oh, he wanted your help. With a pretty face like that, he probably tried to swive it out of you." Felix licked his lips.

She wasn't sure she'd be able to keep her food down. "I didn't have any wealth on my person when he took me from the castle. None. He helped me avoid marriage to Torwyn."

He cracked his knuckles, one at a time. "You listen to me, pretty bird. You were with him. You know something. Capturing you will help restore me to my place in Blackthorne."

"How would that help you? What do you need?" She would use any bit of leverage she could get. She wasn't totally power-less. She'd just never used her powers to attack someone, had never considered it, even.

"What I need is some respect. Instead, all I get are half-truths and excuses, including from you. Didn't you like your lunch? Wasn't it up to your standards?"

She didn't know how to answer him. Over his shoulder, she spotted the long table. Several dishes remained. The serving girl had left the pitcher of ale on the edge of the table.

"Marlowe, the princess needs some persuasion." Though Lord Sullivan only stood a few feet behind her, each step sounded ominous as he moved closer. He squatted down behind her, placing one hand on her elbow and the other, rather curiously, on her bound hands. He tapped them twice, then moved his hand to her other elbow. Then he pulled her to stand, half-supporting her by her arms as she wavered upon being on her feet.

Zara's mind spun with terror. Any chips she had, she feared she'd already used. As the feeling started to come back to her limbs, pain shot down her legs. She sucked in a breath and tried to keep her eyes on Felix.

"There now. I bet I can make you remember." Felix slapped her. "Where did you stay?"

Tears stung her eyes. She reached for the pitcher with her powers, spilling the ale across the table. She brought it closer, at the last second, picking up speed and smacking Felix in the back of the head with it.

"Ow!" Felix rubbed at the back of his head, glaring around the room. "I'm the master of this house."

The pitcher crashed to the floor, shattering. She'd just broken one of her weapons.

Felix slapped her again, undeterred by the broken earthen-ware at his feet. "Where did you stay?"

She shuddered. "The camp at Blue Flax."

"After the raid?"

How had he known about that? How could she get him off track and escape? "I don't know." Felix gestured to Marlowe, and, cursing under his breath, he pulled her arms back, enough so she felt a pinch in her shoulders. "Ah! A house. A great house. We rested there."

Felix grimaced and slapped her again. He still might ransom her, but he would probably blame the rebels for her injuries. She was a fool. Over and over again, she'd assumed a safety she obviously didn't have.

"That would be Omara's. After that?"

"Felix, enough," Marlowe said through gritted teeth.

"I don't know!" Marlowe's grip on her shoulders eased, though he still held onto her. Were any knives still on the table?

"Another estate." Her mind blanked. It took all of her concentration to search the table. All she found was a plate. The silverware was gone. "Farther north."

She pulled on the plate, unfocusing her gaze while she swung it towards them. She pulled harder and it glanced off his shoulder before hitting the floor.

"Girl! Get back to the kitchen! I'll deal with you later."

Felix was unfazed, but focused on her.

Marlowe murmured something to him but to no effect.

Something about the baron gave her pause. Callum had never said anything about Marlowe, but Jeffors had had an odd way of talking about him. He was one of Gracchus' closest advisors, quite close with Prince Adrian too. What was he doing here?

"What does little Callum want?"

Zara answered truthfully because anyone who knew the prince knew how he felt about his family. "To regain the throne for his family."

"And who might that be?"

"What?"

"For whom does he fight? They're all dead. At least except for some ridiculous rumors that surface every couple of years."

"I don't... I don't know." Again, he was getting so close, and she couldn't think of a way to lie that he'd believe. She was terrible at lying. Felix glared. "For himself, I suppose," she finished quietly.

"What was that?" He put a hand to his ear, cocking his head to the side, and Zara's stomach dropped to her toes.

"He sought the throne for himself. To avenge his family."

Felix snorted. "There was a lie. You do know something. I bet he told you everything. Every little detail. Why wouldn't he? He finally had a bitch in his bed who knew he was a prince. Someone to confide in. Of course he'd spill every secret. You probably ate it all up too."

As he spoke, Zara knew she had to escape. Again, Marlowe held her arms firmly but not tightly, his gaze, as she could see out of the corner of her eye, straight ahead. Quickly, she reached out with her magic and loosened her bindings. As the rope slipped, she caught it with her fingertips. Marlowe stayed stock still, outwardly seeming to be listening to Felix.

Felix must have been waiting for her to say something to his accusations. She decided to give him the response he was looking for. Thinking of her beloved Mondelac Castle in flames, she squeezed tears from her eyes as she dropped her head, shaking her shoulders as she did so, the sides of her face burning from his slaps.

"I'm so ashamed! He did tell me things. All about his plans. I thought he wanted my help." She mumbled this slightly, then raised her head as Felix stepped closer. Tears slid down her cheeks as she cast her gaze around the stones in front of her. Taking the ends of the rope in each hand, she wrapped a length around each hand, careful not to show movement in her arms.

"You're a dumb slut like all the rest. You spread your legs, hoping you could be the one to save him." Felix cackled. "Jameson! Go fetch something to write with. I think our princess has things we need to record. I don't want to miss this."

The other guard left the room. This was her moment. The hall was empty but for her, Felix, and Marlowe. The serving wench had retreated to the kitchens.

"I must be! I... I thought he would marry me." She wrenched this from deep within herself, aching over the words, even though she knew she needed to say them. She rolled her eyes as she looked in Felix's face. "He has grand plans to take back the throne. He's raising an army and he's raising allies."

Felix licked his lips again. "Stupid. So stupid. King Gracchus has his last remaining hope."

That caught her up short. She hiccupped and sniffed, hoping to drag out more from him. "His last hope?" She went for the jugular. "He's so arrogant. He thinks he has what it takes to defeat Gracchus."

Felix grunted, stepping right up to her. Slowly, Marlowe released her arms and stepped back, so subtle Felix paid him no mind.

"He'll never win. Neither he nor his precious brother."

She flinched. "Isn't Duncan dead?"

Felix grabbed her ear, pulling her up. "Enough with your lying." He let go for a brief moment and rubbed his hands together in front of his body. Tears of pain stung her eyes and she blinked them away, terrified he would torture information out of her.

She stared at him, panting, her face stinging. He grabbed her jaw, pulling her face forward. "He's found him, hasn't he?"

Tears streamed down her cheeks, and she nodded.

He smiled, looking excited.

"Well, then. Your lost prince is in for a surprise." He squeezed harder, and Zara's teeth cut into her cheeks. "Gracchus is on his way to get Duncan and will now have Callum too."

The shock wave that went down her spine was what finally did it. She couldn't let him. Felix wouldn't just return her to her family and pretend like he hadn't kidnapped, starved, and now tortured and beaten her. At the glassy look in his eyes, Zara saw her own death.

She let one end of the rope go and brought her arms forward, quickly securing the end again around her other hand.

"No. You can't have him." She reached up and pressed the rope against his windpipe, while sweeping her left foot around the back of his ankle, tripping him. As they fell to the floor, she tightened the rope across his neck. Blood seeped into her hands as they pressed against him, her knuckles grinding into the floor, and she guessed he had hit his head hard when he fell. He struggled against her, scrabbling against the stones. Using strength she pulled from her nocturne power, she pinned his arms with her knees and pressed as hard against his windpipe as she could.

A pair of hands circled Felix's neck but she didn't let go of her rope. Marlowe squeezed, his fingers white with strain.

"Let go," she bit out.

The baron released Felix but hovered over him.

She squeezed as hard as she could, holding on while Felix's legs kicked and he tried to dislodge her.

Finally, he stilled and his eyes bulged, his face purple. He went limp beneath her.

"He's dead."

Marlowe released his hold and stepped back, smoothing his coat back in place and mopping at the sweat on his brow.

Zara climbed off of Felix and looked around for the other guard. She dropped the rope on the floor.

"Jameson won't be bothering you," Marlowe said.

She spotted him lying in the doorway in a pool of blood, a dagger sticking out of his neck.

"Is that yours?" she asked Marlowe.

"It was… a favorite."

He helped her up and held her until she stopped shaking.

Marlowe tilted his head at the doorway and said, "Your friends are outside."

CHAPTER THIRTY-SIX

Z ara fled the room, searching through the hallway for the exit. Her limbs felt jittery. She turned corners until she found the main hall. She raced across the flagstone to the entrance.

Her fingers shook and she fumbled with the massive door. On the other side, a familiar group of soldiers stared back at her from the courtyard. It was a group of Emburian rebels, including Jeffors, Viola, and Ranulf. Off to the side, just past Jeffors' shoulder stood Varro, the time-stopping nocturne she'd met in Vespertine.

"What are you doing here?" She ran out into the courtyard. She needed to put as much distance between herself and that hall.

"Princess. It's all right now." Jeffors pulled a handkerchief from his pocket.

She accepted his handkerchief and wiped her face, cursing at the trickle of tears. Her hands wouldn't stop shaking.

"We rode all night after we got the message you were here."

Marlowe.

She took deep breaths.

Jeffors glanced at her soiled dress and swollen cheeks. "We came to take you back to L'Ortagia."

"Is Callum with you?" She didn't see him, but she wasn't sure if this was the entire group of soldiers.

"He already set sail," Jeffors said. "Viola, give her your cloak."

A scratchy but familiar weight settled around her shoulders. "Here. We brought a carriage this time too."

"Get the princess settled. We'll meet you there." Jeffors signaled to his men to follow him into the manor house.

"Wait."

Jeffors patiently turned back to her.

"Felix is dead."

Jeffors winced. "What did you say?"

"There's no point in going back in. I killed him."

"Is anyone coming after you?"

"I don't know. They kept me locked up until today." With Marlowe working both sides, she didn't know how much she could say about his involvement.

"Viola will get you settled. There's something I have to do." He turned and left, ducking into the still open door, followed by four of his men.

Varro approached her at the side of the carriage. "Your Highness, a word?"

CHAPTER THIRTY-SEVEN

"Why are you here?" Zara asked Varro.

She sat in the carriage across from him. Viola stood guard outside. They'd rest the horses as long as they could. It looked like they'd arrived moments before she'd stumbled out of the manor house.

The courtyard was eerily quiet. Zara strained to listen for more of Gracchus' knights to arrive.

"The king's forces are spread thin. We have a few moments before General Millerton returns."

"I heard Felix's men found you and I wanted to help." He tipped his head. "You found a way out on your own."

"Mostly," she said. She pulled Viola's cloak tighter, certain she'd never been as cold as she was now, even in the summer heat. She fiddled with the packet of bread and cheese Viola had given her.

"Here." Varro handed her a flask from inside his coat.

She took off the lid and sniffed. "Did you add anything to this? A special nocturne brew?"

"Nothing that would hurt you." Varro laughed. One of the

earrings along his left ear caught the light, sparkling in the late afternoon glow. "No. It's whiskey."

Zara took a sip and clutched the flask to her chest. "Thank you. What do you want?"

Varro removed a timepiece from his belt. He spun it on his palm. "Before you leave Embury I wanted to know what the lordling said about recognizing us."

Zara watched his hands. They were ink stained but nimble. She gazed at his face, certain his bloodshot eyes matched her own.

"I pleaded your case. He wanted to confer with Jeffors. That is where we left it."

Varro blew out a breath. "We can't wait any longer."

"I know." She took another sip from the flask. And another. Finally, the warmth hit her. "Once he has his brother, he'll come around."

"You aren't sure of that," he scoffed.

"No, but clearly Jeffors trusts you. And Callum trusts no one as much as Jeffors."

"We need more assurance than that." Varro flipped the watch as easily as if it were a coin. "I have a proposal for you, my fellow lady nocturne. But first, tell me, are you going after him or going home?"

Zara sat straighter against the seat. "Home, hopefully for reinforcements."

"Excellent." He turned the watch over and flipped open the back, revealing a small, flat compartment, just big enough for a tiny packet. He shook it out. "This is for you."

She held out her hand. "What does it do?"

"It will be familiar to you. Take it when you need it most. It will…enhance your abilities."

Zara laughed. "I won't be using them for what I have in mind. I can't use them to get home faster, or to convince my mother of anything she doesn't want to do. I can't use them to sail to Casparre faster, can I?"

Varro shrugged.

"Stop talking in riddles. I've had it with men spooling out what they want. Just tell me."

"Madam, I want to come out of the shadows, fully, even without having to offer anything as incentive. Because it is right."

Zara rubbed at her forehead. She held out her hand, waving off his offer of whatever was in the back of the watch. "You have my word that I will make it happen."

Varro squeezed her fingers, closing his eyes briefly.

She gave him back his flask. Weariness tugged at her. She was picking up strings that Callum had left. First with Felix, and now with Varro. Maybe she was being presumptuous. Maybe once he had his brother back, Callum would cast her off. She had to try though.

Varro slipped from the carriage and said his goodbyes to the soldiers.

A whistle echoed across the courtyard stones.

Viola approached the carriage window. "We're leaving. Keep the curtains closed if you can."

Zara pulled one side shut and reached across to grab the other. Her hand brushed against a smooth metal object lying on the seat. Varro had left her the watch with the hidden compartment. She tucked it into a pocket of her gown.

CHAPTER THIRTY-EIGHT

Callum stood at the helm of the ship, anxious to reach port in Casparre and disembark. The next test would be whether they could secure papers to cross into Marenburg, a country that was curiously closed to most visitors. He was relying on Matteo's network of spies and couriers, but he trusted the young man implicitly.

He also had Zara's letter of introduction. Still, he knew he wouldn't feel safe until he had rescued his brother and was on a ship back to Embury.

The winds had been strong, and they'd arrived a day sooner than they planned.

"What business have you in Marenburg?"

"I am a merchant. I brought wine and ale."

"You think we can't make our own?"

Callum tamped down his impatience, remembering the warnings he'd heard about how notoriously difficult the Marenburg department of tourism could be. "No, of course not. I was actually hoping to trade for some of the fine spirits I've had from Marenburg vintners."

"We already have several established agreements." The clerk

sniffed disdainfully. "What you offer would have to be exceptional."

Callum eyed the government worker, certain he'd fall short of whatever exceptional would be and wondering what it would take. He already regretted his disguise and the setup, but had to keep trying.

"I wish to exchange between our countries as I have recently done in L'Ortagia. We provided wine for the royal wedding that, sadly, was not to be."

"What did you say?"

Callum swallowed. "That we experienced wonderful hospitality when we stayed in L'Ortagia. I had hoped to extend that in my travels to your country."

A dreamy look came over the worker's face, his lips softening until it seemed like he could swoon. Callum knew that expression. And he had a guess who had inspired it. He put his elbow on the counter and cupped his chin in his hand. "Did I mention I met the princess when I was there?"

"Which one?" The clerk matched his posture like they were compatriots.

Just to be safe, Callum said, "Oh, both. Although I spent more time with Princess Zara. She was very interested in our wines, declaring them 'exquisite.'"

"She did?" The clerk practically wiped drool off his lips. "I only saw her once, in a parade through our capitol on one of her state visits, but she was so lovely, so regal."

Callum nodded, warming to the topic. "It was a brief meeting, as she was personally selecting wines for the banquet that night, but she made an impression on me."

"She has that way, yes. We'd hoped the queen would make a match for her with one of our princes."

"Actually, she gave me the idea to travel to your country. Her Highness mentioned she and the prince were considering traveling to Marenburg together." Callum ended with a small shrug.

"Well, then, we mustn't disappoint the princess." The clerk reached under the counter for a ledger, setting it in front of himself. He made a notation and the day's date. "Dear sir, how long do you plan to stay in our country?"

Callum smiled. "Hopefully, a few weeks. Long enough to see the leaves change in the autumn."

The clerk nodded , warming up for another speech on a compelling aspect of his country. Excellent. He'd use any guidance he could get.

After an impassioned treatise on autumnal points of interest, the clerk signed and stamped Callum's papers with a final flourish. "Good luck on your journey."

DAYS LATER, one of Matteo's couriers delivered a letter. It had come from Embury, through both human and nocturne transport. Callum tore the seal. He read the words twice, not believing what was scrawled in the lines of script. He had an address for his brother, confirmed by two sources, and the identity of the rebellion's highest-ranking spy in the usurper's command.

Callum shook his head. Duncan was in grave danger. But at least now he was being kept close by.

Callum grabbed his sword and Zara's letter and rounded up the group of soldiers who'd accompanied him.

Duncan was a short carriage ride away.

Callum had guessed at those in Gracchus' court who would betray the king, but he hadn't been sure. This, at least, was a welcome surprise. He relished the idea of the king being betrayed by one of his own. He had no idea how the man could stomach such a close association to the king, but he was grateful.

They arrived at their destination and got out. The building was old, enclosed behind high walls. It was a jail filled and maintained by one of Casparre's magistrates.

In the end, it took little more than Zara's letter, and bribing the guards with wine.

Callum strode down the dark hallway, listening to the sounds of men bickering, sliding furniture around their cells, and the sickening rattle of chains. He tried not to breathe in the stench of unwashed bodies. After so many years and false leads, he held onto hope that he'd see his siblings again. If he'd survived, maybe they had too.

But every time he'd been disappointed.

"Down at the end, sir," one of the guards said.

No sounds emerged from the last cell. Callum stood in front of the open door, squinting at the light coming in from a small window too high to reach. A man, his arm in a rough sling, sat against the far wall, his head tipped to his chest as if he was sleeping. His hair was long, caked with blood on one side, but streaked blond. His clothing was in disrepair, his boots scuffed, his face in shadow, half covered with hair. One hand was slung over an updrawn knee.

Callum's face heated. His heart pounded, nearly drowning out the sounds around him.

He took a step forward.

He knew those hands. They resembled his own and his father's: broad fingers with a bend at each pinky.

"Duncan?" He asked. On careful steps, so as not to alarm him, he crossed to the man.

He shuddered, perhaps caught in a nightmare. Everything about him looked rough and weathered.

"Duncan, it's me," Callum said gently. He crouched beside the other man, hands shaking as he saw his brother's nose. It had the smallest bend in the middle, from an accident when they were little and loved to chase each other with play swords.

He squeezed his brother's shoulder.

The man's eyes snapped open, bloodshot but blue as the Catarine Sea off the coast of Ballyreine. His gaze seized on Callum, and he shook his head, tears welling. "Cal?"

"I'm here, Duncan." Callum clutched the hand hanging across Duncan's knee. After a pause, Duncan squeezed back. "You're alive."

He wanted to crush his brother close to his chest. He was here. It was Duncan. His brother was alive.

"I am," Duncan said. He coughed, wincing against injuries he'd sustained.

"We have to get you out of here. They granted me a few minutes, but you're leaving with me." Callum stood, readying to call the guard back.

"They won't let you. I've already tried. They're holding me for…"

"Don't say his name. I found you and I won't leave your side until you're safely away from this place." Callum felt frantic. The king was due to arrive in Marenburg any day, if he hadn't already.

"I'm tired of running, Cal." Duncan's tone was low, almost as if he was speaking to himself.

"I'll carry you out of here myself." Callum's heart raced. The walls of the jail cell seemed to be closing in on him. "Guard!"

"It's no use." Duncan brushed his sleeve against his face and blinked up at Callum. "Thank you for coming for me."

"I never stopped looking," Callum said.

Boots rang out across the stone floor, the sound sharp, like they had metal heels.

"Quinnah?" Duncan's voice was a rasp.

"A few years ago, there was a rumor that she'd survived. Since then, nothing."

Duncan's head dipped forward again. He looked like he aged another ten years. His eyes were almost sunken in his face, both darkening with bruises. "Maybe it's for the best if she's gone."

"Don't say that."

"Gentlemen," the guard said. He must have stayed close enough to Duncan's cell that they hadn't heard him returning. "Herr Risenbach is here to release you… to his custody."

Callum turned to the man entering the cell, ready to offer his hand. Risenbach gave him a cold stare. "We have reason to believe you would like to be our special guests. I've been corresponding with your father's successor." He kicked at a piece of straw that covered the toe of his boot. "The two of you together will make a nice welcome gift for Gracchus."

CHAPTER THIRTY-NINE

August 6
Mondelac Castle
Kingdom of L'Ortagia

Z ara, Jeffors, and their small group of soldiers arrived at Mondelac Castle's gates just past midnight. Yves, the head of the castle guard, ushered them into the courtyard without waking the entire castle.

"You should be the one to tell your mother you're home," Yves said. He was understandably quite protective of the queen, but no less so of she and Sidony. "She's barely slept since you left."

"I'll speak to her, but I'm asking for an emergency small council meeting."

"At this hour?" he asked. Had his graying hair gotten lighter in her absence? She'd put the people who cared about her through so much. The courtyard was too dark for her to judge the damage from the fire, but from what she could tell, all of the major buildings within the walls still stood.

"If we wait until morning, she'll get bogged down with the

rest of her schedule." If her mother had her way, she would let her wait a month before addressing her concerns. Zara had to meet with the full council, and Sidony, before her mother could rearrange their priorities. She and Callum were out of time. "What I have to discuss with the council can't wait."

Yves crossed his arms over his chest but relented, escorting her and Jeffors to the meeting room outside the queen's apartments. Before he left to wake the queen, Zara pulled him into a quick hug. "I'm sorry to have worried you."

He squeezed her shoulders, his barrel chest a comforting weight against her cheek. "I wish you'd told us sooner. The not knowing was difficult."

"Of course it would be." She pulled back and looked him in the eye. "Please trust that I was out of options."

Yves pressed his lips into a firm line. "A lot has happened since you left."

"Then let's bring them all together so I can be caught up." She caught his hand. "Thank you for watching over everyone while I was gone. Are any Emburians still here?"

She'd heard rumors that Gracchus had kept a presence at Mondelac, but she wasn't sure if that was true.

A strange look passed over Yves' face. "Prince Adrian just left. He took his men with him. You missed him by a few hours."

"He was still here?" She glanced at Jeffors. "Gracchus must have called him back to Embury."

"It's best if your mother explains," Yves said quickly. "I'll get everyone assembled."

He left. It seemed that there was a lot to discuss.

Jeffors waited with her. He paced the length of the room, worrying his thumb on the hilt of the small dagger he kept on his belt. Zara shook the travel dust from her borrowed gown before searching for writing implements. She had several points to make and she needed to ensure she covered them all.

Note-taking kept her from joining Jeffors to pace the room. She had to try this option.

Daven, Master of Swords, Emmanuelle, Chief Diplomat of Foreign Affairs, and Lord Forrenti, Exchequer of Coin and Currency arrived before the queen. When her mother entered the room, Zara approached her and curtsied.

"I see that you are in one piece." Her mother's gaze was like iron. "If we'd known where you were, we would have sent for you sooner. And provided better accommodations for your return journey."

Zara lowered her head. "I want to speak to the small council. And Sidony."

"And who is this?"

Zara brought Jeffors forward. "Mother, this is General Jeffors Millerton of the Emburian rebel army. General Millerton, Her Royal Highness, Queen Isabeau of L'Ortagia."

"General Millerton, thank you for escorting Zara home. I assume you were also involved in her initial trip to Embury."

Jeffors hesitated, glancing at Zara.

"Mother, I want to wait until Sidony gets here."

"Very well. We'll begin once Sidony arrives," the queen said from her seat at the head of the table in the small council chamber. She gestured to her lady-in-waiting. "Sylvie, fetch my youngest daughter immediately."

Sylvie left and Zara paced by the doors. She'd taken to wearing Callum's ring on a thin chain, tucking it unto her bodice. She pulled it free and rubbed her thumb across the dark stone. She felt closer to him in that moment.

It wasn't long before footsteps sounded on the other side. Zara stepped back and opened the doors with her powers, the rush of air giving her a renewed sense of purpose. The doors were enormous and heavy. Until she'd really honed her skill, she'd never have been able to move an object so large.

Sidony had clearly been pulled from her bed. She wore a

green silk robe over her nightclothes and her hair was in a knot on her head. She seemed to carry herself with a renewed sense of purpose, of ease.

She gave Sidony a hesitant smile. Her sister rushed toward her, hugging her fiercely.

"Zara?"

She hugged her back, nodding.

"Good," Isabeau said from her chair. "Now that you are here, Sidony, we can begin. Sylvie, that will be all."

Once the lady-in-waiting left, Zara again used her powers to shut the massive doors. Her temples throbbed at the exertion, but it was worth the effort.

Sidony glanced at the doors in wonder.

The instant acceptance of her powers and her return filled Zara with gratitude and a touch of guilt. She'd left her sister here, alone, to deal with Torwyn and the aftermath of her leaving. They had much to discuss, but she'd been right to trust her with her secrets. Sidony had been up to the challenge.

"That's enough dramatics for the evening, Zara. Please, be seated."

Sidony leaned close and touched her arm. "I've been worried about you. Are you well?"

Again, that care and concern humbled her. The queen cut her off before she could reply.

"Yes, that's the question we'd all like to have answered. Be seated. You called this meeting in the middle of the night. There'll be time to catch up with one another later."

The queen sat at the head of a rectangular table made of polished mahogany, inlaid with ash. Her family crest was laid out in the woodwork. Along the queen's right side were her advisors: Yves, Daven, Emmanuelle, and Forrenti.

Zara strode to a spot opposite the queen at the other end of the table. Sidony went to Zara's immediate right, with Jeffors next to her.

"Let me begin with introductions." Zara placed her hands on the table, keeping her back straight and her voice modulated. She had to retain control and convince the small council to back Callum. "To my right is General Jeffors Millerton. He leads the army of whom you would call the Embury rebels. In Embury, they are royalists."

Silence greeted her announcement, although Sidony smiled and nodded at Jeffors.

Jeffors, whom Zara knew to be relieved to finally have an audience with the queen, greeted the room. "Thank you, Your Highness. I'm pleased to meet all of you."

Zara finished the rest of the introductions. The icy reception from the small council seemed to be directed at the general.

"You snatch her from her own home and then sit here as if nothing happened?" Yves bit out.

"Yves, hear them out," the queen snapped.

"Yes, Highness." The captain flexed his jaw.

"Jeffors is under my protection," Zara warned.

"It's to be expected," Jeffors said. He nodded at Yves. "We were desperate to stop the alliance between L'Ortagia and the usurper. I urged Callum to abduct your princess."

Yves shot to his feet.

The queen spoke to Yves and Zara turned to Jeffors.

"Why antagonize him?" Zara asked Jeffors in a quiet voice.

"If we are to sway the council to our side, they need to know with whom they are dealing. From what you've told me about the captain, I thought it best to be honest."

Zara nodded. "You understand him perfectly." When provoked, Yves had a fierce temper, but it quickly dissipated. If she could lay out her request, he might be the first person on the council to back her.

Red-faced with anger, Yves returned to his seat.

She took a deep breath. "Thank you all for agreeing to meet.

My purpose for this meeting is to protect L'Ortagia. During my time with the rebels, I learned that one of the supposedly deceased heirs, Prince Callum, has been living in hiding since the assassinations of his family and King Gracchus' rise to power. The rebels seek to reinstall King Angus' heir to the throne of Embury. We need to support them in this cause."

At her side, Sidony tensed.

"You called this emergency meeting before we could discuss what happened to you, where you have been, and how you are returned to us. How am I to know that this man isn't somehow coercing you?" The queen lifted a finger from where her hands rested on the table, indicating Jeffors.

"General Millerton is my guest. He helped to bring me home." Zara knew the queen would be the hardest to convince. "I'm under no coercion from him or anyone else."

Daven asked, "Princess Zara, are you asking us to believe that after weeks of captivity, you returned unharmed? There was no ransom, no assurance of your safety, aside from a letter we received from you mere days ago. Do you know why you were kidnapped?"

"It was in order to stop my wedding." She paused, assessing the faces at the table. Most wore pinched and expectant expressions. Did they assume the rebels had abused her? Her appearance was not up to L'Ortagian standards, but she had to convince them that the rebels were better allies than Gracchus. "I assure you that I was unharmed during my time with them."

Sidony fidgeted in her chair. The hairs on the back of Zara's neck stood up. While she'd been gone, she'd assumed things had continued at Mondelac like they always had. Something had changed. What had Sidony had to do while she'd been gone?

"You are aware that your sister has wed Prince Adrian?" the queen asked her.

"I heard of their betrothal," Zara said. She hadn't wanted the news to be true. She turned to her sister. "The wedding already happened?"

"Yes. The day before yesterday." Sidony blushed, her eyes pleading for understanding. "It was a love match."

Zara sat back in her chair. A dalliance wouldn't have been surprising given the attraction between the two. What would this mean for their alliance?

"Things moved forward without you," Sidony said. She twisted the tie of her robe. "And you were gone for so long."

Zara pressed a trembling hand over her heart. What had she done? "Were the terms the same as my arrangement?" she asked the queen.

"Better, in fact. I managed to maneuver a few changes since Gracchus was unable to rescue you." The queen's satisfaction was palpable.

Had she escaped only to put her sister in danger? Dread slithered through her. "Then I'm too late. It's done. I couldn't stop it."

Sidony touched her hand. "I wanted to wed him."

Zara's head swam. "That's not possible." Adrian had fought Callum for her, but what did that mean?

"Oh, but it is." Her mother gazed at Sidony with what neared contentment, for her. When she faced Zara, her expression turned flinty. "Would you like to hear how much she wanted to? You insisted your sister attend this meeting. Let's hear what she has to say."

What had Sidony done? Surely their mother had forced her to wed Adrian. Maybe they could still annul the marriage.

When she faced her sister, ready to comfort and protect her, Sidony sat straighter. "I *wanted* to marry him. Prince Adrian is kind and thoughtful. I believe we are well-suited."

Had her mother turned Sidony against her? Was she the only one who saw how dangerous Adrian was? "The prince can be quite charming. He even tried to protect me from Callum, fighting for me. But he's his uncle's lackey. Everything the rebels said about the king's spy is true. He's surely involved in the king's misdeeds. Perhaps it's not too late to seek an annulment for you."

"I only know his character from what he has shown in his treatment of me and others. Since you were gone for weeks, without any word, we needed the alliance, and I agreed to the marriage. Willingly. Happily. Adrian is a good man."

Sidony did not seem like a woman coerced. She seemed... happy. Maybe there was more to Adrian than Zara knew. Him being so close to his uncle was a very bad sign.

"Yves said the prince left. Shouldn't he be by your side?"

"He had something urgent to attend to." Sidony was visibly pained. Perhaps she believed her husband's excuse.

There was nothing for it though. "Sidony, this brings me no joy. I tried to get here to stop the wedding. Prince Adrian serves at the usurper's command. I know you think he's a good man, but he isn't."

Sidony looked visibly pained. "What are you accusing him of?"

"The prince is a trusted advisor of the king," Jeffors said. "The usurper uses him to rout threats against the crown."

"Every man and woman serves at the pleasure of their monarch. Why is this any different?"

"Because the rebels assert that Gracchus had the previous regent—including his queen and three children—assassinated," Zara said, exasperated.

Her accusation was met with silence.

"There have been rumors of this for years," Isabeau began. She repeated the usurper's alibi.

"Whatever Adrian did was done out of loyalty to family. He gathers information. He would never hurt anyone."

They went around again about Adrian's character. Zara was swayed, in part, by Sidony's defense of her husband. Maybe she knew something about him that explained his loyalty to Gracchus.

Finally, her mother brought the argument around to the other side of the MacKinnon family tree. "If the man who took you is who he claims to be, why hasn't an Emburian court reinstated his title? His throne?"

"The usurper bribed the courts, Your Highness," Jeffors explained.

The queen threw up her hands. "I didn't call this meeting in the middle of the night to debate legal issues in a neighboring kingdom. My heir is returned, and I want to know where she was and why she was gone for so long. If the prince serves the king, then at least he has his priorities in order, which is more than my heir can accomplish."

Her words stung. Exhaustion from the past few weeks dragged at her. "I'm afraid it's all tied together, Mother."

"You can't be serious," the queen said.

Part of her lived to thwart the queen's wishes. Being back in the small council room brought that home to her. She'd tried obedience and making herself into what she'd thought would earn that approval and it had all been for naught. She'd known it the moment she stepped out of her room with Callum, that she needed to stand on her own. If she was every to reign effectively in her kingdom, she had to be willing to disagree and stand up for what she believed in.

In this instance, it would be in the middle of the night, in a ratty borrowed gown, with death at her heels. She couldn't help but find the dark humor in the moment.

With a quirk of her lips, she said, "I also came back on behalf of Callum MacKinnon, one of the Lost Princes of Embury."

CHAPTER FORTY

"The one who kidnapped you?" the queen snapped. "Who you seem to be defending?"

Zara nodded. "Though I'll not have the rebels changed with kidnapping because I went willingly."

Sidony blew out a breath. It was clear that her sister had kept her secret, though it had probably cost her.

"He kept you long enough to convince you to help his cause," the queen said. She sat back, Zara's admission apparently giving her plenty to consider.

"Aye," Zara said softly. "Thought I'm not pleased with his methods. That's what I'm here to improve upon."

"Did they hurt you?" her mother asked.

"The rebels didn't." Now was not the time to discuss her ordeal with Felix. Nor would she bring up how Callum's refusal to take her to Marenburg still stung. "In many ways, Prince Callum was good to me."

Sidony frowned in concern. Her sister knew her so well.

Jeffors spoke. "Your Highness, one of the soldiers who was tasked with bringing a message to the court as to the princess' safety was captured. It was weeks until we knew you hadn't received word. My apologies."

Daven nodded, apparently satisfied.

"As if being kidnapped—or rather, inelegantly snuck out of her own home—isn't bad enough. We'll have you examined to determine your health, daughter. I don't want any surprises in the coming months."

Zara knew it was coming but chose not to react to her mother's comment.

"I am petitioning the council for recognition of Callum MacKinnon as surviving Prince of the House of MacKinnon of Embury, and to offer L'Ortagia's support for his claim of sovereignty."

"You claim the rebels are led by one of the lost princes of Embury?" Lady Emmanuelle seized on an important first step of Zara's campaign.

"I saw for myself he wasn't another pretender," Zara said.

Jeffors stayed quiet, likely because the council would not necessarily believe his assertions.

"You only met him once, daughter, when you were children. How can you be sure?"

"I saw his ring, he told me of the massacre of his family and how he escaped. He remembered details of our family visit that an impostor would not know. And, most tellingly, he strongly resembles the young man I met several years ago. It is Callum."

"Couldn't he fool you?"

"I spent weeks in his company and with his soldiers. They are loyal to him, due to his birth, yes, but also to the man he has become."

Jeffors nodded.

"Then why hasn't he petitioned us for recognition before now?" Lady Emmanuelle asked.

Zara gave a brief, rueful smile. "He has. He was refused an audience."

"What would L'Ortagia have to gain in acknowledging his existence and claim?" Forrenti, pragmatic as always, finally spoke up.

Zara answered, "L'Ortagia has always had a history of supporting our allies. The royal house of MacKinnon should be no different."

"Gracchus is also a MacKinnon," the queen said.

"Distantly, though he was in the line of succession, obviously. You've heard the rumors that he acquired the throne by ill means." Zara swallowed the euphemism, trying hard not to sound brash. "He orchestrated the assassination of King Angus and Queen Maeve, as well as Princess Quinnah."

"Have you lost the ability to count since you were rescued?"

Zara cast a look of disappointment at her mother. "Not at all," she answered in a measured tone. "Not only did Prince Callum escape, the rebels believe they have located Prince Duncan."

A hush went over the room. The survival of King Angus's oldest child, as Zara had expected, garnered special attention.

"And where is this prince? Why has *he* not made a claim to the throne?" Lady Emmanuelle asked.

"His survival has only recently been verified. He is being held by one of our allies, in Marenburg."

The queen's expression changed, going from sarcastic and chiding to thoughtful and strategic. Zara counted another on her side, surprised the queen had changed her mind so quickly. She knew her well, though, and royal birth was highly valued by the queen.

Forrenti steepled his fingers under his chin. "Princess Zara, I think now might be a good time to outline all that you are petitioning the small council for."

"Very well. I petition the small council to recognize and honor Callum and Duncan MacKinnon of Embury's claim of sovereignty to the throne. I also petition that L'Ortagia renounce Gracchus as the usurper and pledge our support and troops to the MacKinnons should they be needed to retake their rightful places as king and royal heir. And there's one more article to the petition: I would like to lead a peaceful L'Ortagian delegation to Marenburg in order to petition for both princes' release."

"Callum has been captured," Zara continued. "Though not by Gracchus. I intend to travel to Marenburg to negotiate for his release."

"It's too bad you didn't get here two days ago. You could have traveled with the king," her mother said.

Zara could no longer let the council be swayed to ignore the threat Gracchus posed. They clearly hadn't grasped what it meant that one of the princes had survived such an ordeal. "Callum typically goes by the name of Ash. He lived in hiding for a few years and then among the rebels. Is it that surprising the rebels would rally around him?"

"How would I know the inner thoughts of a rabble band of vagrants?" the queen said.

"Mother, you go too far. Callum is Angus and Maeve's son." Zara laced her fingers and rested her hands on the table. "We've neglected the turmoil our neighbors in Embury have endured since the royal family's deaths. We can no longer stand idly by."

"It is quite a leap you are asking us all to take, Zara," Sidony said.

Zara needed Sidony to believe her. "The usurper plotted to kill the royal family."

"What evidence do you have?" Daven asked.

"Those are serious charges against a king, Your Highness," Yves said carefully.

Lady Emmanuelle's mouth hung open in shock. "The stories of the Lost Royals are true?"

"It is one thing to state that a dead princes has returned," her mother said crisply. "It is quite another to make such accusations."

Forrenti lowered his head as if in prayer.

The discussion continued with each person talking over the next.

"Enough," the queen said. "The courts have already cleared Gracchus of any involvement in the royal assassinations. The matter at hand is Zara's return and our involvement in our neighbor's budding civil war."

"Zara, why didn't Callum bring you home earlier?" Sidony asked, eyes wide. "Why not stand by your side and make his case to our mother weeks ago?"

"He had his reasons. I don't agree with them, but you have to understand his position. And as he's being held prisoner in Marenburg, he's unable to speak for himself now." Zara stared at each member of the small council in turn. "I won't have L'Ortagia allied with a false king. Prince Callum needs to be freed. We have to take this step."

Emmanuelle added, "I think this has the potential to clearly rile our association with Gracchus, but in the long term, we risk our own sovereignty by not supporting a legitimate and rightful heir."

"Perhaps we should also consider what to ask in return for our loyalty to the house of MacKinnon." Forrenti threw the gauntlet. Zara had only to name the price.

Jeffors broke in first. "I believe that Prince Callum would seek Princess Zara's hand in marriage."

Everyone spoke at once. Their reactions were largely positive. Zara kept her eyes on one person at the table.

The queen took her time, as if coming to a difficult decision. "So, daughter, what do you say to the prince's suit?"

"I will discuss it with Callum." She held up a hand, not wanting to seem ungrateful or needlessly stubborn. "I'm amenable to it, but Callum and I will have the final say."

"Very well." Isabeau inclined her head. "Have a safe journey."

For the first time since setting foot in L'Ortagia again, Zara relaxed.

"Mother, both of your daughters are now a part of Embury." Zara strove for a conciliatory tone. "I refuse to let us be pulled into a war and be on the wrong side. L'Ortagia will side with the rightful king."

"Then you need to leave tonight," Sidony told Zara. She twisted her fingers in her lap and this time Zara spotted the wedding ring on her finger. "You should leave for Marenburg right away."

"You support his claim?" Relief filled her.

"I support L'Ortagia and my family." Sidony swallowed. "You have to leave before my husband returns."

Sidony was right. Adrian couldn't know what they were planning, couldn't know Zara had returned to Mondelac.

"Go, Zara," the queen said. "Go save your prince."

She and Jeffors had done it. Tears stung and she blinked them back, nodding. They stood, joined by Emmanuelle who'd be joining them on their trip to Marenburg.

Zara hugged Sidony, loath to leave her so soon.

"Be safe," Sidony said.

"I will."

CHAPTER FORTY-ONE

Home of Herr Risenbach
Casparre, Marenburg

"Brother, I keep waiting for a change in their routine." Callum stood at the barred door, peering through the narrow window to see along the corridor. Sconces burned, but the light didn't carry far enough for him to make out the distance to the stairs. The rest of the doors in this wing of the building were closed. He was still surprised they kept him with Duncan, though his brother was not in a talkative mood.

He grunted in reply.

Ever since Duncan had been thrown into the upper apartments with Callum, his older brother had slid deeper and deeper into darkness. Duncan had always been moodier than himself, but this was far worse than he'd ever seen him. Duncan barely looked at him. Callum continued acting as if there was a normalcy to be found. That, and checking in with Duncan about how he was doing, was what kept him hanging onto hope.

Certainly the rooms they were kept in were nothing to complain about. They were political prisoners, a fact which heartened Callum to a certain extent, since it validated their status. It was also, shrewdly, an effective means of holding them without them coming to harm, until officials determined their fate.

When Callum had first arrived to free Duncan, Duncan had been kept as a prisoner in what was little more than a dank cage. These new accommodations offered more freedom, and having Duncan with him marked his brother as a political prisoner. It at least allowed him to receive medical care, which he had needed badly. While it looked as though his body would heal, Callum worried for his brother's mind.

No one had told them what was going on beyond Callum's arrest and their subsequent imprisonment with Risenbach. Without being able to get a message back to the rebels, Callum did not know how they would free themselves.

"We'll die if we stay here," Callum said.

"Aye," Duncan said softly.

"Gracchus finally caught up with us." Callum turned away from the window, restlessly scanning the room for a means of escape. Again. "He'll come for us himself this time. Having the throne will make him bolder."

"Realized that the moment the cell door slammed shut behind you, brother." It was the longest sentence Duncan had spoken since they'd been reunited. Callum paused and glanced at him, but Duncan wouldn't meet his eyes.

No matter. Having some of his family back, even for a scant few days, meant everything to him. He didn't want to push. So, they waited. And he planned.

"Maybe we can get some fresh air later," Callum said.

"I doubt they'll let us leave the rooms." Duncan sat near the fireplace, staring into the coals.

"Care to move the furniture for a bout of wrestling?"

Duncan shook his head.

"Do you want to play chess?" It was a game the boys had learned from their father. "I'll bring it over to you." Chess seemed a rare luxury, almost as if their jailers had forgotten to remove the board from the rooms.

He set the board on a small table close to his brother and waited. "Duncan?" he asked softly.

After a moment, Duncan said, "Aye."

"Come on, then."

Duncan turned his chair and got settled, careful not to rest his reset arm down on the chair. He peered at the board and moved his first piece. Callum noted with satisfaction that Duncan's gaze was fixed on the board. He hoped his brother's innate sense of competitiveness would kick in. Callum needed him.

He reached down and responded to Duncan's play.

He wasn't sure how long his brother had been imprisoned, either here or wherever he'd been kept previously. He'd assumed Duncan would tell him when they reunited. But he hadn't said a word about how he'd survived the assassinations.

Callum remembered Duncan as a muscular lad, but his arms had grown even more brawny, as if he had been working as a laborer wherever he'd been before coming to the Marenburg cell. His dark blond hair hung about his eyes, his shoulders rolled forward as he slouched in the chair. He made a distressing picture, looking like coiled strength that had been broken too many times. Callum related, even if it was more in spirit than in body.

Callum stood after his next move, not wanting to pressure his brother into conversation and still unsure how to help him, but desperate to try. He looked out the window, grateful to have one that looked out on the front of the townhome where they were being kept. He squinted at a line of carriages that ambled down the street.

A cough from the other side of the room interrupted his thoughts. He went back to the board, briefly debated his next move, as his brother had become more aggressive with his chess playing than Callum remembered, and moved another piece. He'd take any show of spirit from Duncan, even if it meant losing yet another chess game to him.

"Do you think they get many visitors?" Callum asked.

"I have no idea," Duncan answered. "Although even when I was being kept in the cells, I had a few."

"How long were you in there?"

"Two months."

"How did you end up there?"

"You aren't ready for that story," Duncan said in a flat voice.

Callum swallowed, fear tingling along his arms at what that could mean. "How long ago was your arm broken?"

A long pause and Callum almost wished back his words, fearing he asked too much too soon. "Three days before you arrived. One of the guards tried to hurt someone. I got in his way…" His voice trailed off, and Callum guessed that was all he would say for the moment on the subject.

"That sounds like you. How does it feel now?"

"It's better. I've had worse. Your move."

Instead of deciding on another move, Callum went back to the window to look out; he heard what sounded like carriages outside.

Sure enough, several carriages formed a line in front of the townhome. He counted the visitors getting out and was struck by the number of officials wearing red, a distinctly L'Ortagian color. His heart sped up, fingers pressed to the glass while he waited to see a certain figure.

"One moment. I'll be right there."

Callum spotted Jeffors, but doubted his own eyes for a moment. As the small crowd clustered around the front walk, a dainty foot emerged from the last carriage and landed on the small step, an embroidered stocking on the ankle, and then the lush fall of a silver gown with a scarlet sash.

Zara stood at the front gate, like an avenging goddess.

Hope and a flare of pride burst in the center of his chest. "My move, eh?" he said to his brother.

CHAPTER FORTY-TWO

Zara looked over the line of townhomes as the carriages ambled along, faintly surprised but relieved that Callum and Duncan were being kept close to the capitol. The morning meetings with Marenburg diplomats had gone well. She appreciated that her mother had kept ties between the two countries so close.

Either Callum had lost her letter or the officials had, because they had no recollection of receiving it. Once she returned with him and Duncan, she'd send a stern warning that L'Ortagian letters of introduction needed to be honored.

There were only a few more details to review before Callum and Duncan could be freed. There was a curious lack of representation from Embury officials at the meetings. Zara was unsure exactly how Gracchus had managed to manipulate, extort, or pay the Marenburg guards to arrest Callum. Throughout the morning, there had been no acknowledgment the king was involved in any way. She wouldn't truly believe their negotiating had worked until Callum and Duncan were actually released.

Though the building was one of many along a street of

modest residences, Zara still felt a tingle of trepidation as she looked at the bland facade. She did not want to celebrate something until it really was done.

But what kept her awake at night was how close Callum and Duncan were to death, again. That drove her to move the meetings along this morning and demand to be taken to the prisoners once negotiations had been completed. She couldn't rest until they were out.

Callum and Duncan were being kept in one of the suites on an upper level instead of in the cells in the two prisons the city maintained. She had no idea what their actual conditions were like, or whether they had been injured when taken into custody. The Marenburg officials had been annoyingly vague in describing how and why Callum had been captured.

She adjusted her traveling bonnet and stared at the front windows, hoping for a glimpse inside. Surprisingly, Callum looked down at her from one of the upper-level windows. Her breath stuck in her throat for a moment as she tried to read the look on his face. He managed one of his half-smiles and Zara nodded. Her own delegation understood how much he meant to her. She didn't want her personal feelings to be known by anyone on the other side of the negotiating table.

Carefully, with her powers, she gently pushed against the window where he rested two fingers against the pane. She slid the bottom window up, at least the width of two fingers, letting in a small breeze. It was a pity they were on an upper floor. Otherwise she could just release them from the room through the window.

She wanted Callum to notice what she was doing, to understand what it meant. This far away from him, he might think another nocturne had opened the window. It was long past time she told him. If they had any hope for a future together, he needed to know.

At the front door, the official announced her, calling out her full title.

WITH A SINKING FEELING, Zara looked around the sitting room they'd been lead to as she realized the residence was likely somewhere Gracchus's influence extended. She turned to Lady Emmanuelle, her Chief Diplomat of Foreign Affairs, who had accompanied her and asked the other Marenburg officials to leave the room.

"Perhaps you're tired, Your Highness, and would like to resume our discussions tomorrow?" Risenbach, one of the attaches, with a long, thin nose and close-set eyes, inclined his head toward Zara, looking vaguely sympathetic.

"No, thank you, sir. This will only be a moment, then we can resume and complete our task."

Risenbach sniffed and left the room.

Zara and Jeffors sat across the room from each other, he staying to the back of the heavier negotiations, which had frustratingly been reignited in the afternoon. What had started out as details had escalated into a full-blown rehashing of everything that had been agreed upon earlier in the day.

She took a sip of tea and looked around the room, trying to gauge what was different. Though the officials present lacked true, final authority, Zara saw that the chief diplomatic officer, who had signed off on Callum and Duncan's release, had not traveled with them. And, ultimately, the officials present were in charge of the person who held the keys to the locked room upstairs.

Once cleared, she turned to Lady Emmanuelle and said, "I need you to go back to the capitol and bring Lord Henrick along with his guard. They are going to try to stall until I fear someone else will show up and remove the prisoners."

Lady Emmanuelle took Zara's hands and nodded. "Yes, Your Highness."

"And take two of our officers with you."

"Are you sure?"

"Yes, I'll be safe."

Lady Emmanuelle left with two guards, and Zara called the others back to try to complete the transfer. Jeffors passed a note to her. It read: *They must leave with us today.* She nodded, her confidence shaken but not deterred.

Risenbach started in again. "So explain to us exactly why we are to hand over the Embury exiles?"

"They are not exiles. They are under the protection of the L'Ortagian crown."

"You are risking the very long history of amiability between our countries by interfering in this matter," Risenbach said.

Zara felt the shift in tone. "We went over this earlier today. We are here on a diplomatic mission, whose goals have already been approved by your superior officer."

"The kingdom of Marenburg has many such allies and alliances. Surely you see you are getting involved where you are not needed."

The talk was getting alarmingly out of control and off topic. The veiled threats, the tone, and the lack of continuity with what had happened this morning in Lord Henrick's office all reeked of Gracchus's influence. She urgently needed to free Callum and Duncan. And unless Lord Henrick made a personal appearance at the townhouse, she and her delegation would be leaving without the two princes. She had to stall.

"I'd like to visit the prisoners. I want to be reassured of their safety." Jeffors spoke from the corner of the room.

She gave an inward sigh of relief and stood. "An excellent suggestion."

She'd finally found something that seemed to agitate their hosts, who all shifted in their seats.

"We don't have time for a visit today," Risenbach said.

"Don't be silly. Prince Callum is my intended. I demand to see to his welfare."

The four remaining soldiers stationed behind her stood, as well as the rest of her delegation.

"A visit wouldn't be appropriate." Risenbach's displeasure was evident from the ripples across his forehead. "We won't be able to grant your request today."

"I wasn't asking. I have the signed agreements and we've waited three hours. Take us or we'll find them ourselves. And when I return home, I'll be sure to communicate to the queen that it was you, Herr Risenbach, who refused us."

He sniffed and rose slowly. "Follow me."

CHAPTER FORTY-THREE

As they climbed the stairs, Zara noted that for every member of her entourage, the Marenburg officials had a similar representative, including soldiers flanking their steps. She couldn't remember when L'Ortagia had held political prisoners, but she did not believe they were ever so heavily guarded.

Nor was Marenburg known for being particularly aggressive. Historically, they tended to stay neutral as long as possible. Most of her dealings were when adversaries and allies came to Mondelac, not having to press her suit away from her own advantages.

The hallway was surprisingly dark given the time of day, lending a dreariness to this wing of the residence. They approached a door that had a small window, and one of the guards produced a key, opening the door without any announcement to those present within. Another sign of disrespect, although she doubted Callum would care.

As they entered the room, the two men seated by the fireplace turned and, seeing her, quickly stood. Zara couldn't help it. Her eyes drank Callum in. He looked thinner in the brief weeks they'd been apart, his skin pale and his hair longer than he usually kept it. He did not appear to be injured, but she knew he would not want her to know if he'd ever been hurt.

She checked an urge to run to him. It didn't help that he stared at her like she'd hung the moon.

The man behind him, Duncan, was not in good shape. He looked much older than his seven and twenty years and wore his arm in a sling across his chest. He also had purple bruises below his eyes and a small cut on his chin. His long hair hung in strands down to his shoulders. He barely resembled the handsome blond prince she remembered, but she was glad to see him alive.

Jeffors had trailed her guard leading into the room, so was the last to make it to the apartments. He immediately went over to Callum and greeted him. Callum pulled him in for a hug. He turned and introduced Duncan to him, and Jeffors fell to one knee, his head bowed. Duncan spoke in a low voice, but it managed to carry across the room.

"You honor me, General Millerton."

Zara couldn't get a clear look at Callum's face, but she no longer wanted this reunion done in an official capacity with a room half full of hostile witnesses. She turned to Risenbach. "Leave us."

"I'll do no such thing."

Callum lifted his head, about to speak, but Zara handled it.

"Leave a guard if you like. Mine will be posted outside the door, which will remain unlocked." She held out her hand.

"So be it." Risenbach handed the set of keys to her and left the room. "I'll be back in a quarter of an hour."

The L'Ortagians goggled at the sight of the princes. She was relieved that any proof of their existence would be a formality.

"We'll be downstairs, Your Highness. Congratulations on your upcoming nuptials. The prince is a lucky man indeed." With that announcement, which quieted any discussion going on between the Emburian men, Zara's delegation left but for two of her soldiers, who posted themselves outside the door.

Callum reached her in four quick strides. He hesitated as if he wanted to embrace her, hands twitching at his sides, but then he bowed instead.

"You don't have to do that," she said. Again she resisted touching him, wanting to clutch him close.

"It's just to start." He kissed her cheek. "Did Risenbach say nuptials?"

"He did. We have matters to discuss."

He leaned in. "I don't deserve you being here. Come and meet my brother." He led her over to Duncan, holding her hand. Zara squeezed his fingers, wishing she had bargained for more time. She and Callum had so much to say to each other. Events were forcing them to move forward before they had resolved their issues. Now wasn't the time, however.

When Zara faced Duncan, her breath caught in her throat. The vitality that Callum so naturally exuded was absent from Duncan. The light that had shone briefly in his eyes as he spoke to Jeffors had faded out. He stood before her a shell of a man, hulking and disheveled, but seemingly clean. Zara tried not to let her shock at his demeanor and appearance show on her face. He'd been through enough already.

She curtsied and murmured a warm greeting. Their encounter wouldn't have made an entry in the books on protocol Zara, and likely Callum, had studied.

"Zara, my brother tells me you are one of the bravest ladies he's ever known."

She blushed at his praise. "Your brother has scaled mountains and crossed a sea to find you. I thought you might need my assistance in getting home."

Callum tipped his head.

"It seems that we do." Duncan's gaze flickered, like she'd gotten a glimpse of his longing for home and family.

Once she had them safely away from Casparre and on board her ship, they could discuss Duncan's trials and all that the MacKinnons had lost. It was best to tackle the practical side of their leaving instead.

"Will you be able to travel with us?"

"Oh, aye. This?" He gestured to his wrapped arm. "It's nothing."

"He's surely had much worse," Jeffors said quietly.

"I gather you've been through quite an ordeal. You have the queen's support, Duncan, and mine."

"Thank you." A little spark seemed to energize him for a moment. "You are affianced?"

Zara squeezed Callum's hand. "We're discussing options."

"All the more reason to bring you home," Callum said.

Duncan's gaze passed between them. Had Callum not even told him of their agreement with Byrne?

"We'll talk later," she said. Her emotions were frayed from the long day. "Now, do you know anything about your capture that will help us in freeing you?"

Callum glanced at Duncan before answering. "Only that they seemed to be expecting me."

"How many guards are posted?" Jeffors asked.

"A dozen, though we weren't sure if it was because of our visit today," Callum said.

"They are balking at letting us go?" Duncan asked.

"Yes." She lowered her voice. "Their chief diplomatic officer assured us this morning we could secure your release. Then, you saw how it was going. We're sending for him."

"Good."

"We are also keeping all possible options open," Jeffors announced.

"In the last few days, the situation has gotten unpredictable. I fear we are only waiting here to die," Callum said.

"Don't say that," Zara said. His words echoed her fears. "We are getting you out and bringing you home."

Jeffors turned to Duncan. "Can you fight, if it comes to that?"

"Not very well, but yes."

Callum shot his brother a worried look.

"It won't come to that," Zara said. Her words belied her growing unease. Seeing their conditions made her feel better, in some ways, but given Duncan's bruises and broken arm, the princes weren't safe here.

"Madam, it usually comes to that." Zara usually appreciated Jeffors' honesty, but in this moment, she wanted to leave the men with a sense of optimism.

"I have been through my own...hardship," Zara said. An image of Felix's swollen face flashed through her mind. She stared at each man in turn. "We didn't come all this way to leave you here. My ship is in the harbor, ready to leave as soon as we board her."

Like before when entering the apartments, Risenbach did not bother with a knock or a greeting. He came into the room. "That was your fifteen minutes."

Impulsively, before her resolve leeched out of her and left only a gnawing fear, Zara leaned up and kissed Callum's cheek. She squeezed his arm, wishing her glove would disappear so she could feel his skin and soak up his warmth. He clasped her hand and held it against his heart before letting her go.

"I'd say I was amazed at your courage, but I already knew you possessed it in spades, Princess."

Duncan nodded at her, again seeming to shrink when Risenbach was in the room.

She made her way down the stairs on her way to the parlor. Risenbach didn't waste any time.

"You might as well head back home and save yourself the

trouble," Risenbach sneered. "I saw that you sent your staff out. Tell me, do they hope to bring Lord Henrick here?"

Zara swallowed but kept eye contact with him.

"He left on holiday and won't be back for several weeks," Risenbach said.

"He didn't mention anything to me this morning about leaving."

His eyes got even colder. "While I waited in the hall for you, we got a note from his office. Here, if you don't believe me." He passed it over, and she read the note quickly, seeing that it echoed his words.

She decided to concede the battle. With a drawn-out sigh, she said, "Risenbach, I'd like to retire to my hotel and reconvene in the morning. Please have my carriage brought around. I trust you can communicate to Lady Emmanuelle that we have decided to fold for the day?"

Risenbach practically rubbed his hands together. "Oh, but of course. Of course."

Zara walked out the door, unwilling to even wait for her carriage to be brought around. Jeffors was at her side.

"We're coming back first thing."

"I know, Your Highness. I figured as much."

CHAPTER FORTY-FOUR

The following morning, a footman opened the townhouse door where Callum and Duncan were being held. Zara, Jeffors, and Emmanuelle were ushered through before they could even say why they had returned. Risenbach was nowhere to be seen, even though it was his residence.

"By order of the king, you are to release the prisoners into our custody at once."

The official took the missive from Zara and scanned it, then gestured for them to follow him upstairs.

"Welcome back, Your Highness. The prisoners are likely sleeping at this hour, but I'm sure they will gladly be ready to leave."

Zara frowned at the back of the official, completely ill at ease with his congenial manner. None of this situation felt normal or right, not the hostility before and now not the overly laidback manner with which Callum and Duncan's release was being treated. Zara tried to stay focused on the task and not be so concerned with the means by which it was being carried out.

This time, the official knocked on the door before opening it. Only silence greeted them from the other side.

Jeffors signaled to the official to precede them into the room.

As they followed in behind him, Zara tried to stifle a scream. The room was empty. No sign of Callum or Duncan remained.

"We're too late," Lady Emmanuelle said.

"Why didn't the guard send for us?" Zara asked. She went to the window where Callum had stood just hours earlier.

"Because they slipped out somehow." Jeffors rounded on the official. "Tell Risenbach, he'll regret this."

THE CARRIAGE LUMBERED ALONG, with Callum feeling every rut along the vehicle floor. His hands were tied behind his back, his ankles bound as well. Uncaring of his broken limb, the soldiers had similarly trussed his brother, though Callum noted Duncan didn't make a sound. He'd found his brother, only to watch helplessly as he was beaten before him.

He was reasonably sure Duncan's jaw was cracked and his shoulder dislocated. Gracchus's men had landed several hits to his abdomen, beating him until he spat blood.

Sitting in the carriage, Gracchus was surreal, a living nightmare. Salt and pepper hair, more white at the temple, along with eyes that missed nothing. The usurper remained still and silent, stared at them with interest and hostility, but made no move to speak to them. Nor did he strike either Callum or Duncan. A few times he even peered out the window, as one would do to mark the passing of scenery. It was frighteningly normal and obscene at once.

They'd traveled a little farther and then Gracchus used a cane to tap the top of the carriage, bringing it to a stop.

"Ah, we're here. Not the way you used to travel, but it'll do, I suppose."

When the door opened, Callum saw they'd reached the docks.

Gracchus got out and two soldiers reached in, hauling Callum and Duncan over their shoulders. They carried them up the gangplank of a large ship. Each step felt like thousands.

How could the king travel so inconspicuously? Perhaps part of it was due to the hour of night and to being in a foreign land. Even if he had more recently made allies here, which it certainly seemed he had, he still would not necessarily be known in such a way as to be recognized if he did not want to be.

Callum knew how Gracchus's schemes worked. A hollow ache in his stomach reminded him of the sick fear he'd had long ago. Here he was again, feeling helpless and hopeless as his family was threatened. Gracchus might toy with them for a few hours, maybe even a few days, but the king meant to kill them. They'd likely never see Embury again.

His stomach threatened to empty as they were carried up several flights of servants' stairs. They finally entered a hallway and paused before a door. Once they entered the room, Callum guessed it was a suite since carpet broke the sound of footfalls. The guards set them down.

Gracchus settled into a chair opposite them and someone brought him a drink. At first glance, it would appear they were settled into a discussion in the seating area. Guards were stationed around the room by the exit points, and each prince had a guard assigned to him.

"You boys stay there." Gracchus chuckled at his own joke. "We have one more guest to arrive. Then I'll finish what should have been done long ago." He took another drink and smiled.

CHAPTER FORTY-FIVE

"Jeffors, I don't want to go back to my hotel room. There's nothing we need there."

"Your Highness, we need a safe place to regroup and plan. A carriage isn't it. We don't know where they've been taken. Your suite should work much better. Besides, everyone will be meeting there in a few hours," Jeffors answered. He offered his arm as they went up the grand staircase, then turned to go down a hallway.

"I should never have left. I should have locked myself in with them until Henrick arrived to let us all out."

"That would have been a very long wait. I'm sure Callum and Duncan would appreciate the sentiment, but you don't know that it would have been safe for you to stay. Gracchus could have taken them anyway."

They were almost to her door. "Thank you, Jeffors. You've been so kind."

Jeffors inserted the key and turned the knob. "At your service."

Zara nearly bumped into him, he'd stopped so abruptly. "Jeffors? What is—?"

"Zara, we need to get out of here."

"What is it?" Zara peeked over Jeffors's shoulder and saw that her room had been ransacked. Written with paints from her cosmetics was the word "Mine," all over the mirror in her hotel room.

CHAPTER FORTY-SIX

"We have to get them back." Zara picked her way into the center of her room, scanning the destruction.

Jeffors took a step toward her. "Let's get you somewhere safe."

She raised her gaze to his. Her clothing was strewn on every surface. Even the sheets had been yanked off the bed and tossed onto the floor. "Does Gracchus have a spy among us? How has he been able to stay a step ahead?"

"Your Highness, please." Jeffors looked out into the hall, gesturing to someone. He spoke softly and Zara only caught the end of what he said, asking for a few moments alone. He turned back to her. "I've sent for Lord Henrick. We need to meet with his representative right away."

Zara sank onto the floor, her skirts billowing around her hips. She'd come so far, running away from the man who would destroy so many people's lives, and yet here he'd done it again. "How do you keep fighting him? This is impossible. All I want to do is help Callum and his brother. They've suffered enough. And that monster found a way to hurt them again."

Jeffors closed the door. "Zara, we haven't any other choice. He has to be stopped."

Zara's hands fluttered at her sides. She didn't even have tears. "I've made all this worse. I'm sorry. We had a plan and now..." She gestured to the destruction around her.

Her life had never been so out of control. They'd been so close to saving Callum and Duncan. So close to being able to envision a future with him, of her choice, as herself, fully.

Jeffors squatted beside her. "Madam, we need to leave this place. Staying here is only making it worse. That's why Gracchus does this, leaving chaos in his wake. He wants you off balance."

"It's working. Maybe you should go on without me." She didn't say it as a ploy for sympathy. She meant it. The rebellion had been side-tracked by helping her. And she'd failed the second thing she'd tasked herself to do. "I've made it worse. Gracchus has both of them. Just go."

Jeffors stood and brushed his hands on his pant legs. "I'll give you a few minutes and then I'll send in a guard for you. Come with me. You've traveled this far. You know what the king is capable of, the type of soldiers he favors. We need every ally we have and that includes you."

"Where do you think they could be?" she asked. She pulled out the chain where she kept his intaglio ring, holding it close as if it could signal where Gracchus had taken them.

"My guess is he's getting them out of Marenburg." He went to the door. "Two minutes. Zara, be brave. That brought you this far."

The door closed behind him and Zara was alone. One of her stockings slipped off the bed and landed next to her night rail.

She'd straightened it with her nocturne powers with less effort than a blink.

Zara sat up straighter. She wasn't the same woman who had

run out of options for getting out of a royal marriage. She was faster and stronger now.

She couldn't leave Callum and Duncan to Gracchus. She'd known that even as she'd slumped onto the floor. It was the sense of sheer uselessness that crushed her.

Jeffors had said they needed all the allies they had here in Marenburg. But Zara had been holding back on them, out of habit and out of her old fears. She'd opened a window, but that was more of a parlor trick. Her telekinesis could do so much more. She reached into the pocket in her skirt where she kept the watch Varro had left her. She got it out and checked the latch on the hidden compartment. It sprung open easily.

She stood and straightened her skirts, closing the watch and tucking it away, tucking away the necklace with his ring. She would follow Jeffors' lead and do it with everything she had, including aide from a loyal ally.

THEIR CARRIAGE TOOK them to the docks. "You're sure they're here?" Zara asked Jeffors.

The port teemed with activity. A row of ships with their masts tied, crews loading or unloading, nearly filled the line of docks.

"Gracchus won't want to take any chances. Diplomatic means of removing Callum and Duncan were leaning in your favor. He's looking to escape." Jeffors held up a spyglass to search along the wharf.

"What are you looking for?" Zara asked. They had to be close on Gracchus' heels. "Could they have left already?"

"I know how the King of Embury likes to travel. Got him." Jeffors put the glass down and gestured to the second-to-last dock. "Near the end. With a fresh coat of paint and practically screaming his colors."

The brig near the end gleamed black in the morning light. Its deck crawled with sailors as they hurried to untie the large ropes holding the boat to the dock. Zara rapped on the roof of the carriage. "To the second to the last, Coachman."

Their small but fast curricle sped down the narrow bit of space along the face wall. Zara checked the marina. If the ship got out too far, the sails could take it out of the port and she'd lose Callum and his brother. "Jeffors, we're going to miss them."

The carriage stopped and Zara nearly lost her seat.

"Apologies! The path is blocked," the coachman cried from the front of the carriage.

"We'll have to run. I sent for help from their Embassy. We need to stall the ship." Jeffors's face was tight with strain. They were so close.

Zara alighted from the carriage behind Jeffors and ran down the dock. The ship was untethered, oars dipped into the water to push it out into open water. She had seconds.

She focused her powers, pulling back on the vessel. The ship stopped, water swirling around the hull.

"Row harder!" the captain commanded.

Jeffors joined her and called out to the captain, demanding he stop.

Zara scanned the deck for a sign of King Gracchus. She spotted him just over the captain's shoulder, his gaze pinned to her and Jeffors. He waved his hand.

A woman appeared at the edge of the prow, brandishing a bow. She notched two arrows in quick succession, hitting the very narrow space between where she and Jeffors stood.

Jeffors half-turned to her. "If you have any extra ideas, now is the time." He moved to stand in front of her, protecting her from the archer.

Jeffors called out to the captain again. Zara tuned out their heated conversation. She had one chance.

Zara grabbed the watch and popped open the back. The tiny envelope slipped out but slid deeper into her pocket. She pinched it between her fingers and pulled it out, emptying the contents in her other palm. Four tiny crystals, like flakes of blue salt, shimmered in the dawning light. She swallowed them, wincing at the strange taste. It didn't matter. She'd drink bilge water to stop that ship.

She didn't feel any different. Hopefully, whatever Varro had given her would work immediately.

She used her powers to pull the boat forward. It inched closer in the water, but it was hard to tell if that was just due to it bobbing from being pulled back and forth.

The archer adjusted her stance and raised her bow, keeping her aim on Zara and Jeffors. Gracchus stepped closer to her, speaking through gritted teeth. He was too far away for Zara to hear him over the rest of the din along the wharf.

The archer shook her head but fired another arrow. It went wide, hitting a barrel at the front of the face wall.

The oars went back into the dark water and Zara lost her hold on the ship. Pain streaked across her forehead. Her muscles ached with strain. She pulled on the boat until she got dizzy. She shook her head. She needed something to block the boat's departure. The waters in the marina were clearing of ships. They had yards to go before they could catch the morning breeze and escape.

Gracchus stood next to the archer and gave her a mocking salute.

Zara wanted to scream that he was a coward, but she had to focus every ounce of energy she had on pulling the ship back. She stepped around Jeffors and squeezed his arm. "Let me."

He stayed close, still calling to the captain and the sailors. "I order you, in the name of the rightful MacKinnon heir, to return this ship to port!"

Gracchus spoke to the archer again. Two more landed at her feet with a loud thunk.

"She's going to stop missing. Zara, get behind me!"

"Not yet," Zara said. Sweat poured down her back. "It's better when I have a clear view."

Her stomach turned over, clenching hard, and she swayed on her feet. Whatever enhancement had spelled the crystals must have finally hit her system.

Zara scanned the ship, her gaze locking on the loosened sails. *There.*

Channeling her powers, she blew the sails wide. The ship tilted in the wind then continued pulling away.

She opened all of them, turning her powers to catch the breeze and pull the ship back.

More yelling hit the periphery of her awareness. She dug deeper, sinking into her nocturne powers, channeling every learned effort and attempt. She lost her vision in her left eye, but she kept going.

Arrows peppered the deck and the water in front of her. Jeffors slid closer but let her have a clear view of the ship. Zara waved the arrows aside, her hands vibrating with the force she used to pull the vessel back. The oars tipped up and were pulled in. Zara gave them a passing glance. Someone inside had finally obeyed Jeffors's order.

The sails snapped against the mast, hauling the brig towards them. She almost overshot their slip when the ship careened, nearly smashing into the side of the dock. She eased up and held the ship, sweat pouring into her eyes. Her temples throbbed.

Jeffors caught her as her knees buckled. "You did it. We've got them. She finally ran out of arrows too."

Zara blinked at the ship through hazy vision, now still in the water, Marenburg officials using grappling hooks to hold it in place. "There. Never again."

There was more shouting on the deck. Callum and Duncan appeared, both racing toward Gracchus.

"Is the ship secure?" Zara asked. Her vision faded to mere pinpoints. Her legs wouldn't work and her tongue felt thick. No wonder Callum hated Varro's spells.

"We've got them now." Jeffors gave her a gentle shake. "Zara?"

Her last thought was "Good," before everything went black.

CHAPTER FORTY-SEVEN

Below deck had been controlled chaos. That gave Callum a sliver of hope.

The crews' shouts carried into their tiny cabin. The captain and first mate, or possibly more of Gracchus's guards, yelled for the crew to hurry their departure. Gracchus had sat with him and Duncan, his expression of quiet gloating making the hairs on the back of Callum's neck stand up.

The man turned to a side table, tossing out the contents from a small satchel he carried at his belt. Bile rose in Callum's throat as he recognized what the usurper was doing. He tried to scry his—or their—future. He must not have liked what he saw because he scowled and angrily swept the bones and rocks back into the bag, mumbling under his breath.

Once the ship pulled away from its moorings, Gracchus left them and locked them in.

Callum struggled against his bonds, managing to kick a chair over. Duncan got his feet loose, but with his injured arm, couldn't do much more to loosen the ties on his wrists.

The door opened and two young soldiers, a boy and a girl, crept in.

The boy stopped before Duncan. "Are you the true king?"

Duncan nodded. The boy took off his gag. "I heard them say that the king planned to take you to the middle of the sea and put you where you'd stay lost forever."

"Already came back from the dead," Duncan said.

"Hurry! You know it's him." The girl shushed him and quickly untied Callum.

She looked familiar. Her auburn hair perhaps, or the freckles across her nose reminding him of Viola.

"Where are you from?" he asked her.

"Summerly. The king took us when he destroyed the village. He believed we were nocturnes." She rolled her eyes.

They could be Viola's cousins.

They led them into the hall. "Go that way. There's a window big enough for a man to fit through. You can jump overboard and get to one of the docks."

"Thank you."

"If they catch you, don't tell them it was us." The children ran the other way.

Duncan cocked his ear. Through the shouting, Callum made out Jeffors's voice. "The rebels are here. We have to find a way to help them."

"Down here." Duncan led Callum to the bottom of the ship where the rowers toiled. The men strained against the oars.

"Fight her off!" The head oar's man yelled. "We've got more of us than her. Put your back into it and row!"

Duncan approached the head oarsman and knocked him out. "Take your oars out of the water and pull them in. We are going back to port."

The crew, mostly Emburian, froze at Duncan's words. He sounded so much like their father Callum felt a chill.

Once the oars were pulled in, the ship swung forward as if caught in a tide. Duncan leaned on him before catching himself against a beam.

More shouting sounded from the shore. Grappling hooks thundered across the deck above their heads.

The ship swayed to the side before stopping.

"He's not getting away from me," Duncan said.

Callum led the way to the deck, trying to disarm the men instead of attack them. He focused on finding Gracchus and making him pay for what he did.

They reached the deck and chaos reigned. Callum examined the ship, noting the hooks, managed by Marenburg officials as well as Jeffors, holding a limp Zara. It didn't look like she'd been hurt, but they were too far away to tell for sure. Arrows, dozens of them, lined the deck at her feet and the barrels waiting to be loaded onto the last ship left in the marina.

Jeffors shook Zara but she didn't move. "No!" He scanned the deck and spotted Gracchus, furiously spouting orders to the captain and a small group of soldiers.

Duncan stormed across the deck, shrugging off the guards' attempts to stop him. The men tried to block his way, but their hearts weren't in it.

Callum rushed the king. He grabbed Gracchus and threw him to the deck. He crouched over him and punched him. He might have been yelling, he wasn't sure. Gracchus squirmed, twisting his body underneath, but Callum wouldn't let go. He hit him until he heard the sickening crunch of his nose break. The man's skull must be made of iron because Callum had already split his knuckles.

Marenburg officials stormed the deck and someone pulled him off of Gracchus.

It all happened too quickly for Callum to take it in. Jeffors was at his side somehow, holding his arms. "She's fine. She took something from Varro that made her pass out. You got him. You got him."

Duncan clapped him on the back. "It's over. Your princess brought us back."

CHAPTER FORTY-EIGHT

They settled into the L'Ortagian ship Zara had waiting at port. Zara told the captain to set sail, the route to either L'Ortagia or Embury to be determined in the next few hours. She left Lady Emmanuelle and Jeffors to discuss it. She wanted to get out onto the waters of the Catarine Sea.

Duncan and Callum were treated for their injuries, both princes under L'Ortagian guard.

Gracchus was being held in a Casparrian prison for the next week. At least that was how Risenbach explained it to her before she kicked him off her ship. The archer had disappeared, along with several of Gracchus' crew. Zara had wanted to question her.

She checked on Callum and found him in his brother's room. "Let Jeffors sit with him. He's safe now. Come, get some rest."

She and Callum walked to her cabin, Zara's head on his shoulder.

~

In Zara's cabin, Callum laid her down and rolled her to her side, trying to get her gown off. She roused enough to help, and Callum tucked her in and called for her maid to take her dress.

The L'Ortagian delegates were wary of him and Duncan, but Zara had told them to get to know the both of them and assured her delegation of her safety with him, and they'd started to look less skittish when he joined them for meals onboard the ship.

Lady Emmanuelle took the least amount of time to win over, perhaps due to her experience and political skill. With a sharp eye, she congratulated him on his upcoming nuptials. She'd handled the Gracchus situation with cold-blooded expertise, rounding up Marenburg officials to take Gracchus and his men into custody, alleging crimes against two royal families. Callum doubted they'd be able to keep him long, but he appreciated the head start.

Lady Emmanuelle had also carried the message back from her meetings that Lord Henrick would be personally handling diplomatic relations pertaining to Embury with his people, putting his support behind Duncan's sovereignty and right to rule.

Callum undressed and climbed into the narrow bed with a sleeping Zara, tucking her against his chest. As he pulled the coverlet around them, he looked down at her, finally resting, and realized he owed all these changes in his life to her. And yet, thinking back, he couldn't see how he had could have possibly earned her love and loyalty. She had taught him so many things and been willing to sacrifice so much for him.

It had taken him far too long, but he was finally ready to fully let her in. He'd wasted too much time believing he didn't have it in him to handle loving, and potentially losing, another person after his family died.

But in those days in the cell with Duncan, he realized he'd had a different kind of family for years now. The rebels had shown him loyalty, companionship, and laughter. They'd weathered losses together and managed to make the most of what they had. He'd thought he couldn't let someone else in until he had his family back, but he'd been so wrong. He'd already found space in those empty places for Jeffors and Viola, Ranulf, Liam, and Matteo. They numbered in the dozens. He already knew he could survive loss and re-assemble the pieces. He just hadn't trusted himself enough to be able to do it again. And he'd almost lost Zara in the process of protecting his heart.

He set to figuring out how to make her happy because he was hoping to build a life with her. Zara was everything he had ever wanted. And somehow, she was back in his arms again.

She stirred in her sleep, lifting her head. "Callum?"

"Sleep, love. I've got you." He twined a lock of her dark hair around his finger.

"I've got you too." She patted his chest and lay back down, falling asleep again.

CHAPTER FORTY-NINE

Callum woke to the sounds of a bath being prepared for Zara.

"Sorry to wake you," she said. Two servants poured water into a copper slipper tub.

He pulled on a pair of breeches and kissed her cheek before attending to his morning needs.

"Impressive." He eyed the large basin, now nearly full, once he returned.

"It comes with the ship." Zara stood to the side of the tub, wearing a dressing gown that covered her from her neck to her toes.

The servants filed out and she dismissed her maid.

"Shall we talk while I bathe?"

"Do you want me to help?" he asked. His lips curled.

"Not just yet."

He slumped back into the bed but didn't lose his grin.

"You're going to watch me get in, then?"

He stilled. "Whatever you like."

She hesitated, then dropped her robe. "I like." She stepped

into the tub and hummed. Sinking down, she rested her arms against the sides.

"I've missed you," Callum said. How had she grown lovelier since they'd been apart? He could watch her bathe for eternity and not tire of the view.

She slid him a glance, the steam pinkening her cheeks. "In what way?"

He sat up and stretched, the sheet falling into his lap. "Lots of ways."

"Be more specific." She started washing with her usual air of efficiency, but her gaze strayed to him over and over. He'd hurt her by leaving and even now, it seemed she wasn't sure where they stood.

"I missed talking with you, sharing our days. You made everything brighter, brought me hope when I was lost."

She blushed harder, her lips quirked. "Helped you find your inner poet, evidently."

"Princess, you don't know how hard it was to let you go," Callum said gruffly.

"I needed to leave. It was time for me to return." She rinsed a small cloth and paused. "And I knew you had to see if it was really Duncan."

"I regret how we ended it at Ballyreine." He sighed. "I had no right to bring you into the mess my life had become, but once you were there, it terrified me that something would happen and I wouldn't be able to protect you."

"You have to stop blaming yourself for their deaths."

"I know," he said softly. "I've held onto it for so long. It... wasn't my fault. I know that now."

"Did you get to talk to Duncan about it?" she asked.

"Duncan has been quiet. I think we will, eventually. But he's been through a lot."

"If you blamed yourself, it's possible he did too. He survived by himself these last few years, right?"

"More or less." He ran a hand over his face. "I can hardly imagine being that alone. At least I had my friends."

"You did." She washed her face, pausing when she caught him staring at her. "Does he know what happened to Quinnah?"

"He used to have leads on her but they dried up a few years ago. He fears the worst but said she was supposed to have someone looking out for her."

"Who?" Zara asked. "Did they escape together?"

"He wouldn't say. Said her safety meant he couldn't tell me more. Risenbach's place never felt safe enough to talk in."

"Of course."

He ran a hand through his hair. She was giving him another chance. He had to show her how open his heart was to her, how they could build a future together.

"After we spoke with Byrne, I didn't want to pressure you. Marriage between us was a difficult topic. I had to give you room because I wanted you to get there without me influencing you."

"Your feelings for me wouldn't have been a bad influence."

"Zara, I'd already convinced you to leave home for me. I wanted to be careful with you. You were the one who made the rest happen. A royal wedding between us would have done even more, but I felt selfish bringing it up."

She nodded.

"Then I found that I liked being able to share things with you. Things I hadn't told another person."

Zara looked away. "I liked that too." She gripped the sides of the tub. "As you might already know, there's something I need to share with you."

He knew what she was getting at, but it was an entirely different matter to see her perform a trick for him.

Her eyes narrowed and bubbles rose from her bath. They drifted up and formed a cloud over her head.

"I'm a nocturne. My power is telekinesis." The cluster of bubbles rotated slowly.

His grinned at her display. "Princess, you're incredible."

"I meant to tell you. Truly. I'm sorry." The bubbles popped, tiny droplets pebbling the water in front of her. "I kept it a secret for so long, it was hard to know how you'd handle it."

"Don't apologize for that. I don't blame you for keeping it from me. These weeks away from you have given me time to think. I've held on to my bitterness about how Gracchus used nocturnes to aid him in the assassinations. I've wasted too much time keeping them at bay. They are my people, deserving of respect and protection, as much as any other."

"I should have told you sooner, and then there never seemed to be a good time. I hid it for so long that I didn't trust you with it." She blinked, swiping at the corner of her eye.

"I will spend every moment trying to earn your trust. I love you, every part of you."

She stilled for a long moment. "We already had so many obstacles, I couldn't stand it if this thing that made me happy to use again, would change how you felt about me."

"I wish you'd told me but I understand."

"It's something I'm proud of." Zara leaned forward to wet her hair.

"As you should be," Callum said, drawing closer to her. "Can I help you with that?"

She arched a brow. "Yes, please."

CALLUM KNEELED beside her tub and filled a pitcher of water. "I think I fell in love with you the day we left your castle."

"Truly?" Her voice cracked.

"Truly. Somewhere along the halls and stairs of Mondelac." He poured water over her head, careful not to let the soap get in her eyes. "I wanted you with me but had no idea how to make it work. What was I supposed to do? Keep you in hiding until I could figure out a way to defeat the usurper? I couldn't do that to you. I had no right."

"I might have lost my heart to you then too. But I needed to see what I could do on my own. Standing up to my mother and leaving with you was only the beginning. Once I went back and convinced her to help you, I realized I should have been handling myself that way all along. I've always wanted to be needed, but it's when I'm standing up for what I believe in that I think I can do the most good."

He stared at her, his gaze softening.

"I'm not some pretty doll you can put on a shelf when you don't want her. I haven't gone through what you have, but I know pain and compassion, hurt and kindness too. You kept me out after I showed up to help you. I risked so much, and then you acted as if you could easily let me go."

"I'm sorry, Zara. I'm so sorry. You were the one person who had nothing to do with all the shite my life had become. I loved that about you and it scared me like little else could. I want us to be together, in whatever way you'll have me."

Zara coasted her fingers along his temple and down his cheek. "Either get in here with me or help me dry off."

Callum laughed softly and reached for a drying cloth. "Here."

He was on his feet, offering a hand to help her out of the tub. She stood and pulled him close, kissing him with all the passion in her heart, all the misery she'd felt, finally breaking free. He kissed her back with equal fervor, brushing the two tears that slid down her cheeks with his thumbs.

With his arms around her, she kept warm in the cool air of the room as she stood dripping wet. Finally, he pulled back and wrapped her in the towel.

He lifted her out of the tub and carried her to the bed, sitting her on the edge.

She adjusted the towel around herself but felt more exposed than she'd ever been. "Callum, wait." She rested her hand against his chest. He'd said those three little words, but they hadn't decided anything between them. She couldn't go back to how it was when they were in Embury. "What is this?"

Callum got on his knees before her. "What do you want it to be?"

"I want it to be real. I want this to be about us, just us, not what we can do for each other or what's advantageous for our countries." There. She'd laid it out for him.

"You and me? Zara, I want that too. I've always wanted that."

She grinned at him and leaned down for a kiss.

"We should discuss our betrothal," she said softly.

"I've been meaning to ask you about that." He ran his hands along the tops of her thighs and down the sides. "That was part of your agreement with the queen?"

"I promised nothing, but we needed to help convince my mother to go along with the plan."

"Zara, I'd have rather asked you myself. Maybe I can convince you now?" He tilted his head, a glint shining from his whiskey-colored eyes.

She stared at him, marveling at how precious his features had become to her, how much she adored him.

"Wait."

He paused, a thumb rubbing along her knee.

"I want to do this." A little spark burst in her chest, warming her from the inside. She spotted the necklace she wore hanging from a hook by the bed. She slid off the bed and grabbed it, slipping the ring from the chain. She patted the spot where she'd been sitting, indicating for Callum to take her place.

She knelt and clutched his intaglio ring.

"Zara?"

She took a deep breath and hoped the drying cloth stayed put.

"Callum, you were there when I needed you. And then you kept me safe as best you could. I would not be here if you hadn't believed I had more to offer than my hand in marriage. You treated me as an equal from the very beginning."

He shrugged, as if to say "of course."

"I think I've carried a tendre for you since we met years ago. That you came rushing back into my life—as if out of my dreams—is really no surprise."

He winked at her.

"Don't distract me." She had an excellent view of him sitting inches from her, shirtless and in breeches.

He shifted on the bed, muscles flexing deliciously. He tweaked a strand of hair by her ear. "I love it when you're earnest. Keep going."

"I admire you for your loyalty and courage, for your cunning and affection for others. Knowing the person you've become, for bringing out the best in me, I'm asking for your hand."

"Marry me, Callum." She held up his ring. "I promise to be honest and true, to fight for you and love you until my dying breath."

He reached for her. "Leaving you was one of the hardest things I've ever had to do." He settled her on his lap, his face against her neck, and clutched her close. "I never want to do it again."

"I know." She stroked his shoulder, careful to avoid the bruises he wore. "Callum?"

"Yes," he said softly. He took the ring from her palm and slipped it onto his finger. "I'd be honored to marry you."

She held his hand to her chest and kissed him for all she was worth. He kissed her back until they were both breathless.

"I'm glad we made that official," he said once he pulled away.

"Me too." She brushed at the water that had dripped along her neck.

He laughed and set her on the bed. He reached for a cloth, then settled behind her. "Here, let me comb your hair."

"Sure." Callum started working on the long mass, blotting the dripping water. Her body hummed, a pleasant warmth coursing her skin as he touched her so gently.

"I'm not going to ask how you learned how to do that."

"I had a little sister, you know."

She smiled. "That you did." It would take time, but she could come to trust him again.

He lifted her hair and kissed the back of her neck. "Princess, you are more resourceful than I realized. And powerful. What you did with the bubbles—but an entire ship? Love, that's incredible."

"I wasn't going to let him hurt you and Duncan again." She lifted a shoulder. "I didn't know I was that strong. I had some help. Varro gave me something that enhanced my power. At least, that's what I think it did."

"In exchange for what?"

"Nothing but a promise." She let the words hang between them.

His hands stilled on her hair. "I have to make it right with the other Emburian nocturnes. Find a way to make their inclusion in the rebellion official."

"Yes, you do."

"I'll meet with Varro as soon as we return. It's long past time."

"If Duncan disagrees, what will you do?" she asked.

"Make him understand."

"Good." She turned and angled her head for another scorching kiss.

He kissed her soundly, pulling her the rest of the way around to face him. She tucked the towel against her chest, but it was hopelessly tangled. She made a frustrated sound.

He chuckled and kissed her nose. "I love you."

She met his gaze. A dark lock of hair fell across his forehead in a dashing manner. She smoothed it into his hair. "I love you too."

His grin was like the sun shining across the sea.

Oh, this man.

"Come here." He pulled her on top of him and lay down, settling her against him, astride. She squirmed against his arousal, before finally sliding off her towel.

"Callum…"

He kissed her neck, pulling her up along his body while his lips traveled down. "Zara, would you mind if I showed you how much I've missed you?"

She gazed down at him, an answering need rushing through her. "I was hoping you would."

He laughed and wrapped his arms around her. "Should we run away together, after the wedding of course?"

"We could." She tapped her fingers on the pillow beside him. "Or maybe we should stay and have everyone we love around us, to remind us we aren't alone."

He snagged her hand and kissed the tips of her fingers. "An excellent plan, Princess."

THE END

ACKNOWLEDGMENTS

This story noodled around in my head for a long time. I started reading romance during an old school era and had a fun time trying to put twists on familiar tropes. Writing and editing this story was only possible with the help and support of many, many people and the (unrelenting) patience of my husband and kids.

Thank you Evie, Olivia, and Lainey for always being there for me. To my sweet friends Dave, Saira, and Sharon, thank you for your encouragement. It means so much to me.

Thanks to the Yahoo Romance Critique Group for your helpful critiques of early versions of this story. Thank you also to Miranda Dubner for giving me a roadmap toward a better story.

Huge thanks to the Mermaids, the Golden Heart class of '16, for being so supportive. A special thanks to Tracy Brody for hosting me at my first Writers Retreat. Loved hanging out with you! I am so grateful for our friendship.

Thank you to my editors Jessa and Christa, my proofreader Liz, and my cover designer Kim. I feel blessed to work with all of you. You are so talented, professional, and understanding.

Thank you to my beta readers Colette Dixon, Jaycee Jarvis, Diane Lloyd, and Yvonne Weers. I really appreciate your detailed reading. Your ideas and suggestions were so helpful and made the story stronger.

Thank you to the readers who told me they were looking forward to this story. Wow!

Thank you, Ryan, as my first reader and holding-it-all-together spouse. I hope you love this story. Your early enthusiasm for it kept me going when I wasn't totally sure what I was doing. And, lastly, thanks to my awesome kids for being so sweetly enthusiastic and encouraging. I love you so much!

ABOUT THE AUTHOR

Ainsley Wynter's writing is inspired by a love of fairy tales, social justice, and superheroes. She's been reading romance since junior high and credits the genre with getting her through tough times.

Ainsley is the author of the fantasy romance series *The Lost Royals*. Her debut novel, *Kissed at Midnight* is the first book in the series. *Once Upon a Princess* is her latest release. She was a 2016 finalist in paranormal romance in the Romance Writers of America's Golden Heart® contest, as well as a 2017 finalist in the unpublished Single Title contemporary romance category of the Maggie Awards.

Ainsley lives in the Midwest with her wonderful husband, three rambunctious, sweet kids, and three (mostly) cuddly cats. When she's not reading, writing, or procrasti-tweeting, she enjoys dancing, Real Housewives, and the occasional excel spreadsheet.

Sign up for Ainsley's newsletter at AinsleyWynter.com to be the first to hear about her new releases and tips for self-care.

Thank you so much for reading this book. If you enjoyed it, please consider leaving a review.

ALSO BY AINSLEY WYNTER

Kissed at Midnight

Princess Sidony of L'Ortagia serves as the queen's hostess, leaving affairs of state to her sister Zara. During a masquerade ball, Sidony kisses a handsome stranger only to discover he's Prince Adrian of Embury, a man with a fearsome reputation and the emissary sent to arrange her sister's marriage. Worried her actions will damage the budding alliance, she convinces Adrian to forget the incident...even if she cannot.

Adrian roots out traitors in his uncle's kingdom of Embury using his magical abilities. When he's sent to arrange a wedding for his cousin, a kiss in the moonlight gives him a taste of what he's been missing. Sidony is everything his life is not: laughter, warmth, and passion. But the king maintains an unbreakable hold over him, hiding his family in exchange for Adrian's loyalty to the crown.

After Zara disappears on the eve of the royal wedding, Adrian's orders are to stay and maintain the alliance with L'Ortagia. But Sidony's effect on his powers and his heart becomes too strong to deny. When he has a chance to rescue his family and throw off his royal ties, will he take it, knowing he'll have to leave Sidony? Or will the dark prince abandon his past to be with the one woman who brought his cold heart to life?

COPYRIGHT

Published in the United States of America.
Ebook ISBN: 978-1-7335898-1-9
Paperback ISBN: 978-1-7335898-2-6

Cover design by Atlantis Book Design
Editing by Jessa Slade of Red Circle Ink
Copy editing by Christa of EditorChrista
Proofreading by Liz Lincoln

Ainsley Wynter Press
PO Box 22041
Lincoln, NE 68542
www.AinsleyWynter.com

❀ Created with Vellum

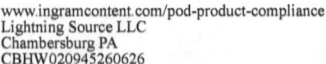